Blood Sword

Book 3 in the Danelaw Saga

by

Griff Hosker

Published by Sword Books Ltd 2022

Copyright ©Griff Hosker First Edition 2022

Contents

Dedication

To my editor and wife of 50 years, Eileen, thank you for everything. Most of all for putting up with me all these years. Here's to the next 50.

Real People used in the book

King Sweyn Forkbeard - King of Denmark
King Æthelred – King of England
Edmund Ironside- his son
Ælfheath – The Archbishop of Cantwareburh
Abbot Ælfmaer – Abbot of the Augustine monastery in Cantwareburh
Harald Sweynson – the eldest son of the King of Denmark.
Cnut Sweynson - second son of the King of Denmark
Lady Ælfgifu – a Saxon noblewoman
Lord Ælfhelm – her father
Thorkell the Tall – Jarl of the Jomsvikings
Hemingr – Thorkell's brother
Æthelstan, the son in law of King Æthelred
Oswy - the son in law of Eorledman Byrhtnoth
Thurbrand the Hold – A Northumbrian lord who controlled southern
Northumbria
Uhtred the Bold - A Northumbrian lord who controlled northern
Northumbria
Ealdred – the eldest son of Uhtred
Findláech – Mormaer of Moray (the father of Shakespeare's Macbeth)

Prologue

Agerhøne 1009

Our clan had been raiders but we had tired of war and enjoyed a season or two of peace and trade. That is not to say that all the Danish drekar became peaceful traders. Men still sailed to the land they now called England to raid. Their weak king, Æthelred, was a poor king who tried to pay off the Vikings, both Norse and Dane, who plagued his land. It was foolish for the more he paid the more he was raided. All of us agreed, when we sat in the mead hall to feast, that the sensible thing would be to build up an army that could fight us. While we had become more traders than raiders, we all practised the art of war. My sword, Oathsword, and my dagger, Norse Gutter, were kept honed and I grew no merchant's paunch. I used my spear, Saxon Slayer when we practised a shield wall or wedge. I think we might have changed from a warrior like clan to a trader clan had not the land been devastated by the twin scourges of famine and a disease that wiped out every pig within fifty miles of our home. Mary, my wife, and the Christians in our clan all blamed our lack of piety for the disasters. I knew that there was no arguing with such an idea but if their god had decided to punish us, he was hurting the Christians every bit as much as those who adhered to the old ways. Whatever the truth of the matter the result was still the same. The old and some of the young died and our families needed food. A warrior cannot stand by while his family starves and so we did something about it.

The jarl, Sweyn Skull Taker, my foster father, called all the men to the mead hall. He held a Thing. Even as we all trooped in, we knew that there was only one choice for us. Where did we raid?

I sat with my cousins, Sweyn One Eye and Alf Swooping Hawk although we normally just called him Hawk. Lodvir was the leading warrior after the jarl and he sat at his side. He was the hersir of Ribe and I had been given the honour of the title of hersir of Agerhøne. That I was young was overlooked because of my skill in war. The young warriors who liked to follow me and the sword that had once belonged to King Guthrum were as close to me as they could. All of them were happy at the prospect of war. They were young and wished for the chance to test their skills.

"We all know that we must raid but we have choices. Do we head for the land of the Franks? Should we raid the Hibernians, the Scots and the Irish? Or do we sail across the water and join Thorkell the Tall and the Jomsvikings?"

Men shouted out their thoughts while I just listened.

"The Hibernians are poorer than we are. Their animals are weak and they have no gold."

"What about Man? There is honour in fighting them."

"The Franks are not as strong as they were. The Norse have now conquered so much of their land that they have a leader in Duke Rollo who can challenge even kings."

"England is closer."

I remained, like my cousins, silent. The one man we trusted more than any other was Sweyn Skull Taker. He had said nothing and we would wait for his words. The thrall with the ale brought it over and poured some in my horn. That was another effect of the curse that had been laid on the clan, we had fewer bees and there was not enough honey for mead. The ale that came from the barley was not as good as it once had been. Were the gods, rather than Mary's one God, really punishing us?

When Erik Arguer and Harald Broken Nose began to fight, Lodvir banged the pommel of his sword upon the table and shouted, "This is a place for words and not fists. I will come there in a moment Erik and Harald and you shall feel my wrath."

I smiled as the two men obeyed instantly. There were few men who would face Lodvir.

Sweyn Skull Taker stood and nodded, "Thank you, Lodvir the Long. I have heard your words, would you like to hear mine?" There was an almighty cheer. This was the way it normally went at a Thing. Men would talk but it was just so that they could give an opinion. Sweyn Skull Taker was wise as well as being the best warrior in the clan and he had listened to the various arguments. "The shortest voyage is to England. Thorkell the Tall is already there and he occupies most of the warriors of Æthelred." He gestured to me, "My foster son, Sven Saxon Sword, served King Forkbeard when he rescued Prince Cnut's future bride from the Northumbrians along the Humber. I have heard the story from the crew and from Sven. I believe that this river gives us the best chance to raid. We can travel deep within the land, even as far as Jorvik. We can take our drekar and make a longphort where we will. If Thurbrand the Hold tries to fight us we can defend our ships, our treasure and the animals that will feed our people." There was a cheer for the idea appealed. "There is something else. The people of that land

2

had a famine some years ago. Since then they have resown their fields and their crops, according to Aksel the Swede, grow well as do the pigs. The part of Northumbria that we raid has many pigs." There was another cheer. "And if we exhaust the land before we have enough then we can sail north. The Dunum is also a long river and has not been raided for some time."

Sweyn Skull Taker was wise. He had thought all of this out and even had a plan should his first one fail. He was a true leader of men. The hands and dagger hilts that pounded the table told him he had the approval of the clan. We would raid along the Humber and its many tributaries. The rivers of England would be as our roads.

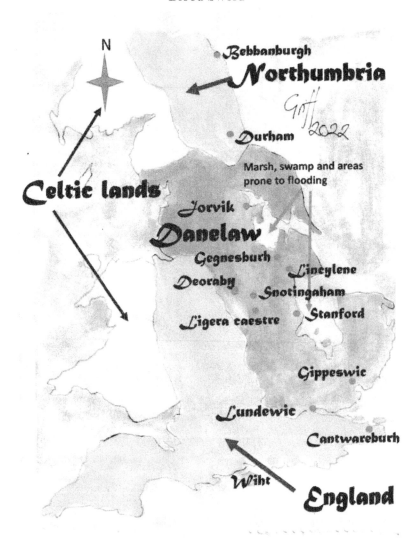

England at the start of the 11ᵗʰ Century

Chapter 1

The days when I was a young warrior relegated to sharing an oar at the prow were long gone. I was a warrior of renown. I had fought in battles and used Oathsword to win great honour for both the clan and for me. Sweyn Skull Taker had me with his sons close to the steering board of our drekar, *'Sea Serpent'*. The three of us were close and we were all different. The three of us had married but our wives were as unique as we were. Frida, Hawk's wife was the daughter of Aksel Østersøen the rich Swedish merchant who had come to Ribe. Sweyn's wife was a contented Danish woman who was happiest on her farmstead with her children while Mary, my wife, well, she was a force to be reckoned with. She was a Christian who tried to convert everyone in our clan. She had succeeded with many, mainly the women, but the men, knowing that their hersir, me, was still a pagan, just humoured her. Hawk did not need to go to war for Frida was Aksel's only child and I knew that he had enjoyed his one moment of glory when he had leapt amongst the Norse at the Battle of Svolder. I was not sure how many more voyages he would have in him. Sweyn was the singer of songs and he enjoyed battle for the chance to immortalise it in words, and me? I knew that my fate was tied up with the sword I had taken in my first battle. The Norns had spun and my destiny was bound not only with the sword but King Forkbeard's second son, Cnut. I knew that no matter what my wife believed or what I hoped, the spinning sisters would decide my future and only a fool fought the fates that were the three sisters.

We had five drekar and four knarr. It meant we had more than two hundred and thirty men. Not all were warriors. Some were going to war for the first time. It had been some years since we had been asked to raid. That had been in Wessex three years ago when we had fought at Sandwic. The three of us who occupied the front oars each had a mail byrnie and a good helmet. Only those before the mastfish were so well armoured. At the prow, the youngsters going to sea for their first raid had a leather byrnie, a spear and an old helmet handed down from some father or grandfather. When we fought it would be those who sat before the mast fish that would be in the front ranks and fight the better warriors. The youngsters would hope to take a sword. The Saxons and the men of Northumbria had good swords. Many of the Northumbrians were descended from Viking raiders and knew how to use their weapons. However, I believed that their blood had been diluted too much by the Saxons, and they had lost that edge their forebears had enjoyed.

Mary had been torn, as I prepared to leave. She knew that we needed the food but thought that we should buy it and could not understand the need to take it. As I pointed out to her, the whole of our land had been blighted by this pestilence and those who lived across the water would charge a king's ransom. Whilst inside I might have agreed with her, I would say nothing for that would have meant going against the clan. To them, those who lived across the sea were sheep to be plundered and shorn whenever we needed. Mary had been one of those sheep and I had taken her as a thrall. Each time we raided the land of her birth then relations between us were strained. My departure was a chilly one although my children were excited for me. Gunhild wished for a present. She might have been brought up a Christian but she would be happy to have something taken on the raid. Steana was desperate to come with me. Fortunately, all the other boys going to sea for the first time were older than he but I knew that the next raid would be a different story. Bersi was too small to even contemplate coming but like his siblings, he wanted a present.

We chanted as we led the line of drekar and knarr westward for the three-day voyage across the sea. Sometimes the winds were against and sometimes they were from the east. The length of the journey might vary from two to six days. It helped the young warriors learn how to row and the familiar songs, sung in the mead hall, helped them. It did not harm to remind them of the great deeds done by the warriors of the clan. Many were still on one of the drekars. Griotard and Lodvir were astern of us in their ship and when our words drifted over to their vessel, I knew that their crew would sing with us.

Sweyn Skull Taker was a great lord
Sailing from Agerhøne with his sons aboard
Sea Serpent sailed and ruled the waves
Taking Franks and Saxons slaves
When King Sweyn took him west
He had with him the men that were best
Griotard the Grim Lodvir the Long
Made the crew whole and strong
From Frankia where the clan took gold
To Wessex where they were strong and bold
The clan obeyed the wishes of the king
But it was of Skull Taker that they sing
With the dragon sword to fight for the clan

6

Blood Sword

All sailed to war, every man
The cunning king who faced our blades
Showed us he was not afraid
Trapped by the sea and by walls of stone
Sweyn Skull Taker fought as if alone
The clan prevailed Skull Taker hit
Saved by the sword which slashed and slit
From Frankia where the clan took gold
To Wessex where they were strong and bold
The clan obeyed the wishes of the king
But it was of Skull Taker that they sing
And when they returned to Agerhøne
The clan was stronger through the wounds they had borne
With higher walls and home much stronger
They are ready to fight for Sweyn Skull Taker
From Frankia where the clan took gold
To Wessex where they were strong and bold
The clan obeyed the wishes of the king
But it was of Skull Taker that they sing

The winds were favourable and we did not have to row for long.
Even so, some of the younger warriors, who had not acquired the
hardened calloused skin of a veteran would need to use a salve or,
perhaps, simply grease.

As we stood by the mast fish drinking ale from the barrel we had
brought, the others asked about the river we would raid. I had been
there a couple of years earlier to rescue the Saxon maid, the daughter of
an important Northumbrian noble, and the future wife of Cnut when she
was of an age. I knew that I had made an enemy of the Northumbrian
who lived there. Thurbrand the Hold had pursued us and almost caught
our knarr. He would remember the Danes who came and stole his prize.
The land he ruled was north of the river and I had advised the jarl to
raid south. That was not because we were afraid of a fight, far from it,
we relished one, but the lands to the south were more fertile. They lay
just north of the Five Boroughs where the first Vikings had set up their
home. They had chosen well for it was a fecund land and flat. We
would see horsemen from far away. Driving animals and boarding them
on knarr was never easy.

Hawk had changed since his marriage and it was no wonder. His
home was palatial and dwarfed his father's, the jarl's. They had servants
as well as thralls. This would be an interesting test for him for despite
his position he had raided less than any of us veterans. I knew that I
would be the one that others looked to. I would have to put my family

from my mind. To do anything less would be fatal. I had learned that Oathsword was not only a weapon that inspired others, but it was also a burden to be carried. I did so willingly. Hawk was the son of the jarl and men would look to him but for different reasons. I hoped he would not falter. When you fought in a shield wall every warrior relied on those around him. I had, before I had been made hersir, also been the hearthweru of the jarl. Sweyn and Hawk still were. They would be the ones who flanked Sweyn Skull Taker. I had my own hearthweru and when I fought, they would be the ones on my flanks. I would not be able to help Hawk.

I knew he was nervous as he stared west and sent questions at me like arrows from a bondi archer. "The men we fight, they are not Saxons?"

I shook my head, "They have Viking blood in them but it has been mixed. Do not underestimate them for it will not be like fighting in Wessex and Thurbrand the Hold has a reputation as a fierce warrior. If he musters all his men then we will have a hard fight."

"But you think that it should be easier south of the river." He sounded almost desperate. I doubted that he would encourage his sons to become warriors. I wondered if that would disappoint my foster father.

"The day it seems easy is the day that you die. cousin. Every time I draw Oathsword and Norse Gutter I know that I am risking my life, we all do. You cannot guarantee that you will survive but, like me, you now have children and your blood will continue through them." I patted my sword, "This sword is like the blood of our people for it sought me out. The Saxon who had it before me had no right to it. It was the gift of a king to a Dane. If I die then the sword should be passed to one of our clan."

Sweyn One Eye asked, "Your sons?"

I shrugged, "Perhaps, Steana will soon begin training as a warrior but the sword will choose." I looked him in the eyes, "I do not intend to die on this raid but I sail knowing I could. There is a world of difference between the two."

Sweyn looked at his younger brother, "You and I guard our father. If you cannot do that, Alf, then this should be your last raid."

He looked from his brother to me, "What will my father say?" His words told me that this would be the last time he came to war with us.

Sweyn shrugged, "I know not but for this raid, you must be hearthweru and that means risking your life for our father's. There is no halfway."

For the rest of the day he was lost in his own thoughts. I took Sweyn to one side, "If you wish a couple of my men to take the place of Hawk…"

"No, Sven, the Norns have spun. Our father is still a mighty warrior. Lodvir and the others will be on the raid. I am not worried but I am a little disappointed. Is this the same youth who took such a prodigious leap into Norse warriors?"

"As you say, the Norns have spun."

Thorstein the Lucky waved me to the steering board. His son Lars was with him learning how to be a helmsman, "The jarl said that you reported the mouth of the river to be as wide as the sea?"

I nodded, "To my mind, it is as wide as the Tamese, if not wider."

"Good, then we can risk it at night. By my estimate, we should see their coast by the middle of tomorrow afternoon. We will step the mast and row inshore. That way we will remain unseen."

Sleep always came easily to me when at sea. It is the motion of the drekar that does it. Some of the new warriors found it hard for the sea could spray up and douse them. Perhaps I had been made to be a sailor or the fact that I slept beneath an oiled cloak that kept me dry. I also managed to sleep after the break for food at noon and when Karl, one of the new ship's boys, came to rouse me I woke refreshed. I drank deeply from the ale barrel knowing that it might be some hours before I would do so again. We all worked together to take down the mast and lay them on the mast fish. It was not a quick task and while we did it we were vulnerable to attack but the seas appeared to be empty and the breeze kept pushing us towards the smudge on the horizon that was England. That done we took our oars and began to row. We would not be able to sing once we entered the estuary but we had another hour or two before then and so Sweyn started a chant of his own creation.

The king gave commands and all obeyed his mighty words
The sword was charged to sail to the east
To rescue the girl that was held by the beast
On a knarr, they crept like hunting birds
Oathsword, the blade of the Danish king
The Saxon sword the skalds all sing
Oathsword born for Sven to swing
Oathsword, death will bring
Along the Hull through darkest night
With Royal prince aboard the knarr
They sought the hall and Thurbrand's lair
With drawn swords they went to fight

Blood Sword

Oathsword, the blade of the Danish king
The Saxon sword the skalds all sing
Oathsword born for Sven to swing
Oathsword, death will bring
Agerhøne sent her bravest men
To help the prince his bride to fetch
And take her from an evil wretch
They crept through the boggy fen
Oathsword, the blade of the Danish king
The Saxon sword the skalds all sing
Oathsword born for Sven to swing
Oathsword, death will bring
The night was rent with cries of pain
Oathsword slew and the guards they died
They sailed to reach the river wide
To reach their Danish home again
Oathsword, the blade of the Danish king
The Saxon sword the skalds all sing
Oathsword born for Sven to swing
Oathsword, death will bring
The red sailed ship brought Saxon swords
Sweyn One Eye loosed his arrows well
Saxons died and in the sea, they fell
Then Sven led the men to climb aboard
Oathsword, the blade of the Danish king
The Saxon sword the skalds all sing
Oathsword born for Sven to swing
Oathsword, death will bring
As the red sailed ship began to sink
Sea Serpent brought hope from the eastern land
Oathsworn warriors, Agerhøne's band
All had been saved from the brink
Oathsword, the blade of the Danish king
The Saxon sword the skalds all sing
Oathsword born for Sven to swing
Oathsword, death will bring

I was embarrassed that the song was about me but I knew it was the right thing to chant for we were aboard *'Sea Serpent'* and sailing the same course. By the time we stopped singing, darkness had fallen and we were entering the vast estuary. Thorstein intended to sail close to the south bank of the river and to that end, the ship's boys clung to the gunwale on the larboard side to peer into the darkness for the signs of shoals or the bank. With a light from our stern, we would lead the other ships of our fleet along the safest route. Thorstein the Lucky was well named and we encountered no obstacle. Half of the rowers rose and went to rest. We now had a familiar routine. We would sail slower but we would still make progress with men always at the oars, taking shifts to keep the ship moving against the current. Sweyn went first and after an hour he returned to relieve me. I drank some ale, ate some food and then lay down to close my eyes. I would not sleep but the hour of rest would help. The ship's boy came to rouse me when the hourglass was turned and I relieved Sweyn.

By dawn, we were fourteen miles upstream and it was time to stop. We had, by Thorstein's reckoning, another twenty odd miles until we reached the place where the Ouse met the Trent. That was where we would raid but as Thorstein had found an empty and desolate section of the river with bogs and mudbanks to guard our larboard side, we halted to sleep properly.

After six hours we were awakened and ate raw, freshly caught fish. Fish from foreign waters might be the same as those we caught at home but they all had a different taste. Refreshed we took to the oars and headed upstream. We could have chanted for the river appeared to be empty but sound travels on such open land and we remained silent. Sweyn Skull Taker prowled the drekar like a wolf seeking sheep. He went to the prow and pulled himself along the figurehead to peer into the distance. When he came back just before dusk with a look of joy on his face, then we knew we had found the mouth of the Trent. We had a rough time as we left one river to find another and the drekar bobbed alarming up and down as the two rivers fought like leviathans. I knew that the knarrs we had brought would be struggling. With fewer rowers and being less streamlined their crews would be exhausted by the time we began raiding. We rowed for two hours up the river and then stopped. The river had narrowed and we could, if we needed, make a longphort to bridge the river giving us access to both banks. This time, when we stopped, my men and I were sent ashore along with another group of scouts sent by Lodvir the Long. Wearing just our leather byrnies and with just our swords we leapt ashore and headed away from the river. Haldir and his scouts went downstream.

We found fields with crops growing. The men who lived here liked to dig ditches to provide drainage. We had been told that the river was prone to flooding and so we followed the ditches. I led and when I smelled woodsmoke I stopped and drew my sword. We were scouts and had to remain hidden but we needed to know what lay close. From what we had heard there were no burhs in this part of the land. They were further south but there would be a thegn who ruled this land and he would have a home that was fortified. We hoped that it would not be close but we had no way of knowing for sure without using our eyes.

I saw the spiral of smoke rising from the dwelling and we headed towards it. The farmer had planted a hedgerow to protect his vegetables from the east wind and we crouched behind it. The farm was not a large one but I saw the barn and heard the sound of animals within. We watched patiently and counted the occupants. There were four women although two looked like young women and one was an old one. There were eight men and as three had thrall collars we deduced that there were just five men whom we would have to battle. The men I had with me could take them but we were not here to raid. We were here to watch. When they returned indoors, we headed back to the river but went back a different way. We saw that they had some cattle in a field. They had a dog to guard them. As we smelled their scent, I knew that the wind was taking our distinctive aroma towards the river.

By the time we reached the drekars, the longphort was almost in position. It would not take much to move one vessel to complete the bridge across the river. I saw Haldir and his men approaching along the riverbank. We reported directly to Sweyn Skull Taker and Lodvir the Long. The other captains were there but they took their orders from their jarl and his right-hand man. Kindling had been placed ready to light a fire for us to use to cook but they awaited our reports.

Pointing to the southeast I said, "A mile or more away is a farm. Five men and three thralls are there. They have cattle and from the noise we heard I am guessing pigs in the barn." It was live pigs we needed. The cattle we would eat for cattle were harder to transport than pigs.

"Good. Now rest. We will send others to take the farm." I waved to Gandálfr to fetch my sleeping furs and war gear from the drekar. I was keen to listen to Haldir.

Haldir had similar findings. "There is a farm a mile and a half away. There are four warriors and a couple of thralls. I heard pigs in their pens."

Lodvir looked at me, "The wind is blowing here from the south and east."

I nodded, "And at the farm also."

"Then light the fires. We shall have hot food."

By nightfall, the two farms had been raided and we had a herd of cattle that would keep us fed. The sight of so many armed warriors, Sweyn and Lodvir sent twenty to each farm, meant that there was no

12

violence and none died. There were curses, of course, that was understandable but the families were brought to our camp and secured. Sweyn did not need them as slaves and they were promised their lives. The pigs were perfect. There were two boars and twelve sows. We had three cattle slaughtered and butchered and the next morning one of the knarr set sail for Agerhøne with the precious pigs aboard as well as the carcasses of some of the cattle. The meat would be salted on the voyage back and we could begin rebuilding our herd of pigs.

We questioned the thralls about this land and learned that a few miles south of us was the village of Skumasþorp. It lay just six miles south of us and we knew we would have to take it before we could continue to raid. On the west side of the river, twenty-five miles away lay the important settlements of Tanshelf and Kirkby. Erik Bloodaxe had ruled there before he was made King of Jorvik. Any military threat to us would come from that direction. We now had a map of the area and the next morning we divided into four columns and headed out. Sweyn Skull Taker chose the hardest target, Skumasþorp, and we ran down the ancient track to the palisaded village. This land had been at peace for five years or more. The Vikings who had settled there and married Saxons had changed since Skuma the Dane had landed there and made it his home.

This would be, we knew, our easiest raid. We had taken the only people who could warn Skumasþorp and when we ran towards the spiky palisade, people were still in the fields or collecting fish from their nets. Sweyn was not one of those leaders who believed a warrior had to scream and shout as he attacked. True, it sometimes terrified an enemy so much that they froze, but we had learned that our appearance in the heart of them could be just as effective. The screams came from the women and girls tending the fishnets when they spied their biggest fear, Vikings. The shouts came from the men in the fields. I followed Hawk and Sweyn One Eye as they tore through the open gates of Skumasþorp. The hersir had managed to don his helmet and was standing with three hearthweru outside his hall when we reached him.

Sweyn Skull Taker sheathed his drawn sword as he shouted, "I am Sweyn Skull Taker and if none fights then all shall live."

The hersir was a grizzled old warrior. In his day he must have been a fierce warrior but, without mail and coif, his paunch and grey hair marked him as well past his prime. He shook his head, "I will not be a thrall."

Sweyn took off his helmet, "And you will not be. We take what we need and leave."

The rest of our men had arrived and it was clear that we outnumbered them. When the hersir and his bodyguards dropped their weapons then we knew we had won. While our men began to gather the animals and food, I went with my foster father and cousins into the hall of the hersir. It was not a large hall. We drank his ale and it was good. We had heard that the river made good beer.

"We did not expect a raid for we are of Viking stock, as you are."

Sweyn nodded, "We have endured two years of disease to our animals and poor crops. You were close."

The hersir nodded. It was clear that he understood our reasons. "You know that Thurbrand the Hold will come to fight you?"

Sweyn nodded, "Of course, you are duty-bound to tell him and he will challenge me for the right to raid."

The hersir, whom we had learned was called Dreng, pointed south, "And the men from the towns to the south will not take kindly either."

The hersir was fishing. He was trying to discover how many men we had and where we were based. Sweyn Skull Taker nodded, "We expect that too. I can see that you were a warrior once." The hersir winced at the insult although I could see that he knew it was true. "You know that a warrior who raids and does not expect to fight will lose."

"Aye, you are right and I can see that you are wise. While Wessex and the south suffer at the hands of Thorkell the Tall we have enjoyed prosperity. King Æthelred has little to do with us." He emptied his horn and then asked, "Will you take all?"

"There will be some food left for you and you have the river and the crops yet to be harvested." He gave a wry smile at the portly leader, "It will be a lean winter but you can learn and prepare to defend what you have."

"And that we will."

As the rest of the warriors headed back to the ships, I was ordered to wait a mile from the settlement. Sure enough, a half dozen warriors left the village and headed along the river. My hearthweru and I waited by a stand of trees and as they approached, their attention on the ground, we stepped out, "And where do you go?"

The six were led by a young warrior who had an ancient helmet, leather byrnie, a badly made shield and a sword. He looked belligerently at me and my handful of men, "Out of the way, spawn of the devil, we have been sent to find your ships."

I laughed and pointed back to Skumasþorp, "Go home, follower of the White Christ. We are warriors of the old ways and if we die with a sword in our hands we go to Valhalla. You will beg for a priest to confess your sins."

14

He suddenly launched himself at me. My shield was around my back but my hands grabbed my sword and dagger in a blur of movement that took even my hearthweru by surprise. His attack was too frenetic and holding my sword and dagger like the cross of the White Christ I blocked his sword and stepped to the side. He tripped and fell. Oathsword pricked the back of his neck as my men laughed at him.

"If you are going to take on a mailed warrior, my friend, then you need far more skill than you have. You will return to your village and not seek to find our ships. I have given you a lesson, learn from it. Now go." He rose to his feet and looked from me to his sword. There was a definite kink in the blade. His fellows were already heading down the trail and he joined them.

"Why did you not draw blood?"

"There was no need, Snorri. Believe me, when the land hereabouts is roused then we will bathe in blood."

We waited an hour and then hurried along the trail. We stopped frequently and we disguised the tracks of the clan. They would discover where we were but the longer it took them then the better for us.

Chapter 2

The first two weeks followed the same pattern. We raided and every four days or so sent a knarr back with animals and the food that could be stored. Our herd of cattle kept us well fed. The first knarr returned after ten days away and we sent another knarr back with animals and food. As we had yet to encounter any warriors Sweyn sent Lodvir to scout upriver towards Tanshelf and Kirkby, while we continued to take all from both sides of the Trent. The longphort was working well as it enabled us to cross the river with ease. This did not feel like war and I felt guilty that we were taking from people who were so similar to us.

It was when Lodvir arrived back within half a day that we knew our peaceful raid had ended.

"Thurbrand the Hold is heading here with a large army. He is on the north bank of the Ouse and he brings ships with him too. His best warriors row and the fyrd march. We will be outnumbered, Jarl Sweyn, for there are more than four hundred men coming and at least half will be our equal as warriors."

With the crews of the two knarr missing and the dozen or so men to guard our camp, we had less than two hundred men. Jarl Skull Taker was not put out by the discrepancy in numbers.

"He will need to cross the river and as there is no bridge then that means it will have to be by warships. We discourage his landing. Lodvir position your drekar at the mouth of the river and light a fire ashore. When he comes then throw on damp leaves to make smoke. We will march towards you when we see the signal."

Some of those who captained and crewed the knarrs were fearful for they were not warriors such as we. They were traders and whilst they could fight to defend their ships from pirates they wore no mail and were unused to standing in the shield wall. Sweyn took them to one side while his hearthweru and I gathered those who were not warriors to tell them what they would do.

"None of you will have to stand in the shield wall." The relief on their faces was almost laughable. You can use bows and send arrows over our wall to thin their numbers. Your ship's boys and those from the drekar will send their stones. Can you do that?"

Rurik nodded, he was the oldest of the men before us, "We can, Sven Saxon Sword, but can you hold these men who have such a fierce reputation? Will the Oathsword be enough?"

I nodded, "The Oathsword is just one weapon we shall use. Remember, the men who will stand before you like a wall of iron fought at Svolder, where failure meant certain death for the waters where we fought were deep. We won and when we fight Thurbrand the Hold we will win too and when he is defeated then we can spend another month gathering the food and animals that will help the clan to prosper."

Ebbe Ruriksson asked, "Have we not enough yet? We have sent three knarr filled with animals and food back already."

Hawk knew trade better than any and it was he who answered, "We were blighted by the twin curse of disease and famine. We need new animals that will be resistant to the disease and we need seeds that have grown well here. When we raided Wessex, we won because they had famine in their land. Since then they have prospered and by taking their seed, we reap the benefit of their hard work."

All knew of his father in law's riches and his words assuaged their fear. We gave them lessons in swordcraft but I knew that if they had to use them then we would have lost. We would win because the best one hundred and fifty warriors would defeat their best warriors. It was as simple as that.

We ate well that night knowing that we might have to go a day or two without hot food if we were stalking the enemy. When that was done, we sharpened swords and cleaned our mail in sacks of sand. I then oiled my mail and my sword. I had once thought it a waste of oil but I had seen the effect it had. Mail stayed stronger and blades sometimes slipped along oiled links. Such narrow margins can save a life. We had let the first two families go a week after they were taken and so we only needed a few men to guard our camp at night. I enjoyed a full night of sleep.

Lodvir had the harder task for he had to keep his ship anchored in a notoriously fast-flowing river and ensure that he had enough men on watch. Had he chosen to then Lodvir could have disputed with Sweyn Skull Taker to lead the clan but Lodvir and his friend Griotard were the most loyal of warriors. Sweyn's position was assured. That he was doing a good job was clear when we saw the black smoke rising to the north. There was neither panic nor rush in our camp for we all knew what we had to do. Those guarding the camp and the longphort helped warriors to don mail and as soon as each band of warriors was ready then they set off north and east. I was proud of my crew of warriors for we were the first to be ready and my men and I stood behind Alf and Sweyn One Eye as the rest formed up behind us. I had my spear, Saxon Slayer, in my hand and my shield was around my back. With

Oathsword and Norse Gutter in my belt, I was prepared for whatever Thurbrand the Hold had to throw at us. I saw Sweyn Skull Taker scowl angrily as some of the other ships' crews still tarried preparing themselves. There had been no panic but I knew that he wished them to be quicker than they were. When they were ready, we set off at a lope. I knew why it was important to get to the river as soon as we could. We had to make it hard for Thurbrand to land his men. The Jarl knew not the numbers we might be facing nor their formation. His orders had been simple. We would form a shield wall with a variation on the Boar's Head formation. His best four bands of warriors, mine was one, would form spikes in our line to strengthen it. The bondi archers and those without mail would be at the rear. It meant our line would be, at most, fifty men long. As such it could be flanked. For that reason he had asked me to be the right flank and, when he landed from his ship, Lodvir the Long would be the left flank's guardian. I confess I was not happy. It was not that I was afraid for myself but for Jarl Sweyn in the centre. His two sons were not enough protection.

I knew without looking that my four hearthweru, Dreng, Snorri, Faramir and Gandálfr were close behind me. They were my oathsworn and, along with Lars and Lief Eriksson, Bodulf Therkilson and Diuri Thorstenson we would ensure that the right held. Oathsword would be needed but not until the shield wall had done its job and broken the attack of the enemy and attack they would. I knew that Thurbrand the Hold would remember me. We had bloodied his nose when we had taken Lady Ælfgifu from his hall and he would not forget. Sweyn Skull Taker would have also angered him by raiding lands that were close to his. He would bring every warrior that he could and he would not care if the fyrd fell. He had a ruthless reputation and a land to hold. With Uhtred the Bold as a rival to the north he could not afford to let us raid the fertile lands to the south of his domain. Our line of running warriors was spread out. Some men were running in mail and they were unused to it while others had not kept themselves fit but so long as the leading fifty reached the river before too many of the enemy had landed then we stood a chance.

The land was flat. It was prone to flooding and that made it a very fertile part of this land. It also helped us to see into the distance and we saw the ships on the river. Our scouting expeditions had shown us where Thurbrand was likely to land and Sweyn Skull Taker had led us there. We were converging on the same spot. Thurbrand's ships were almost identical to ours. They had not stepped their masts and that was how I knew which ship was Lodvir's. His men were rowing to shadow the enemy fleet. He was taking a risk for they could turn at any time and snap back at him but his presence would unnerve them. I could see, for we were close to the front, that we would lose the race. Already one of the ships had lowered its sail and that meant it was ready to land men. Each ship would hold between thirty and fifty men. Even fifty men would not cause a problem, but as we hurried to cover the last half mile I saw another two ships lowering their sails.

Lodvir would not be able to land his men for some time and that meant we would have a weak left flank. I saw sunlight glinting off mail as men poured from the first ship that had landed. They were armed in a similar fashion to us. The first ship would contain the best that Thurbrand the Hold had. It was hard to judge numbers but I estimated that there were forty spears ahead of us. We had another five hundred paces to cover as the first ship left to cross the river. It would ferry the fyrd from the north bank of the Humber. As the second two ships disgorged their men the enemy started to form its shield wall.

"Sven Saxon Sword go to my right!"

Sweyn Skull Taker was already modifying his plan.

"Aye, jarl." Pointing my spear I hurried to overtake Hawk.

"Snorri Pig Snout, take your men and go to the right. Halt when I command!"

"Aye, jarl."

We would have a line of almost twenty men. In the scheme of things, it was not a large number but we were the best that Agerhøne had to offer and we would buy time with our blood until the rest could come to our aid. The Norns had spun and the plan of the jarl was almost in tatters. Instead of a solid line with spikes of warriors and two secure flanks, there would be just a handful and two tiny spikes. *Wyrd*.

Thurbrand's men were doing the same as we and they had a double line of almost a hundred to face us. The last three ships were landing men when my foster father decided that we were close enough. We were one hundred and fifty paces from the river. Our one, slim advantage, would be the bondi archers. The men we saw before us were all armed, as we were with spear and shield. We had more than forty men and boys armed with bows and slings. Until their fyrd was ferried over the river it was we who could unleash a missile storm. The archers and slingers had kept pace with us and would be equal to the number of warriors who faced the enemy.

I stood on the far right of the line. I was the least protected of all our men. The shield on my left arm protected Gandálfr but an enemy could attack my spear arm with impunity. As I locked shields, I glanced behind and saw, to my relief, that the other crews were closing quickly with us and soon I felt the reassuring presence of Olaf Longsword's shield in my back. Like me, he was exposed to an attack from his right but I would not be alone. Our narrower line meant that Hrolfr of Heiða-být would be behind him. Both warriors had fought at Svolder. The three of us knew how to fight.

There were more than one hundred mailed and armed men arrayed in a double line ahead of us. Our line was now thirty men long but until Lodvir arrived the enemy would be able to flank us. I could see their ships at the northern bank and men of their fyrd were boarding. Numbers were impossible to assess but once they had boarded their ships, crossed the wide Humber and landed then we would be seriously outnumbered and it would be we who would endure arrows and stones.

Sweyn Skull Taker was not about to give them that advantage and he shouted, "Archers and slingers, do your worst."

The slingers, including Sweyn One Eye's son, Sweyn Sweynson ran to our front while the archers pulled back on their bows and sent their missiles into the air. The enemy with helmets and mail would not need to fear the arrows. Even if they struck the wounds would be slight. However, like us, less than half of their men had mail and if they held their shields above their heads, which was the sensible thing to do, then they would be exposed to the hail of stones from the slingers. The twenty boys knew this was their chance to impress the jarl and as shields were raised and arrows slammed into them they hurled their stones, some from as close as twenty paces. It was they who hit the first of the enemy and four warriors fell. As some shields were pulled around to protect their front so arrows found shoulders unprotected by metal. More men fell. Our lines cheered and that encouraged the slingers and archers. I was not sure how many men were killed but even a wounded man would be easier to defeat. I saw their leader, he had a red shield with a black wolf upon it, turn and look over his shoulder. He was assessing the likelihood of reinforcements. The ships had left the north bank and were rowing across the river. As the man next to him was felled by a stone that struck his face he weakened and shouted, "Charge!"

It was the wrong decision. I was dispassionate enough and had seen enough battles to know that what he should have done was order a shield wall with shields to the fore and over their heads. We were not fighting men led by Thurbrand the Hold. From what we had been told he was a skilled general who had often fought against that mighty warrior, Uhtred of Bebbanburgh.

Sweyn Skull Taker was not about to risk our archers and boys. He commanded, "Slingers to the rear! Well done! Brace."

I put my right foot behind me and planted Saxon Slayer in the soft earth with the long spearhead facing the enemy. Spears appeared over my right and left shoulder and shields were held up to protect our heads. It felt both comforting and constricting at the same time. Gandálfr and the rest of my men planted their spears in the same fashion as I had. Thurbrand's men raced towards us. The slingers and the archers had thinned their ranks and it was a ragged line that charged toward us. The Norns had been spinning for some of us would have four or five men to fight while others might have none. Arrows still flew over our heads and as the slingers joined them so stones fell. The rattle of stones on shields sounded like a hailstorm. There were enough cries to tell us that some men attacking us had been hit.

I braced myself for the spear that would be thrust at me. I dared not raise my shield until I knew if it was aimed at my head or my middle. My men and I had to fight as one. When I saw the spears that were coming were held overhand then I knew it would be to our faces. While that was a tempting target, for none of us had masks, it was also the easiest one to block.

"Raise!"

We lifted our shields as one and there was a mighty crack as spearheads hit shields protected with metal. Although I did not move it I felt my spear as it sank into the thigh of one of the warriors who had thrust at me. I could not see his face for my shield covered it but as we lowered our shields, I saw him sinking to the ground. I pulled my blood-soaked spear back and knew I had given him a swift death. All along our line lay the enemy dead. Alarmingly, however, our shorter line was already buckling. We needed Lodvir's men on our left and he had yet to land. With our formation, the only way to succeed was to break the line. One way was to use shield jumpers. Hawk had done this at Svolder and now I saw men run at us with shields held aloft. As they neared the line they leapt into the air. The aim was to land on a shield and knock the man down; behind the jumpers came a reformed line led by Wolf Shield. The first man who tried to do so realised his mistake and was speared before he could land. The charging line neared us and allowed me to see the river and their ships. I saw that the first of the fyrd had landed. Wolf Shield's reinforcements were coming to his aid.

I now held Saxon Slayer balanced in my right hand. Soon it would be time for Oathsword but, for the moment, Saxon Slayer was my most potent weapon. As Wolf Shield led his line towards us, I saw that they would strike at Sweyn Skull Taker. The lack of Lodvir's men on our left meant that our line was echeloning back. Inevitably the enemy moved to my left and stretched their right flank. As the enemy line met ours, I shouted, "Thrust!" All around me were my men and as one we stabbed with our stout spears. Mine found a weak byrnie with wide rings of mail and it pierced through to flesh; the man fell. Behind him was a warrior wearing just a leather tunic and I rammed Saxon Slayer into his chest. He had no time to bring his shield around such was my spear and then I was through their line, along with the rest of my men. Raising my spear I shouted, "Attack their flank!"

We were now attacking men whose shields were facing us and not their weapons. Some of my men dropped their spears and drew swords and axes. Lars Larsson's axe smashed down to split the helmet and skull of a surprised warrior. As I saw a warrior raise his shield to protect himself from such a blow, I thrust Saxon Slayer into his side. Dropping my spear I drew my sword, "Oathsword!" As it always did a thrill of power raced through my arm and seemed to imbue my men with more energy and courage. Mary would never understand the joy of battle when weapon and man were as one. We fell upon men attacked on two sides. Our left might have broken but the archers and slingers we had brought were hurting those who stumbled over our fallen.

It was at that moment when I hacked across the neck of a mailed warrior that Lodvir appeared. He had not landed but, instead, was attacking the ships ferrying the fyrd. I heard an enemy voice shout, "Our ships! They are taking our ships!"

Men turned and saw one of their ships in the middle of the river. It had been holed and was sinking. It was only one ship but Lodvir's vessel contained warriors while those he attacked had men who were passengers. The enemy broke and as Wolf Shield was slain by the jarl their line broke and they fled back to their ships.

"After them!" Sweyn One Eye gave the command and we raced and chased after the enemy.

Had they still enjoyed a leader they might have moved back steadily and maintained some sort of defence, but they fled and we were able to strike backs with little protection. A byrnie can stop cuts but an axe or a sword that strikes it can break bones. Worse, for the warriors we attacked, the fyrd who had landed were now racing back to the five ships that lay on the south bank of the Humber. A handful of their mailed warriors chose a brave end. They turned to face us and I admired their courage. They were buying time for their fellows to reach the ships. Such men do not fear death and when I spied a couple of Thor's Hammers about their necks I knew that they would die hard for they were not Christians.

"Line!"

My men fell into formation immediately. With Gandálfr on one side and Faramir on the other, the rest of my men formed a wedge. The enemy warriors were using swords and axes. A spear slows a man down when he runs. Two of them had wounds and knew that they would die but they were determined to take us with them. This time they were not warriors seeking Oathsword, they were warriors intent on a glorious death.

"Fight cold!" My command was for my men. I was always cold when I fought. A hot head is reckless and a reckless man makes mistakes. My men had trained with me and knew how to seek weaknesses in an enemy's defences.

The enemy were the opposite and they rushed at us in a wild, almost berserk attempt to slaughter us. As one, our shields were raised to take the blows and I rammed Oathsword under my shield aiming at the wide rings of the poorly made byrnie. The warrior whose axe came at my head went for the dramatic kill. It was easily blocked and the metal studs on my angled shield prevented it from penetrating too deeply as well as directing it down the face of my shield. My sword slid beneath his shield and up. He wore a byrnie but I kept a sharpened tip on Oathsword and I struck with great force. Lodvir's training regime of carrying logs in my youth had made me as strong as an archer. I tore through the links as though they were not there and my blade slipped through his padded undershirt and ribs into his body. His face adopted a shocked expression as his axe fell to the ground. I twisted as I pulled and he fell to the ground. I looked for another enemy but my wedge had done as I had commanded and fought with cold hearts and blood. Only Faramir had been hurt. A sword had scored a wound on his knee but the brave enemy rearguard lay dead.

Our archers and slingers had joined us at the riverbank and as the five ships tried to slip away arrows and stones took a fearful toll. Some mailed warriors fell into the river. They would sink to the bottom. Lodvir and his men continued to send their arrows at the other side of the ships. By the time they were too far away for our archers, the battle was over. One of Thurbrand's ships was sunk and another had to be beached. We cheered as *'Hyrrokkin'*, Lodvir's ship, rowed back upriver. He cupped his hands and shouted, "I had to make a decision, Jarl. I chose to stop the enemy reinforcing those ashore."

Sweyn nodded and answered, "It was the right one! We will collect the mail and weapons. Bring your ship close to the shore. You can take it back to the camp with the wounded and the mail and weapons."

Those too badly wounded to be healed were given a warrior's death. Every enemy who was wounded was slain but mercifully by having their throats slit. There was not only armour and swords to be collected but many warriors had battle bands around their wrists. Some had silver crosses and many had coins in their purses. We did well.

It was late afternoon when we hurled the last enemy body into the river and headed back to our camp. Lodvir would be back first and tell the guards at our camp that all was well.

Chapter 3

We spent just a day recovering for we now had the opportunity to raid on the north side of the Humber and the west side of the Trent. We landed and then enjoyed five days of plundering farms that had thought themselves safe. We captured another thirty pigs and slaughtered twenty head of cattle. We took treasure from farmhouses and sent the people hence. They would head to their burh where the extra mouths would take much feeding. We had to return after five days for we had no more room on our ships. Such was the plunder we took that all the knarr were sent back to Agerhøne. The jarl allowed us two days of rest and we needed it. Faramir's wound had meant he had been confined to our longphort but he was well on the way to recovery when we joined him in two days of lying in the sun without the need to wear mail. Of course, we still kept sentries out and, on the third day, we heard our horn sound. It was an alarm and meant that warriors were approaching. We all dressed and armed ourselves as quickly as we could. The bondi archers and slingers manned the drekar to guard our flank and escape route while the rest of us formed ranks.

In the distance, we saw horsemen and they were mailed; light glinted from their helmets and spears. The Saxons used such warriors. What we did not see was a long line of men following the sixty or so riders. We did not change our formation of shields and spears but we all relaxed a little. If they charged us, they would pay a high price. Horsemen were useful but only if they were backed by archers and men on foot. We had heard of Norsemen led by Duke Rollo who were mailed and charged shield walls but they used many archers and spearmen to attack at the same time.

"It is Thorkell the Tall."

We all knew Thorkell. He led King Sweyn Forkbeard's men in their raids on Wessex but it was Lodvir's sharp eyes that spotted him. We all lowered our spears and unslung our shields. We were not about to be attacked. He reined in and dismounted next to Jarl Sweyn. We knew his reputation. He led the Jomsvikings and they were a band of Vikings that hired themselves out. King Sweyn paid them well. I had seen Thorkell the Tall before but never this close up. He was a muscled warrior without an ounce of fat upon him. As his name implied, he was tall and that was a double-edged weapon. He would be able to see further but would be an easier target in a battle. His mail was well made and the links so small that the wire to make them must have been wound around

25

the smallest of sticks. His long sword hung from his belt and his scabbard was beautifully decorated. You can tell much about a warrior from the weapons he carries and Thorkell's bespoke a mighty warrior.

"It is good to see you, Thorkell the Tall. Have you come to join us?"

He shook his head and I saw that his face was dark. This was not a social visit, "Come, you and I must speak alone."

Although Sweyn nodded he also waved Lodvir to come with him. I knew why. King Sweyn Forkbeard was a cunning man and Thorkell was as clever. It paid to have witnesses.

I handed Saxon Slayer and my shield to Gandálfr and approached the horsemen who had dismounted. These were Thorkell's hearthweru. Hawk and Sweyn One Eye joined me. I recognised one of the warriors.

"Is that you, Bersi Hrolfsson?"

I had met Bersi at the King's court at Heiða-býr when I had been summoned there to be given my instructions for the rescue of Lady Ælfgifu. He had been a pleasant warrior who chatted about my sword and we had got on.

"Aye, it is Sven Saxon Sword. I see," he waved his hand around the camp, "that you have raided well."

"We have."

He came closer to me, "You should know that King Sweyn Forkbeard is displeased."

Hawk said, "Displeased? We raid the English as does he. What has he to be unhappy about?"

"Aye, but without his permission and you do not raid Wessex. He wishes the support of the Danes in this land and this is Danelaw."

Sweyn One Eye had a sharp mind. "He wishes the throne?"

Bersi put his finger to his lips, "You did not hear that from me but you know, as do I, that Æthelred is a poor apology for a king. If you lived in this land, would you wish him to be your leader?" Bersi was right of course. "The north and the east of this land have many with Norse or Danish blood and it is only the west that needs to be conquered. You have angered those of Danish blood and they have complained to Thorkell. Why should they pay Danegeld while one band attacks them?"

Sweyn One Eye nodded, "And that is why Thorkell is here. He wishes us to cease raiding those who will be his allies when he comes to take this land. Our father is being chastised."

Bersi shook his head, "More likely that he wishes you to join us. Your warriors have a good reputation and Oathsword does not taste defeat. You could come south and we could continue to raid the rich lands of Cent, Mercia and Wessex."

He was looking at me when he spoke. "We came here for animals to help us recover after the pestilence and famine. I have no desire to fight the men of the west."

"Do you not wish honour, Sven Saxon Sword?"

"I never sought notoriety or what you call honour. I am not even sure what honour is. Do you know, Bersi?"

He rubbed his beard, "It is knowing that an enemy will seek you out in battle because of your fame. You should relish that. You cannot be defeated while you wield the sword of Guthrum."

I sighed, "Odin spare me from such delusions." I jabbed a finger at Sweyn, "Much of this is down to you, cousin."

"Me?"

"You are the one who weaves the stories about Oathsword. Now men believe that I cannot be wounded while I use it. What nonsense!"

"I never said that in any of my songs about you."

Bersi said, "Your sword is the talk of our camps, Sven. Men dream of holding such a weapon and as for not being wounded," he shrugged, "I heard it and it made sense. Men weave tales about the sword and they are not all Sweyn One Eye's. I fought alongside you and you never came close to being hurt. It seems to protect others too, Hawk and Sweyn here survived Svolder along with you. When you fight men wish to be as close to you as they can so do not be surprised if they think that the sword stops you from being wounded." He cocked his head to one side, "Have you any wounds, Sven Saxon Sword?"

Sweyn laughed, "Then I must stand closer for I lost an eye."

"An honourable wound, Sweyn and one that might have resulted in death had you not been as close to Sven as you were."

I liked Bersi who was an honest warrior but I knew he was wrong. The sword had nothing magic about it. When Mary and I had read the parchments, it only gave us its history. It had been a gift from one king to another. Alfred was known for his piety and I knew from Mary that the White Christ did not condone killing. Why would a Christian god give a sword such powers? It made no sense to me.

Thorkell and Sweyn Skull Taker spoke at length and when they had done walked towards us. Sweyn did not look happy. "Thorkell here wishes to speak to the warband. Sweyn, Hawk, go and gather them." I turned to follow them but my foster father said, "No, Sven, Thorkell the Tall wishes to speak with you alone. I have said that you will hear his words." He looked at King Forkbeard's general, "And that is all. I must go and speak with Thorstein the Lucky."

Thorkell waved a hand and Bersi scurried off leaving Thorkell and I alone so that he could speak, "You are a great warrior, Sven Saxon Sword, and your weapon is the talk not only in this land but everywhere that Vikings gather. Your rescue of Lady Ælfgifu is a legend in its own right and King Forkbeard and his son sing your praises." I said nothing for whatever I said might be misconstrued. "If you and your sword fought alongside me then we could conquer this land. I have told King Forkbeard that this is a plum that is right for the plucking. Think of the honour of being the sword that takes this land for your king."

"The honour is that you ask me and I am humbled that you think I can do this but if I heard my jarl aright, this is my decision and I believe that my foster father will soon sail home to Agerhøne. I will sail with him. I must, politely, decline your offer."

Shaking his head he said, "Think of the gold you would have and the power. If you help to conquer this land for your king you could choose your own title."

"And that does not interest me. I am a hersir and happy with that. I am sorry."

"I confess that I do not understand you but as you are close to Prince Cnut when he comes to join me perhaps he will persuade you to be part of this venture." I was not sure that Cnut would even think of trying to persuade me but I nodded my head.

Our men had begun to arrive. Some of his hearthweru helped him to stand on a barrel so that all could see him. I moved away from the press at the front and headed to the drekar where Thorstein and Sweyn were talking. I knew that Thorkell would ask. Sweyn said as I neared him, "Well?"

"You knew, Jarl, what my answer would be. I take it he told us to stop raiding?"

He nodded, "King Forkbeard is less than happy with our raid. It seems that our king believes that he can tell men what to do. He is our king and he can ask us but I like not this demanding."

Thorstein said, "But you cannot offend him, Jarl Sweyn, can you? Denmark is a small country and if the king decided to punish us…"

I saw that it did not sit well with my foster father who said nothing. "I think that King Forkbeard has his eyes set upon the crown of this land."

I saw that my words had surprised Thorstein but not Sweyn. Just then Thorkell the Tall began to speak.

"Brave warriors of Ribe and Agerhøne, I have heard of your mighty deeds and I offer you the chance to join me in the west where there will be the opportunity of great glory and riches beyond your wildest dreams. Instead of returning to the east, bring your drekar to the island of Wiht where I am preparing for an offensive against King Æthelred. What say you?"

I smiled for he had expected a cheer to follow his rousing words but, instead, he was met by silence.

"You will not be staying here for the king has ordered Jarl Sweyn Skull Taker to present himself at Heiða-býr." He stared over at us, "This raid is over."

Lodvir the Long had stayed with the others and he shouted, "Aye, Thorkell the Tall, and we are loyal men who will follow our jarl and sail home. We have taken enough and showed those who live in this land that none can stand before us. Find other men to do Forkbeard's bidding we are not his dogs of war."

"He is your king!"

"And I do not remember choosing him. His father, we followed but he was murdered. We obeyed King Forkbeard at Svolder but, as I recall, both you and he were a little late in the attack. It was this band of warriors and the rebel Norse who won the day."

I knew that Lodvir had gone too far, "You should watch your tongue, Lodvir the Long."

Lodvir laughed, "Why, will you challenge me to combat to settle this?"

The silence was eloquent. After he had stepped down from the barrel Thorkell said, "Come, my men, we will leave this hotbed of vipers and traitors and we will do as the king asks."

As he mounted his horse, I saw Bersi look over at me and shrug.

When they had departed Sweyn Skull Taker gathered us together, "We could stay here and disobey King Sweyn but it would gain us little more. We have taken more than enough to feed our people and to restock our herds and flocks. We are all rich men and when our knarr return we will sail home."

Lodvir said, "And some of us will come with you to Heiða-býr."

Sweyn laughed, "I think not, for I do not wish war and you have shown, Lodvir, that while you are a brave warrior you are neither a strategist nor a diplomat. You fight battles you know you can win and this one is unwinnable."

We left the Trent ten days later after slaughtering and salting the cattle. We boiled the bones and took those with us too. When we reached our home we would make a bone fire and use the ash to feed the land. We continued to gather animals and food for there was little point in sailing with empty ships. When we left we were laden and we raised our masts and sails for we needed no secrecy. Our fleet sailed down the river. We had to be careful where we joined the Humber for, until the winter storms and floods came, the sunken ships would be a hazard to shipping. Thurbrand's handful of ships watched us from the Ouse but made no attempt to attack us. They were an escort until we reached the sea. I think they feared we would land close to the River Hull where Thurbrand had one of his halls.

On reaching our home we were greeted like heroes. The animals were evenly distributed although Sweyn, Lodvir, the other hersirs and myself were given a greater share. My people knew that they could rely on me to give the offspring from the extra animals. It was what good leaders did and Mary would not have had it any other way. The beans, grain and salted meat were also distributed and the first two days were so busy that none of us had time to turn. Steana and Bersi stayed close to me. I had brought them, much to Mary's annoyance, gifts: a pair of small daggers taken from two of the men I had killed. They were more like eating knives than lethal weapons but to the daughter of a priest, any weapon was to be abhorred. Gunhild was given a necklace of jet I had found in one of the farms we had raided. The rare stone was much prized and this necklace was beautifully finished and polished. My daughter was delighted. Bringing nothing for Mary pleased her. Whenever I brought her a gift from a raid she was angry as I had broken one of their commandments. It was stolen. I had learned my lesson.

When, eventually, the children went to bed and Mary and I were alone she asked me about the raid. I had learned to clean up the reality so that it was more acceptable to her. It was a difficult task as she could see beneath words and detect inconsistencies. This time, apart from the one battle, we had managed not to slaughter great numbers. I had thought about that on the way back. We had managed to keep a secure camp without any attempts to recover animals. I think that was because we had not come as an avenging angel bringing death and destruction. The people would survive.

She nodded when I had finished, "And it is now over? You need not raid again?"

I was able to answer honestly but it was not the answer she wished, "For my part, I will hang Oathsword over the fire and try to learn to be a farmer but King Forkbeard has summoned the jarl to Heiða-býr. I was asked to present myself at the same time."

When Mary was cross or angry her voice was not raised. She never adopted the shrill shrieks I had heard from other wives. Instead, it became low and threatening, like the growl of a dog about to attack. She did so now, "Are you to be at the beck and call of that foul Forkbeard? Will he use you for his own fell purposes until the end of time?"

I sighed, "For good or ill he is the king and his word is law. He could make life difficult for the clan."

"God should be the only one to make laws."

Shaking my head I said, "And how can that be? No, my sweet, we live in lands ruled by men. Kings are just as varied as men and some are good like Bluetooth was and others, like Æthelred, are not good. King Sweyn Forkbeard is a strong king and that keeps our land safe. Would you have another bring an army to take over Denmark? Your land is suffering Thorkell the Tall's raids because they do not have a strong king. If you lived across the water, would you not wish for a stronger king who could protect his people?"

"I just wish to live in a peaceful land. I would return to my home in Norton in the Dunum. There I was happy." She stared into the fire. "When I read those parchments to your mother there were passages when it spoke of a time in the past when there was peace. When the Romans ruled then there were few raids and a strong wall kept back the pagans and barbarians."

I nodded. I had heard of these Romans and when we had raided in Wessex, we had seen some of the buildings they had built almost a thousand years earlier. They had seemed a powerful people and yet they were now gone. How could that be?

I stood, "Well, my love, we should retire to bed for I have to leave on the morrow with my hearthweru and the jarl. I do not wish to go but the sooner that Sweyn Skull Taker hears the judgement of Forkbeard the better."

She sighed, "I have come to love this land, Sven, but I would be less than truthful if I did not say that my heart dreams of a time when I might return to the river where I was brought up and live in my father's home in Norton. I know that it cannot be but I like not this Danish king and I am sure that his ambition will not end well."

I laughed, "Are you a volva now, that you predict the future?"

I had angered her by calling her, albeit jokingly, a witch. She snorted angrily, "You blaspheme. I try to talk to you and you mock me."

I kissed her, "No, my love, I hear your words and I would not wish you to believe that I do not respect them. I do and I will do all in my power to make you happy."

We rode east to the king's hall. I rode next to the jarl and Sweyn One Eye. Hawk had stayed in Ribe to be close to his wife who was due to have a baby soon. My hearthweru would protect us all. We had a couple of horses with our mail, helmets, shields and spears. King Forkbeard liked to greet warriors dressed for war. I think it made him

31

feel more important. Once we left our lands, we saw the devastation caused by the disease and the poor crops. There were empty farmsteads. Thanks to our coin and raid none had suffered as badly as those just twenty miles from the borders of our lands.

"Why does the king wish to see me, foster father? I know that he is angry with us for raiding and I can see why he has summoned you but he specifically asked for me."

"Aye, and I fear it is the sword. Perhaps that is more of a curse than a blessing."

I smiled at his use of a Christian phrase. We now had many Christians in our lands and they were having an effect on us.

Sweyn One Eye shook his head, "No, father, it is the Norns. They sent the sword to our clan and Sven was chosen to wield it. I confess that when it happened, I thought it was a mistake but the sword has moulded the man and Sven here outshines even Lodvir the Long but I agree that Sven's inclusion will be because of the sword."

I wondered if I should simply throw the sword into a deep patch of water. I could have done so on the way back from the Trent. Even as the thought came into my head, I knew I could not. Sweyn was right and the Norns were spinning. Despite my wife's words, I knew the power that the three sisters had. I could no more throw away the sword than abandon my family.

There were fewer warriors at the king's hall. I knew why. Most of the king's men were fighting with Thorkell the Tall. It meant we had more room in the warrior hall. Karl Three Fingers came to greet us and show us to the hall. He was an old friend of Sweyn's and when he spoke, we listened. He waved away the thralls so that the hall was empty as we laid our blankets on the beds there and then began to don our mail ready to meet the king.

"Sweyn, you need not don your mail. Your travelling clothes will suffice." That was a relief. "I see that you have brought those most loyal to you and so I can speak openly. You have angered the king by raiding without his permission."

I knew my foster father well and recognised the signs of anger. It was the stiffening of the shoulders, the narrowing of the eyes and, like my wife, the growl in his voice, "When did a Dane need permission to go a-Viking?"

Karl shook his head, "Those were different days, Sweyn. We have a king now who believes he has greatness within him. He seeks the crown of England. He rules Norway but that is a piss poor land. England is the rich jewel he wants. I speak honestly to you so that you will heed my words. England is a place filled with treachery. Their king is beset on all sides by enemies. Your raid upset the balance of power. The north and east of the land support King Sweyn and your raid might have driven them to support King Æthelred."

I said, "But it did not, did it, Karl Three Fingers?"

He turned to look at me, "No. Thurbrand is unpredictable and your raid was not as damaging to the people as it might have been."

I nodded, "Then all is well and I cannot see why we are summoned here."

He sighed, "The king wishes to show others that raids like yours will not go unpunished."

"Punished? How will we be punished?"

"Sweyn, I am your friend. I am glad that you did not bring Lodvir here for when you are chastised then you will bow your head and be contrite. That will be an end to it. Had you brought Lodvir then there would have been blood."

"And if that blood was King Sweyn's then that might be a good thing for this land."

Fear filled Karl's face, "No, it would not and you know it. There would be war in Denmark and that would only suit our enemies. Swallow your pride and then return to Ribe. You will not be asked to go to war again."

That surprised us all and Sweyn One Eye asked, "Really?"

Karl Three Fingers said, slowly, "You, Sweyn Skull Taker, have a good reputation amongst all the warriors in this land. King Sweyn knows that and he will not give you the opportunity to gain more honour in battles where he watches from afar. Thorkell the Tall is the tool he uses. If you wish to raid again then choose the Franks or the Frisians."

My foster father was a thoughtful man and I saw him weighing up his choices. He would bow his head.

I turned to Karl, "Then why am I here?"

"Prince Cnut spoke highly of you and you have a sword that inspires me. He will wish you to war for him and it will be in the interests of all if you agree." He looked from me to my foster father. The verbal chastisement might turn into something more draconian if I refused. I saw that clearly. It was why Karl Three Fingers had brought us together before we met the king. I felt sorry for Karl. He was in an impossible situation. He did not want to do what he was doing but he thought of his land and his friends before he thought of himself. He was an old-fashioned warrior with old fashioned values. King Forkbeard was a new reality.

We were summoned to meet with the king at his feasting hall. His eldest son, Harald, was not present but Cnut was and I was given a warm smile when we entered. He had grown since I had last seen him and was now a young man as opposed to the boy I had last seen. Cnut's smile was in direct contrast to the glowering looks we received from the king. There were a handful of other warriors there and from the battle rings they wore and the adornments in their hair and beard were high ranking warriors. I smiled to myself because I knew what my two mentors Lodvir and Griotard thought of such adornments. They despised them and both openly said that a real warrior needed not to show off in such a way. We were plainly dressed in comparison.

The jarl knelt before the king and we all bowed. Karl's words had been a warning and Sweyn was doing his best to play along with the illusion that he was contrite.

"I have come, King Sweyn Forkbeard, King of Denmark and ruler of Norway for I have been told that I have offended you by raiding for animals and food. I did not know that we had to ask permission to do so and I apologise."

It struck the right tone and a half-smile showed the king was in a forgiving mood, "I do not mind you raiding other people but the land across the water pays us Danegeld and I would not jeopardise that payment." That was patently a nonsense for Thorkell the Tall was rumoured to be gathering a fleet further north and that he would be launching another invasion soon. "You are forgiven but from now on ask my permission to raid." With an imperious wave of his hand, my foster father was dismissed. I saw him clench and unclench his fists. He was not happy. "And now let us sit and eat for I am hungry. Sven Saxon Sword, I would have you seated close to me as I have words I need to say to you."

I had a feeling I knew what they were. My hearthweru, my cousin and foster father were all shepherded as far away as it was possible and seated amongst the hersirs. It was a sort of punishment. I saw that I was to be seated next to Cnut. At least I could talk to him without worrying about my choice of words. The warrior to the right of the king looked familiar but I knew I had never met him. Then it came to me, he was related to Thorkell the Tall. They had the same features. The King of Denmark was supposedly a Christian and before we ate a priest stood before us and chanted some Latin while we bowed our heads. I knew the words for Mary used them at our meals and so I knew what to do. It was something called Grace and thanked God for the food he had provided. I knew to say Amen at the end and I saw a nod of approval from the king. It was a simple enough act I had performed and did not mean that I was a Christian.

Cnut was keen to speak to me and he asked about Mary and my children. I told him that they were well. "And you, Prince Cnut, I hope that you have continued your training for war?"

He nodded, "I have and I have used my new skill of reading to find out how other warriors in the past won their battles."

I frowned, "As few men speak of Viking battles then these must be those fought by the Romans." He nodded, "We do not use either the same weapons or types of men as they do. It might be a mistake."

He smiled, "Duke Richard of Normandy is of Norse stock and descended from the mighty warrior Göngu-Hrólfr Rognvaldson. They use horsemen, mailed warriors on foot and archers. I can see how we might do the same."

I was not convinced but before we had the chance to speak any more King Sweyn said, "And I need to thank you, Sven Saxon Sword, for the rescue of the Saxon maid, Ælfgifu. Many detractors call us barbarians but your heroic act showed the world that we are not. I would reward you further for your efforts. Now is not the time but soon I shall give you land."

"I thank the king but I was glad to play a part in rescuing such an innocent child." The words I used came from Mary. She had improved the way I spoke and brought nods from not only the king but his priest and the queen.

"I would like to use you and your sword again." He cut a piece of pork from the leg before us and after placing the meat in his mouth pointed his knife at my foster father. "Many told me to punish Sweyn Skull Taker for his reckless raid but I am a forgiving man."

It was a crude threat and I concentrated on the food on my platter. It was well cooked but it tasted like sawdust for I knew that the king was going to issue a command. That it would come in the form of a request was of little comfort to me.

"Thorkell the Tall will lead a hundred ships to punish the Saxons of Æthelred. I have not forgotten the death of my sister and as King Æthelred has made no attempt to apologise or to do penance for the deed, I am sending my able lieutenant to punish him." He gestured to the warrior to his right, "This is Hemingr his brother. Like you, he is a mighty warrior. With such warriors will we cow these killers and abusers of women."

I could not believe his words. He was trying to make out that we were going to help the Saxons when, in fact, all that we were doing was plundering their lands. I said nothing. "I would have you and your hearthweru sail on his drekar," he smiled, "as a personal favour to me. It will mean that Ribe and Agerhøne need not pay as much tax as I had planned for next year."

This was an alarming turn of events. I had expected a request to which I would have had to accede but this sounded more urgent, "You would have me leave from here?"

"Of course. Hemingr leaves two days from now."

"But the jarl needs me and my hearthweru as an escort."

He laughed, "This is not some wild and backward country but Denmark and we have peace and law and order in the land but if it truly concerns you and is your only objection then I will send Karl Three Fingers and his bodyguards as an escort." He smiled the smile of a wolf about to devour a lamb, "That is your only objection, is it not? You would not refuse a request from your king." I was trapped.

Cnut said, "If Sven is sailing, father, may I go with him?"

The king looked at his son and shrugged, "If you wish then you may but I want you as an observer." He turned his attention back to me and jabbed his eating knife at me, "Sven Saxon Sword, my son must not be risked. We have invested much in him and I would not have my plans thwarted. You will fight but Cnut can stay with the baggage."

Cnut frowned. He did not like it but he nodded, "I will watch and learn, father."

I had not had the opportunity to speak to my foster father before the king and queen retired for the night. We had the problem that others would be in the warrior hall and so I suggest we walk by the quay. That none of them were surprised told me that they had observed the king's gestures and our heads close together. We went to an almost deserted quay. The waterway to the sea was a narrow one and there were no drekar there. The watchman recognised that we came from the feasting hall and moved further down the quay.

"Well, cuz, what did our host want?"

There was no easy way to say it and I told them all bluntly what had been said. Gandálfr and my hearthweru knew what it meant for them. They would not get to say goodbye to their families and we would be going to war again.

The jarl banged his hand against a mooring post so hard that the night watchman jumped. "This is wrong, Sven. You are being used and it is the threat of punishment for our people that makes you accede. It is not right."

I nodded, "I agree and if you can find a way out of this then I will grab it with both hands. Can you?"

He said nothing and we watched the small ships at their moorings as they rose and fell with the incoming tide.

Sweyn One Eye said, "It is the Norns, Sven."

I nodded, "Tell Mary... It matters not for there are no words that will assuage her anger."

Sweyn One Eye said, "I will bear the news and suffer her ire. It is the least I can do for you."

As we headed back to the hall my foster father said, "And make sure you return for if anything were to happen to you then I will not be responsible for my actions. Too many men have died because of this king."

I sighed, "Fear not, for I believe that the sword has another purpose for me. I do not feel that I will die in this raid."

Even as I said it, I clutched the Hammer of Thor. Was I risking the anger of the *wyrd* sisters?

Cent 1010

Chapter 4

Dreng, Snorri, Faramir, Gandálfr and I stood and stamped our feet on the hard-packed soil outside the feasting hall as we waited for Hemingr, our leader. It was cold after the warmth of the warrior hall. The horses we had brought from Agerhøne would be taken back by the jarl. We were given five sorry-looking sumpters for the short ride to the ships.

One of the warriors who were there with us chuckled as he saw our discomfort, "I would get used to waiting, my friend. Our leader is a friend of Eilifr who is the brother of King Forkbeard's son in law, Ulf. They are close. Hemingr might be a mighty warrior but he likes this palace. Me? I want to be across the water raiding the sheep." He tapped his mail, "This hauberk comes as a result of the last raid we made in Wessex." He leaned in, "I think this will be the last raid for I have heard that the king has ordered us to hold the land so that he may land and be crowned king of that isle. Then we shall see riches. We will all be given lands and slaves. We will be the richest warriors in history."

The men with him all cheered his words. It was at the moment that Hemingr and Eilifr came from the hall with the king and the three of them took the cheer to be for them. They beamed and raised their hands in acknowledgement of the accolade. Cnut did not come from the hall but led his horse from the stable to join me. He smiled as he said to me, quietly, "My father does not need to go to war to be cheered by his men eh, Sven?"

I did not disillusion the prince but nodded. Their bodyguards brought their horses and the two warriors mounted. We did so too and Hemingr rode next to me, "You and the son of the king will sail on my ship, *'Firedrake'*. You and your men will need to take an oar. We have no room for passengers." It was to be expected but the way he said it made it sound like an insult.

I did not like his attitude and I decided to let him know my feelings from the start, "As I do not go on this raid of my own volition then I will be more of a prisoner than a passenger, don't you think? And, Hemingr, I know how to row. My men and I have just come back from a raid up two long rivers. You need not worry about me. I know how to bend my back… and to fight."

He laughed but it was a laugh without humour, "I had heard you were a feisty cockerel. Let us see how you do without Agerhøne's noisy birds around you. You and the prince may ride at the rear of the column."

It was an insult and I knew it, "Good, for there I will not have your big head blocking the sun and the air will be fresher."

The cold smile left him and he snarled, "Do not push me, boy."

I tapped my sword, "Any time you wish to test my mettle I am here. I fought at Svolder, did you?"

I knew that he did not and as far as I knew had yet to take part in any major battle. His reputation appeared to come from small raids he had led against Wessex and I knew that they proved nothing. He whipped his horse's head around and headed up the road.

Prince Cnut shook his head as he joined me at the rear, "That was not a good start, Sven."

"I care not, my prince, I like you but I feel your father is using me and making me do that which I would not do if I had a choice. We were chastised for raiding and then ordered to raid. Where is the fairness in that?" I shook my head, "He wants my sword and that is all."

We rode in silence and then he said, "I am promised England when we take it."

I turned to look at him, "But that will be when the king dies, Cnut. He would be king of Denmark and England as well as Lord of Norway. We both know that. The putting on of the English crown is a lifetime away." We rode a little further along the road and then I said, "Is that why you came?"

He nodded, "I want to see the land and the people." I saw that he wore plain clothes and a serviceable cloak; he was not marking himself as a prince of Denmark. His next words told me that it was not just because he had been taught to do so by me but he was under orders. "I am not to be addressed as prince. Hemingr has been told that I am to act as your servant. That is why I did not come from the hall with the others. None shall know that Cnut son of Forkbeard goes to England."

I saw then that his father was wily and had thought all of this out.

There were more than one hundred drekar laying at anchor off the northeast coast of Denmark. We were close enough to the island of Svolder for me to see the top of the mast of the sunken *'Long Serpent'*. The King of Norway's ship had broken up after the battle and part of it rested close to the island with the top of the mast sticking from the water. Soon it would be shifted by a storm but for the moment it was there as a reminder of Forkbeard's ambition.

Thorkell the Tall greeted his brother. I was given a cursory look and when their heads went together and they laughed I knew it was at my expense. This would be a long campaign. I gritted my teeth and hoisted my warbag onto my shoulder. Those like Hemingr and Thorkell who led the raid had their ships at the small quay. The rest were loading their men on the beach. We climbed over the gunwale of the almost new longship. We put our bags at the prow. This would not be like our own ship where the younger warriors would be close to the bows. The sailing master would allocate the oars but as Cnut would not be rowing, I wanted him to make a nest at the prow. I had learned, on my first voyages, how to rig a cloak and use chests and bags to make a place that was dry and sheltered. I was told that we were heading for Sandwic again and that meant sailing down the whole east coast of England. With a fleet our size that would take some time and I wanted a place the six of us could call home.

By the time we had made our home the other rowers had boarded. They had chests and because of our unexpected inclusion, we had none. There were enough crewmen for us to have three men for each oar and so the lack of chests was not a problem. The loading of men from the beaches took time and we did not leave until dawn the next day. With Thorkell leading, our drekar tucked in just to his right. Hemingr's own men took the oars first. It was a clear decision to show the rest of the fleet that his ship was a good one and as Thorkell's drekar headed north, towards the Skagerrak, I saw the fleet begin to spread out behind us. The wind was against us and that meant that when we eventually turned to head south, we would not need to row. Our turn to row came after noon and my men and I were placed in the middle of the drekar. Gandálfr was next to me and we took the oar together.

The song the crew had sung on the first part of the voyage had been a song about Hemingr and we did not know it. They changed the chant and I began to sing as we rowed for it was Sweyn One Eye's song and it was well known. All joined in and it helped us to bond as a crew. That Hemingr did not like it was clear. He was not mentioned and it was a reminder that I had fought at Svolder and he had not.

The king did call and his men they came
Each one a warrior and a Dane
The mighty fleet left our home in the west
To sail to Svolder with the best of the best
Swedes and Norse were gathered as one
To fight King Olaf Tryggvasson
Mighty ships and brave warriors' blades
The memory of Svolder never fades
The Norse abandoned their faithless king
Aboard Long Serpent their swords did bring

The Norse made a bridge of all their ships
Determined that King Sweyn they would eclipse
Brave Jarl Harald and all his crew
Felt the full force of a ship that was new
Mighty ships and brave warriors' blades
The memory of Svolder never fades
None could get close to the Norwegian King
To his perilous crown he did cling
Until Skull Taker and his hearthweru
Attacked the side of the ship that was new
Swooping Hawk leapt through the sky
To land like a warrior born to fly
Mighty ships and brave warriors' blades
The memory of Svolder never fades
With such great deeds the clan would sing
They cleared the drekar next to the king
Facing Olaf were the jarl and Sven
Agerhøne and Oathsword joined again
Mighty ships and brave warriors' blades
The memory of Svolder never fades
The bodyguards of the King of Norway
Fought like wolves in a savage way
It mattered not for the dragon sword won
Stabbing and slaying everyone
The king chose the sea as his way of death
And Long Serpent was his funeral wreath
Mighty ships and brave warriors' blades
The memory of Svolder never fades
Mighty ships and brave warriors' blades
The memory of Svolder never fades

Perhaps our singing annoyed him for, after a shorter stint at the oars than I expected we were relieved. It meant that, as darkness fell, we were able to snuggle into our nest and enjoy the relatively calm waters of the Østersøen. We woke to the choppier waters of the sea we called the Danish Sea. I know that the sailors of England called it the English Sea. Its name mattered not for it was the same unpredictable sea no matter what its name. The wind meant that the sail was hoisted and I saw that Hemingr had paid for a beautiful dragon to be sewn onto it. It must have cost him a lot of gold for there were many colours on it. My men and I stood on the larboard side. We would be passing our home in the afternoon and although it would be a smudge on the eastern horizon we would know and we would ask the gods to watch over it and us as we passed.

It was Thorkell who realised that we were travelling too fast and that we risked losing some of the ships that were already falling back at the rear. He reefed his sail and Hemingr was forced to do the same. It made for a more pleasant motion. At full speed, the new drekar with no weed and a good sail fairly flew across the water and it felt like riding an untamed horse with no saddle. We spent the time talking. Cnut had many questions. I was the one who had been raiding the land of the Angles and Saxons for more than fourteen years and so he picked my brains.

"The warriors we fight are badly led but they have good weapons and if they spent the money they give to us on more mail then, if they had good leaders we might not win as often as we do. Remember Thetford, Cnut; but for your brave ride then things might have gone ill for us. Ulfcetel still leads the East Angles and the men of Essex. If we fight him then they will stand and make it hard for us."

Cnut looked downcast. He remembered the battle where so many had died. "Then it is unlikely that I will gain the throne any time soon."

Gandálfr laughed, but it was in a gentle way, "Cnut, your father is healthy and he is not on this ship about to be in harm's way. I think that the placing of a crown on your head is many years away. Do as we do and enjoy the time that you spend with Sven Saxon Sword and Oathsword. I relish the fights to come for I know that Oathsword is a special weapon and its connection to two great kings, one Saxon and one Danish still sends shivers down my side."

I counselled caution, "If we fight Ulfcetel, Gandálfr, then it will be a bloody sword and by the end of the battle will be little more than an iron bar."

Faramir shook his head, "If I wielded the sword then I would be more positive about the outcome, hersir."

"But the Norns did not choose you did they, Faramir? It came to me and since that day my life has not been my own." I turned to Cnut, "And it seems to me, Cnut, that it also tied me to you. My cousin Sweyn was with me the day that I found the sword yet he is not here and he will not have to battle with Ulfcetel but you are. You seem to wish to grab the crown of England, for my part I hope you do not for I can see that I will have to be with you."

"And that is not a good thing?"

"For you, aye, for my family and for me? No. Yet I can do little about it. The three sisters have spun their spell and I am trapped in their web."

43

"I am a Christian and do not believe in these Norns."

My men and I clutched our hammers and I shook my head, "It matters not that you do not believe in them for they are real and there are too many strange things that have happened to me for me to believe other. Now, rest. This voyage will be the only time we will have to do so. Once we land then we march and when you march and fight then there is never enough time to sleep and remember, Cnut, if you are to play the part of our servant you shall not be riding a horse like Thorkell and Hemingr. We will be laden like ponies."

I could see that the youth had not thought of that.

Although the winds stayed with us it was a blustery and showery wind. Our shelter kept us dry although each time we stepped from its shelter for food or ale we came back to our haven, damp. It was not an auspicious start to the raid. We slowed down even more as we neared the Tamese and its estuary. I had learned that we would not sail to Wiht as we had before but land at Sandwic. We had raided there once before and the ports of Meregate, Remisgat and Sandwic would not stand against us. With more than one hundred drekar we could field more than two and a half thousand men. The locals would flee.

When we landed at the ports it was as though we had found a ghost town. The ships at all three ports had fled taking with them as many of their people as they could carry. The rest headed towards the nearest burh, Cantwareburh. Thorkell the Tall had thought all through and we spent just one day collecting horses for our scouts and our leaders then we marched towards Cantwareburh. Some said it was the holiest place this side of Rome and Jerusalem. Certainly, Mary revered the cathedral and its history. It was where Christianity had landed and what we were about to do would have appalled her.

We had landed in the middle of Heyannir and the days were so long that the night was measured in a handful of hours. The fleeing men of Sandwic had warned the city and we were greeted by churchmen who had three thousand pounds in gold for us. They were buying their safety before we could harm them. All we had to do was to promise not to sack Cent. Thorkell took the money but I was not sure that it had bought anything for Cantwareburh but a stay of execution.

We then headed west towards Wiht. For me, this was a familiar country. The burhs we had taken the first time had barely repaired their defences and the sight of such an enormous army made our victory easy. Most places barely put up a fight and we looted their treasure and took their animals. Oathsword was not even needed and Saxon Slayer tasted no blood. I wondered at the strategy. If Thorkell wished to show that he could take the land then we should have moved against Ulfcetel.

He was the only leader we feared. The other important Saxon was Eadric Streona but he kept to the west. He had ordered the building of a fleet of one hundred ships. A measure of his efforts was that the English fleet was closer to Wales than to Wiht. Our own fleet followed us to the island and we made a huge camp there. King Æthelred had abandoned Wintan-Caestre but it was still defended. When we headed north again, in the autumn, we simply skirted it and headed for Readingas and Oxenford.

As we marched north Cnut said, "My father is still bitter about the massacre of Danes. My aunt's death still rankles."

Snorri said, "But we sacked it once."

I nodded, "And I fear that we will sack it again."

As we left another burning town and unburied bodies, I wondered why King Sweyn Forkbeard had felt the need to include me with this army. It was clearly unnecessary. I had slain but two warriors and I had only used my spear. As we headed back to Cent our scouts reported that an army was waiting for us close to Lundenwic. Thorkell the Tall picked his battles and we avoided the waiting Saxons and headed back to Sandwic where our ships were moored. I wondered if the raid was over and we might sail home. My hopes were dashed when the fleet was beached and the older ships had their hulls cleaned while those that had been damaged were repaired. Thorkell and his brother took over the largest hall in the town and kept the gold we had captured there. The hall was ringed by their men. We found a small, some might say mean house on the outskirts of the port. It suited us and we resigned ourselves to winter there. Many of the people had returned to their homes and warily continued their fishing and their lives. They were relieved to be unharmed by us.

Our decision to live apart from the main army proved to be a wise one. More than two thousand warriors with little to do but drink and gamble is a recipe for violence. Some men seemed unable to hold their drink. We only needed to go into the centre once a week to collect supplies and it was while we were there that we learned of a drunken fight that had led to deaths. That neither Thorkell nor his brother had stopped it showed, to me at any rate, that he was not as good a leader as he thought he was. We learned of the fight from Galmr Galmrsson, the captain of a drekar with more than thirty-two oars a side. *'Odin's Breath'* was a well-made ship but she was no longer young. One of his men had been killed in the fight. We had marched with Galmr and his crew when we had raided and we had found that we had much in common. His clan were not rich and the raids were seen as a way to enrich their families.

45

"Hrolfr was a stupid man who could not hold his drink. He also gambled and his decisions were not wise ones. He lost money and then objected. He claimed he was cheated. As another three felt the same way it might have been true. A warrior called Thrum ran the game and he has a band of men who follow him. They beat the four to death, first with their fists and then with staves of wood. I know not about you, Sven Saxon Sword, but I have enough treasure to take back to my home. I like this not."

"I agree, Galmr, but we are bound, for good or evil, to stay with this fleet. We cannot leave."

"Aye." He smiled, "You and your men are more than welcome to join my camp. Now that Hrolfr is gone the dark heart is gone and the wood is good."

"I thank you for your offer, Galmr, but we enjoy the peace and solitude of our little home, but when we march, if you would allow it, we will march with you."

He beamed, "And we would be honoured. My men are in awe of your sword. You have a reputation and it seems to me that it is well deserved."

The fight had an effect on Cnut. When we spoke, he told me how he would organise his men. "They need rules, Sven, you have them as does Sweyn Skull Taker. We will never win over this island so long as they think us barbarians. This petty raiding does little to win the land for us. The gold we were paid is not enough. We must bring them to battle and sooner rather than later."

He brooded about the way the raid was going and at the end of Mörsugur, he asked us to escort him to see Thorkell the Tall. As we entered the hall, I saw why Thorkell had not interfered. His men were as drunk as the ones we had passed in the streets of Sandwic. He and Hemingr were relatively sober but the only other ones who were not drunk were the men guarding the king's gold.

"Ah, Prince Cnut, how goes it in your monastery?"

I knew that many of the others mocked us for we appeared to them like monks. We did not abuse any of the local women as the majority of men did and we did not drink to excess. None of us enjoyed gambling and our only recreation was the game we played with carved pieces of bone. We called it stone war and we learned it from Cnut who had learned of it from a Rus Viking who had returned from Miklagård where he had served the Emperor there. He called it *chatrang* but as we could not get our tongues around that we made up the name stone war. I enjoyed playing the game as did the others. The months we had spent in

Sandwic had seen us become almost addicted to it. I could see why Thorkell thought of us as monks.

Cnut was smooth and he merely smiled, "Perhaps being in a monastery is not a bad thing, Thorkell the Tall, for it brings us closer to God."

Thorkell knew that only Cnut, of the six of us, was Christian and his wry smile was clear evidence of that. "So what brings you here, my prince?" His voice was heavy with sarcasm.

"I wondered when you planned on bringing the English to battle."

"They will not fight us and flee and besides it is winter."

"And since when has winter stopped us from fighting? Besides they will not expect it. Ulfcetel will fight us. He never shirks from war and Danish blood runs in his veins."

He sighed, "When spring comes, we will raid but I do not see the point of poking Ulfcetel with a stick."

Cnut then said something that showed me how much he had grown, "Are you afraid of him, Thorkell the Tall?"

The Jomsviking stood and said, "No man accuses me of cowardice."

I held my hand lightly on the pommel of Oathsword and said, quietly, "Lord Thorkell, Prince Cnut is young but he is of royal blood. May I ask you why you do not fight Ulfcetel?"

I was teaching Cnut how to speak to men like Thorkell. I had asked almost the same thing but in a different way. Thorkell backed down. I do not think he was afraid of me but my use of the royal connection must have had an effect.

"We may well fight Ulfcetel but our aim is to get as much gold as we can from this land. When we have impoverished them then your father will have an easier task ahead of him. I thank you, Prince Cnut, for your suggestion and I will give it some thought."

When we reached our home I said, "Thorkell is a dangerous man, Prince Cnut. Be careful. What would we do if he decided to claim the throne of England?"

"He would not dare do that."

"And what is to stop him? How many ships remain in Denmark with your father? How many men are there left to come here and, if Thorkell took the crown, wrest it from him?"

My words had an effect. Cnut stared into the fire and then said, "Let us play stone war. It helps me to think."

Chapter 5

I know not if it was Cnut's words or had always been planned by Thorkell the Tall, but in spring we left Sandwic and marched north. The men of Lundenwic and the valley of the Tamese thought we were heading for them. They did not raise the fyrd but manned their walls and barred their bridge to us. We headed upstream and crossed the Tamese well to the west of Lundenwic. We headed through Essex towards Gippeswic. The port had not been raided for many years and when we neared it, they manned their walls. I think that Cnut's words had stung Thorkell into action for he decided to attack the wooden walls but he also chose to punish Cnut for he had me lead one of the warbands assaulting the walls. We had marched north with Galmr and Thorkell followed me with the rest of his men. If he thought it would create a bad feeling then he was wrong. I was not afraid of the task and both Galmr and I knew that being the first into the town would give us the greatest treasure. I think it was Cnut who was the most affected by the decision. He saw that Thorkell was punishing him for his accusation. Cnut could do nothing and would have to watch us as we charged the walls.

They knew we were coming and were prepared. The walls bristled with weapons and when we saw, in the morning light, that some of those on the walls had neither helmet nor spear then we knew that they had used every man and youth that they could. In an attack like this, you worry only about your own part in the attack and we had been given one of the smaller gates. None of my hearthweru used axes and I had to rely on three of Galmr's crew who were axemen. Every leader had his own method of attack and as we stood awaiting the horn to launch ours, I spoke to Galmr's crew. "We do not run for that could result in a fall and if one falls then so will others. We may not be the first to reach the wooden wall of Gippeswic but we will all arrive together and it is our numbers that will win the day." I saw nods of approval from some of the older men in the crew. "We will march in a wedge. I have the best mail, shield and helmet and my shield will be at the fore. We will march and chant." I smiled, "In my experience, it helps to keep the beat. If there are obstacles before us then I will halt the wedge and my men and I will clear them."

One of the younger warriors, Eirik, asked, "The wielder of Oathsword will clear a ditch?"

I laughed, "Aye, for I do not wish to be impaled by a stake. The axemen will be protected by the tallest warriors as they hack at the gate. The defenders will drop rocks to try to deflect us from our task but as I have seen no smoke, I do not think they have heated water or oil." Some of the younger ones had not thought of that and hands went to either hammers or crosses. "Once inside we stay together and seek the richest looking house or warehouse. We will reap the reward for our courage. Now form up."

I held Saxon Slayer and felt Gandálfr and Faramir push into my back. One of the axemen was behind them and my other two hearthweru guarded him. His shield covered Gandálfr and Faramir as well as giving me some protection. The padded head protector I wore beneath my helmet was well made. Mary had knitted the outer and then packed it with cured sheep's wool. It might be the difference between life and death if they dropped rocks upon us. Four hundred men had been chosen to make the initial attack and Thorkell kept the rest ready to follow up when we made our breakthrough. The horn sounded and I began the chant as we moved steadily forward.

Bluetooth was a warrior strong
He used a spear stout and strong
Fighting Franks and slaying Norse
He steered the ship on a deadly course
Njörðr, Njörðr, push the dragon
Njörðr, Njörðr, push the dragon
The spear was sharp and the Norse did die
Through the air did Valkyries fly
A day of death and a day of blood
The warriors died as warriors should
Njörðr, Njörðr, push the dragon
Njörðr, Njörðr, push the dragon
When home they came with byrnies red
They toasted well our Danish dead
They sang their songs of warriors slain
And in that song, they lived again
Njörðr, Njörðr, push the dragon
Njörðr, Njörðr, push the dragon

We appeared to be the slow ones for most of the other warriors ran towards the walls, screaming war cries and threats. I knew that Thorkell would make some disparaging comment to Cnut about our lack of courage but I cared not. I knew what we were doing. My plan was vindicated when the warriors next to us were brought up short by a number of things. The warrior who had raced ahead of his comrades was not mailed and the arrows that slammed into him brought him down. His falling body brought down another three men and, encouraged by their success, those on the walls of Gippeswic sent arrows and stones at the men. Others tripped and fell allowing us to overtake them. That is not to say that we were immune from the missiles although the disaster to the crew next to us did draw the majority of the missiles towards them. An arrow smacked into my shield but the metal pieces embedded there prevented its sinking into the wood. More alarmingly were the two stones that pinged off my helmet. My eyes were looking down and the top of my helmet was the strongest part. Even so, the blows made the metal ring.

Gandálfr said, "They must be Christians and are trying to make your helmet sound like a bell, hersir!"

The axeman behind him, Haldir, said, "Then I will make a prettier tune on their skulls when we have taken their gate."

To my relief, there was no ditch. There might have been at one time but new buildings had sprung up and the ditch had been filled with rubbish. The cacophony of arrows and stones from slingshots increased as we neared the gate but we now had a good rhythm and we reached the weathered wood intact. I held my shield above my head and my hearthweru did the same. Haldir was a short stocky man and he used the space created by Gandálfr and Faramir to allow him a swing at the gap between the two gates. He was a skilled axeman and the blade barely shaved the wood of the gate. It made a dull sound when it hit the bar that held the gates. He took eight blows and then stepped back to allow a fresher blade and warrior to take over. He knelt and used a whetstone to put an edge back on the axe. Stones were dropped from above but we were beneath the lintel of the gate and had angled shields. That combination meant the stones did little damage. A skilled axeman is a wonder to behold. He can use his weapon, apparently so cumbersome, with the deftness of a lady sewing a kyrtle It was the third axeman, Siggi, who cracked his axe through the bar. I was close enough to see the effect of his strokes and I said, as he raised his axe for the final strike, "Ready! Push!" As he hacked down, we put our mailed weight against the gate and it sprang open.

There were men waiting for us but they were met by Sven Saxon Sword and his hearthweru. It was an unequal battle for we were all mailed and five ran as one. With Saxon Slayer held close to my shield we ran, like a human spear, at the centre of their line. Often success in battle comes from knowing that you might be hurt, even killed, but carrying on anyway. The five of us were outnumbered but with heads peering over shields we must have appeared as something inhuman to the men of Gippeswic who awaited us. As I pulled back my arm to drive Saxon Slayer into the middle of the mailed man whom I had chosen to strike, I knew that his spear would come for me. I had seen that he held his spear over his shield and the blow would come for my head. I lowered my head a little to protect my eyes with the reinforced brim of my helmet. The top of my helmet was rounded and polished and, as Saxon Slayer punched into the warrior's shield, his spearhead screeched and scratched off my helmet. It did not slow me down much and the weight of our mail and bodies, allied to my powerful spear thrust knocked him not only backwards but also from his feet and he lay on the ground unable to rise. I gave him a quick death and Saxon Slayer drove into his throat. Their thin line broken, the gate's defenders lay dead or dying. As I withdrew Saxon Slayer I glanced over my shoulder and saw the reserves pouring through the shattered gates. The men on the walls were now impotent and they raced to get to their homes and their families. They would have to pass through our army and they would die. The town was ours. We spread out to clear the square behind the gate of any enemies and it was eerily empty. More of the men who had been waiting for us to clear the gates poured past cheering and shouting my name. They would clear the rest of the town and get to the ships and warehouses that lay by the water.

Gandálfr pointed to a large two-storied building with a long low building attached to it, "Hersir, that looks a likely target."

Nodding I pointed my spear and shouted, "Galmr, the hall!"

We ran towards what was clearly the home of a rich merchant. Aksel the Swede had a similar one and I knew that the building attached to the hall would be filled with goods and treasure. Gandálfr and I burst through the door as though it was parchment. The two surprised guards lay spreadeagled on the ground. They had made the mistake of standing too close to it.

Pointing Saxon Slayer at the throat of one I said, "Keep your hands from your weapons and you shall live."

He nodded but the other tried to draw his sword. Gandálfr skewered him like a stranded fish. I heard a scream and saw the merchant's wife, at least I assumed it was his wife, as she cowered behind her husband. He shook his head and spoke to me in Danish, "Do not harm us. We would have our lives."

Nodding I lay my shield and spear down and took off my helmet, "Faramir and Snorri secure the rear gate." I knew there had to be a second way into and out of the building and I wanted whatever was in the hall and warehouse for us.

After securing the thralls and the merchant's family our men searched the house. I went with Galmr and my hearthweru to search the other buildings and we found, in the warehouse, vast quantities of pottery. The Frisians who had settled there more than two hundred years earlier made fine pottery and one of the other buildings contained the workshop that made the pots. As Galmr and I wandered around the huge warehouse we discussed our find. "It is not like the mint we have captured." King Edgar had set up a mint in the town forty years earlier and was the main reason for its choice by Thorkell. "It is not as if we can carry it away with us. By its very nature, it is fragile. Perhaps we should destroy it."

Galmr sounded disappointed but my mind was working out a way to make coin from this find. "Do not be so hasty. We will be spending at least a week here. Who knows what may come our way? We will eat well and in comfort." I knew that warriors such as we appreciated food and shelter almost as much as gold. Of course, the warriors who preferred drink and women sought those out and those first days were filled with the screams of women and the drunken laughter of warriors. We were restrained and the merchant and his wife began to appreciate that life could have been worse for we treated them well and allowed them to use one of their rooms where they felt safe.

Cnut joined us that first day and he was appalled about the excesses of many of the men, "How can my father expect to rule this land when they see us as barbarians and abusers of women?"

"And now you may see why I did not wish to come. This is a time for you to learn, Cnut. Use it wisely."

Neither Thorkell nor his brother came to thank me for gaining entry into the town. Our assault had been the only successful one and the other men sent to take the gates now lay dead. Had we not managed to break the gate then it would have taken much longer and we would have lost far more than the thirty men we did lose.

Most of the ships that had been in the harbour had fled at our approach and when Galmr, Cnut and I went with my hearthweru to see what we might salvage from the boats that remained we found only a few snekke and small ships that would not serve our purpose. We were about to leave when Snorri spotted a sail in the distance, "That is a knarr, hersir and she looks to be heading here."

Galmr snorted, "Then the captain is a fool. He will lose his cargo."

"Perhaps not. Let us wait. Who knows, we may be able to reap some benefit from this?"

When it was half a mile from shore Snorri said, "I recognise her, hersir, it is one of Aksel the Swede's traders, *'Lady Anya'*."

Were the Norns spinning?

There were a dozen guards left by Thorkell to watch the quay and they began to nock arrows. "Hold, this is a friend."

One of the men snorted, "And who are you to command us?"

"I am Sven Saxon Sword and you will heed my words."

The other recognised my name and one pulled back his friend's arm, "Aed, this warrior wields the Saxon sword of King Guthrum. He may look young but he has a fierce reputation."

The warrior stepped back and bowed his head, "No offence meant, my lord, I was just obeying orders."

I saw Cnut smile and he said, quietly, "I can see how having an ally like you, Sven Saxon Sword, might be a wise choice when I seek to better myself."

The Norns were spinning. The captain of the knarr was another Swede, Ulf, and he wisely kept his ship forty paces from the quay choosing not to land until he understood the situation. I was not wearing a helmet and I shouted, "Ulf, it is I, Sven Saxon Sword. What brings you here?"

He cupped his hands and shouted, "We hoped for a cargo but I can see it was a wasted journey."

"Not so. We have a cargo of pottery. It belongs to Galmr and me. Would you take it back to Aksel and ask him to sell it for us? He can have a quarter of its value."

Aksel chose his men well and Ulf made a quick decision. He realised that what could have been a wasted voyage might now prove to be a good one. We were just as quick and before Thorkell could get to hear of it we had our men bring the chests of pots and load them aboard the knarr. By noon she was heading east and Galmr was happy that when the war was over, he would have money waiting for him at Ribe. We trusted each other for we were now shield brothers and such ties last a lifetime.

The one who was less pleased was Thorkell the Tall. I was summoned two days later to the hall he had commandeered. "Why did you send back plunder we had taken? It was not yours."

I nodded, "I believe that when we raid, we take for ourselves that which we win. The men Galmr and I led took the risks and won the gate. Would you have been able to send the pottery safely home?"

I had him there and his face told me so.

"However, if that is the rule then, from now on we will surrender all our plunder to you and I will watch to see that others do the same. Is that satisfactory?"

His eyes narrowed, "You are a clever young warrior. Some say, too clever. I will watch you, Sven Saxon Sword, for I do not like clever young warriors who use their tongues like snakes."

"Good, for you can never have too many men watching a warrior who is always placed in danger."

It was all nonsense of course. Every warrior had taken from the men we had slain and the houses we had occupied. It was not in our nature to share. I also knew that the bulk of the coins we had taken from the English mint would find their way into Thorkell's purse. When we raided with Sweyn Skull Taker then we did share everything equally but that was understood before we raided because we raided as a clan. This was different, here we obeyed the commands of a king.

The mail we had taken was given to the warriors in Galmr's band who did not own a byrnie. My hearthweru all had the best of byrnies, helmets, shields and weapons. We even found a couple of good swords. Since Oathsworn had chosen me every warrior hoped that the sword he took from a dead enemy would be another such sword. We sharpened our weapons and we repaired the byrnies and shields that had been damaged and, a week after we had taken the port, we set off to continue our raid but we had travelled barely twenty miles when our scouts reported that there was an army heading for us. Ominously it was led by Ulfcetel Snillingr whom we had last fought six years ago. When we had fought him then, he had almost won. That the army approaching meant business became clear when we learned that King Æthelred's son in law, Æthelstan, was with the army as was Oswy the son in law of Eorledman Byrhtnoth the hero of the Battle of Maldon. They had raised the Cambridge fyrd and brought many warriors from the north, west and east. We marched towards them but I knew that the wily general would have already chosen his battlefield. He would use every advantage he had.

Thorkell was no coward and he was a good general so we marched quickly to meet the English. It was one thing to let them pick their ground but quite another to give them enough time to make it better for themselves. I knew where Ulfcetel would choose. It would be the place he so nearly defeated us before, at Thetford, or as close to it as possible for that was close to the land he ruled. It was as we headed north to meet them that we had desertions. There were few but it was a lesson to Thorkell and, when we were just twenty miles from Thetford and had made a defensive camp, I was invited with other leaders to meet with him.

Cnut stood at my side and Galmr at the other. Eilifr and Hemingr flanked Thorkell. There were about twenty or thirty hersirs gathered. During the last months, I had come to know them. There were some, like Galmr, that I liked but there were at least eight whom I thought to be nithings and when we stood the two groups were apart. I think that Thorkell recognised the division for he organised his battle lines with that division in mind.

"We face our old enemy, Ulfcetel, and this time he brings nobility with him." He grinned, "There will be rich pickings when this is over. We face the East Anglian Fyrd and the Men of Cambridge."

"How many?" It was one of the nithings who spoke.

Thorkell frowned, "Does it matter? We are better warriors and we are Danish. Would you show fear when the son of King Sweyn is present?" All pretence at disguising Cnut's identity was gone although, to be truthful, we had not made much of an effort in that regard. His dress, his manners, and the fact that he had not drawn a sword nor done much of anything identified him as someone who was different.

"My brother and I will hold the centre with the crews of the ships I brought. Eilifr, you will lead the left with these hersirs." He pointed to the nithings. "The right, Sven Saxon Sword, will be under your control." He was standing at a table and he leaned forward putting both hands upon it. "This will be a bloody battle. I am trusting Eilifr and Sven to hold the flanks. I will bring Ulfcetel to battle. None will leave the field of battle. We either win or we leave our bones to bleach here in this land. Is that clear?"

His brother and Eilifr took out their daggers and began to bang the pommels on the table, "Thorkell! Thorkell! Thorkell!" We all took up the chant but I was not sure how much belief was in the words.

Chapter 6

The Battle of Hringmaraheiðr 1010

This was a flat land but Ulfcetel had managed to find, some four miles south of Thetford, a copsed piece of high ground. The handful of trees was hardly worthy of the word 'cover' and the elevation was little enough but he would have an advantage and as we approached, I saw that he outnumbered us by some margin. However, the advantage was in numbers rather than quality. I shuffled the men of the right flank into three lines. I put the slingers and archers before us and then I turned to view the enemy. There was a sprinkling of warriors. The Saxon housecarls and the Viking warriors were spread out along their lines, no doubt to stiffen the resolve of the fyrd. I saw their banners too. The army was divided into two. One half was commanded by the king's son in law, Æthelstan. I saw the Wessex standard and they were opposite us. The men of Cambridge stood with their royal leader. On the other flank was the standard of Essex; that would be Byrhtnoth's men led by his son in law. I wondered at that for Ulfcetel, who was in the centre, only had his hearthweru with him. It looked like a continuous line but I knew that the two groups would close ranks once danger approached and that might just leave Ulfcetel isolated. The majority of men who faced us had no mail. They each had a shield although some looked to be simply crudely nailed planks of wood with a slight curve to them. They held spears and pole weapons. I did not underestimate the pole weapons. A billhook was a savage weapon and could be more effective than a spear when lines locked. I looked at the men I would lead. Galmr's men were all warriors as were the other crews with us. Thanks to our success more than half were now mailed and all had a shield, helmet, spear and either a sword or an axe. The ones with the least protection were the slingers and the archers. I would order them behind our third rank once the enemy advanced.

Cnut leaned into me and said, "Will they not simply stand there and wait for us to charge?"

"That could be their plan but it is the fyrd we face. They like to run. Sometimes it is away from a battle but at other times, if they are tempted then they can run to danger. The slight slope they enjoy might encourage them to run and once they start they will not stop. If we stand and are silent then they may take that as a sign of weakness. We are in the hands of two men, Thorkell the Tall and Ulfcetel Snillingr. It is a battle between them as to who charges and who stands." I nodded towards the rear. "Now go and stand behind the last line and find yourself a pony. If this does not go then get yourself back to the drekar."

"You think that we might lose and you may die?"

"I am saying that this will be a hard-fought battle and any warrior who goes into battle thinking that he will survive is doomed to die. I hope not to die for I would watch my children grow but I know that the Norns are spinning and the day could go either way. The king charged me with your protection and I cannot fight a battle and watch out for you. Do as I command."

He nodded, "I will go and find a pony but then I will kneel and pray that we will win."

I pointed to the English priests who were blessing the enemy ranks, "Just as they do. Sometimes, Cnut, it is like the game of Hnefatafl that we play. One piece can cancel out another and in the end, it comes down to how hard the men who are fighting wish to win. If I was fighting for the opposition then I would be fighting for my home and I would happily give my life to save my family. We fight for treasure and for a king who is across the sea." Once again my words had an effect. I could almost see and hear his mind working. Once he was gone, I could focus on the battle.

I had Faramir and Gandálfr flanking me and the other two were in the row behind. We had consistency in the weapons of the front ranks. We bristled with long ash spears. Our spearheads were well made. Unlike the enemy, the men with whom I fought were warriors who valued their weapons and cared for them. Saxon Slayer's head was well made, cunningly crafted and had both a tip and sharpened edges. The bindings were new and would not break. It would not let me down. My shield was heavier than most but using oars and the carrying of logs when I had been young had made me strong enough to easily manage it. The boss was but a year old and there were tiny fragments of metal I had taken from the sweepings of the weaponsmith's workshop embedded in the wood beneath the painted leather face. One important task I had after each campaign was to oil the wood and replace the leather.

The priests having finished their invocation to God, the two armies faced each other. Men shouted taunts. A warrior, I recognised him as the drunken, Thrum, stepped forward to challenge any of the enemy warriors to single combat. I saw one Saxon step forward but an imperious voice from the rear made the warrior return to the ranks. Thrum strode along the line as though he was a hero and had already won the battle. Hemingr ordered him back to the lines and his friends all cheered the warrior. We waited. I had an ale skin hanging from my belt and I drank deeply. I reached into the small satchel that hung there and took out some dried meat on which to chew. The act of simply chewing seemed to take the edge off my hunger and helped me to concentrate my attention on our foes. I had heard of battles between Alfred and Guthrum where the armies had faced each other for days before a battle took place. Was this to be another such day?

Thorkell was the one who broke the stalemate. Four of his warriors left him in the centre and came to speak, not to the hersirs but the archers and the slingers. Then the four returned to our leader. After a short time, one of his hearthweru put his horn to his lips and gave three blasts. Suddenly the archers and slingers raced forward to stop just one hundred paces from the front line of English warriors. They unleashed arrow after arrow. Stones clattered against wood, metal and flesh. The enemy archers were behind their warriors and although they sent arrows and stones in reply they were not as effective. Two blasts on the horn made the archers and slingers turn and flee. Twenty of the bondi and slingers who had attacked lay dead on the ground but their attack had been devastating. At such a close range they had slain or wounded more than one hundred and twenty of the fyrd. There were holes all along their lines. Even worse for Ulfcetel was that some of the fyrd, angered perhaps by the attack suddenly launched themselves down the slope and raced after the slingers and archers. I saw some of their thegns try to hold them back but it was like a pot that begins to bubble and then boil over. Once the bubbling began it could not be stopped and I heard the horn of Ulfcetel sound the attack. Thorkell had won the first move of the battle. He had made Ulfcetel deviate from his plan.

I was in command of almost a quarter of the army and I shouted, "Brace!"

Shields were lifted to lock into line and our right legs were placed behind us. I rested Saxon Slayer against my foot, the head poking over the top of my shield. Snorri's spear rested on my shoulder while his shield pressed into my back. We knew that there would be no arrow storm for we had seen their archers behind the rest of their warriors. The wild attack of the fyrd meant it was the lightly armed men with little or no armour who raced towards us and would reach us first. The slight slope made it hard for them to stop. They screamed their insults and their invocations of their trinity as they ran toward us. Some men like a helmet with a face mask but I preferred an open one with just a nasal bar to protect my nose and eyes. I was able to see which warriors would be the first to strike us. I saw a knot of warriors, Saxons by their dress, follow a young leader who had a helmet, a round shield and a spear. The sword that hung from his belt had a good scabbard. The six men who ran with him were as close to him as they could be and I saw that they would strike us. Already the first men had died as our archers and slingers thinned their racing ranks. Unlike the seven who ran towards me, others had reached our lines alone and had been easily slain. The young leader brought his band for me.

"Push!"

I timed my command as the seven struck us. The order was to make the ranks behind push and stiffen us. The effect was as though the seven warriors had run into a stone wall. Saxon Slayer hit the shield of the young leader while his spear hit Gandálfr's. While I did not move, for I was held in place by those behind, the young leader and his men seemed to bounce back. Two had been impaled upon the spears of my men and Snorri's spear had cut the face of the leader. The blood dripped down his cheek but he was brave and as the heavier armed men and the rest of the fyrd hurried to get to grips with us, we had our own battle with these five men from the East Anglian fyrd. He stepped at me and thrust his spear at my head. I raised my shield slightly and took the blow there while I punched upwards with Saxon Slayer. Spears came over our shoulders to thrust at the men and one was speared in the eye. He dropped like a stone. I felt Saxon Slayer meet resistance and I pushed up. Feeling it grate off what felt like bone I twisted and the young leader grimaced as the handspan of metal entered his body. He was brave and must have known he was doomed but he still cursed me and even tried to headbutt me. I lowered my head and his dying head struck the top. At the same time, I pushed with my shield and Saxon Slayer. He reeled back and although he tried to move, his legs gave way and buckled. The last of his men were speared and we now had a small barrier between us and the more solid line that advanced towards us.

"Lock and brace."

A single Saxon ran at us and tried something I had not seen for some time. He tried to use the bodies and the shields as a springboard. He reminded me of Hawk at Svolder. As the dying young warrior watched, the Saxon leapt on the dead bodies before us and planted his foot on Faramir's angled shield. He leapt in the air and I wondered if, like Hawk, his landing might break our line but one of Galmr's men rammed his spear to impale him and then contemptuously threw his body behind us. The next warriors would pose a more serious threat for three mailed warriors with long spears and helmets with face masks led their men towards us. Soon I would have to discard Saxon Slayer as I saw more men rush to reinforce the advancing warriors and when there were two shield walls then swords and axes were the best weapons. For now, however, our spears would hold the enemy at bay and we might inflict more wounds and deaths upon them. A battle such as this, between two equally matched sets of warriors, would be decided by who killed the most.

The initial contact was loud and deafening but few men died in that first coming together. We were all ready for it and there was not the wild confusion that would come after a few blows. I had the luxury of knowing where the mailed thegn would strike so that I was able to raise my shield and block it. He too deflected my strike with the ease of a veteran. Men did die but they were the eager warriors who had little mail on their backs and thought to have a moment of glory, slaying a Viking. I pulled back my arm to strike at the thegn's head. He surprised me by using his spear to block it and then he brought the head of the spear back to crack into the side of my helmet. Mary's head protector did its job. As more men formed up behind those that we were fighting so we were pressed closer together and with men behind me it was hard to thrust. Instead, I inverted the spear so that the spearhead faced the ground and then I rammed it into the thegn's foot, pinning it to the ground. He was not expecting such a blow and, as his head lifted when he screamed and tried to jerk back, I brought up my shield to ram him under his chin. He was rendered unconscious and, had he not had warriors pressing into his back he might have fallen. Instead of going for my sword and while I had no enemy facing me, I drew Norse Gutter. It was the perfect weapon for such a confusing battle and I drove it at the man standing behind the thegn. He did not see Norse Gutter until the last moment and I drove the sharp tip into his eye and brain. One immobile man might have been held by those behind but not two and the two mailed bodies slipped to the ground. The thegn's foot was torn in two by the spearhead and I knew that he would bleed out.

All around me knives and swords darted out to seek flesh. I felt a sword rasp against my mail. Had it struck directly it might have caused damage or a wound but it slid along the oiled links. I had no idea whence came the blow. In a battle like this everyone before you was an enemy. I punched the next Saxon in the face with the boss of my shield and he reeled, his arms flailing for balance. I lunged with the dagger and found his armpit. The wound might not be mortal but when his right hand dropped, I knew that I had rendered him crippled, probably for life. He moved back out of the way and the space he created allowed me to slip Norse Gutter into my left hand and draw Oathsword.

Then I saw Æthelstan gather the remaining mailed men to try to rally the shaken fyrd. He came for me. His armour was well made and he had a good helmet with a face mask. He had chosen a sword as his weapon and that made us equal. He cursed me, "You are the spawn of the devil and I will end your raiding here on this field, Viking."

He ran the last few paces towards me and his move took his bodyguards by surprise. I easily blocked his sword swing with my shield and the blow was a weak one. This was not a warrior who had fought in many battles. I brought my sword from on high aiming for his neck. He raised his shield just as his bodyguards reached us and my hearthweru jabbed and stabbed with spears to keep them from me. My blow, in contrast to his and used with the flat of the blade, made him reel. He had no shield in his back and he was forced to step to the rear. The ground was uneven and slippery with blood. As he started to fall, I pulled back my sword and he raised his shield for protection. I still held Norse Gutter in my shield hand and I dropped to one knee to drive the blade into the eyehole of his facemask. There was a collective wail from his bodyguards and one tried to end my life. I blocked his strike with my sword as Eirik, one of Galmr's men drove his spear into his side. Lars and his brother Leif, along with Diuri and Bodulf ripped into the last of the bodyguards and slaughtered them.

The death of the thegn and two of his bodyguards had given us a slight advantage. Now the death of a mighty lord broke the will of the fyrd and I saw them wavering, waiting for our next move. In this real-life game of Hnefatafl, we now had the initiative. I could not see the rest of the battlefield. All that I could do was to hold my flank and hope that Thorkell and Hemingr would win the battle of the centre.

"Oathsword! To me!"

The order was to make my hearthweru form a small wedge and to stabilise our line. Raising the legendary weapon drew attention to me. I saw, on the higher ground, Ulfcetel look at me. He had yet to commit his reserves and his hearthweru. I wondered if the flaunting of the sword might encourage him to do so. A warrior saw his chance and ran at me with his spear held in two hands. He had seen a gap and my men were still forming up. I was able to watch, almost as a detached observer, as the spear came for my chest. It was the right strike for if I blocked it the head might be driven up into my skull. I turned my hand slightly. To the fyrdman, it would not be noticeable but as he rammed his spear at my middle, I moved the angled shield so that the spear, well thrust as it was, merely slid along my shield. Sometimes you need a dramatic gesture and this was that moment. Oathsword was yet to draw blood, for I had hit Æthelstan with the flat of the sword and the edge was razor-sharp. I used every piece of power my arm possessed and swung it at his neck. The warrior was already committed to the lunge and, even had he wanted to, could not have stopped himself. The sword sliced through flesh, muscle and bone. The head flew from the body, spraying those around with blood. It was at that precise moment that my four hearthweru and Galmr's men reformed the line and as many of the East Anglian fyrd looked in horror at the skull that bounced along the ground, so they thrust and fifteen of their fyrd fell as one. I had killed at least one thegn and all the mailed men who had led the East Anglian contingent were now dead. As I raised my blood-covered sword, the fyrd broke and then ran.

I was a young warrior but I had fought in enough battles to know that there is a time for order and this was one such. There were archers and slingers behind me and I shouted, "Archers and slingers pursue them. Men of the Oathsword let us take Ulfcetel."

It was a bold move but there were no men between the top of the slope and us. Ulfcetel and Oswy, son in law of Brynoth waited there with their one hundred reserves and their bodyguards. Picking Saxon Slayer from the foot of the dead thegn, we headed towards them.

"Keep together!"

Our men began to bang their shields with the pommels of their swords as we advanced up the hill. My hearthweru began to chant, "Oathsword" as they did so and soon it spread along our line and I could hear it further to our left. I kept my eye on the men at the top of the slope. If they chose to advance then their experience and elevation would give them an advantage but even as I watched I saw Ulfcetel make the decision to lead his bodyguards to go to the aid of the fyrd of Cambridge. They faced the greater danger of Thorkell and Eilifr. He waved his spear and I saw a warrior lead the reserves down to fight us. We would be relatively evenly matched but they would be fresher.

Galmr said, "That is Oswy. His father-in-law led the Saxons at Maldon. He will be a stern test for us, Sven."

"All we need to do is to hold them. We have driven a third of their army from the field. We have done our duty. We must keep their attention on us."

Oswy was not leading the fyrd but his own men. Not all were mailed but enough of them were to make this a hard fight. Looking at it now, I can see that he saw his own chance of glory. The East Anglian fyrd had fled and this was his chance to avoid a disaster. If he defeated us then he could go to the aid of Ulfcetel and perhaps he could win the battle. I say this now for he suddenly raised his spear and shouted, "Charge! Destroy the pagans!" His men took up the shout and charged down the hill.

"Halt and brace!" The chants stopped as my voice cut through the air. I locked shields and held my spear before me. We were a much shorter line now but still two deep. The one hundred men who ran towards us were more of a mob than clearly defined battle lines.

It was Oswy and his hearthweru who reached us first and they hurled themselves at us like madmen. The slope, their speed, allied to their weight meant that as they crashed into us, we were driven back but it cost them. Although my helmet was knocked from my head by Oswy's spear Saxon Slayer had driven through the body of one of his hearthweru but was then pulled from my hand by his falling body. Pulling back his spear Oswy thought to end the combat quickly for my hand was still reaching for my sword. I still held Norse Gutter and as I brought my shield and dagger over to block the blow the dagger caught on the wooden shaft and embedded itself there. The head itself slid along my mail. The Oathsword was freed from its scabbard. Pivoting to my right the eorledman's momentum carried him past me and I punched him in the side with my shield as he passed. In trying to keep his feet he lost his spear and, like me, had to use his sword. Mine was out already and I swung, not at his mail, nor helmet but at his head. He blocked the blow, which I delivered with the flat of the sword, but it still hit his head and his helmet fell from his head. I could see his face now. He was a greybeard and of an age with Lodvir. I knew that he would have learned much since Maldon and I took nothing for granted.

The wild charge of the men of Maldon had made this a fight between groups of men. My four hearthweru fought the bodyguards who remained. None would give quarter. My men had all sworn an oath on the blade I now used. A blood oath is the most sacred oath a warrior can swear.

Oswy's curse was delivered as he swung his sword at my shield, "You will die here Viking and I will have your entrails cast to the winds. Foxes and rats will feast on your corpse. I will display your head on my hall's walls."

There was a time for talk but this was not one of them. His sword struck my shield and he had made the mistake of using the edge of his blade. It bit and as we both tore apart I knew that it would no longer be as sharp as it had been. Mine had just had to take the head of one man. My spear might be blunted but not Oathsword. I feinted with the blade's tip as I punched with my shield. Norse Gutter, still held in my left hand, rasped across his sword arm, tearing some links in his byrnie. We were so close that I could not manage a full swing and so I punched the hilt of his sword at his face. Neither of us wore a helmet and his coif could not protect his cheek. The hilt raked a long line across his face. He tried to swing his sword at the side of my unprotected head. I was younger and fitter. I ducked and the sword sailed over my head. I punched him in the side with my shield and then stepped back. Men had fallen; some were dead, some lay dying while others were wounded. I stepped back because I saw I had space there. The battle had spread out from the tightly packed lines of the start and I wanted to be able to move around the older man.

He thought it was fear that made me move back and he roared at me and ran to wreak revenge for his bloodied face. He tried a punch with his shield simultaneously with one from his sword. I blocked both with my shield and used my sword to smash into his knee. His byrnie covered it but I used the flat and it was like a strike with an iron bar. I had hurt him and his face contorted in pain. I jinked to one side and his sword flailed at fresh air. I swung Oathsword at his opened side. The edge tore through the mail links and the padded undershirt. I pulled back and felt it tear through flesh. I raised my sword and as he tried to bring his shield around to protect himself from another blow, I backhanded my sword into his neck. This time the head stayed attached but as his lifeblood arced, I knew he was dead.

His hearthweru did not join the flight but they rushed at me. Perhaps they thought I would despoil his body or it just might have been that they had made a blood oath and were determined to die with the leader they had followed. They hurled themselves at me and my hearthweru who had locked shields around my side. I heard a shout and saw Diuri and Bodulf along with Lars and his brother Leif, race to my aid. I would have good warriors around me and I needed them for I was weary now and bruised. Just raising the shield was an effort but I did so. I held my sword out to provide some added protection to my shield. The Saxon warrior's sword was swinging diagonally as he ran onto my blade. The blow from his weapon was well delivered and as his mailed body fell onto my shield, I felt myself being pushed back. There was no comforting shield in my back and the ground was slippery with blood. I could not keep my feet. I did however keep my head. Instead of falling backwards, which would have been a disaster, I dropped to my right knee and that arrested my slide. It did, however, lay me wide open to two of Oswy's men who ran at me. I did not attempt to rise, that would have been fatal. I swung Oathsword across the front of my body. I was rewarded with a cut to the leg of the one on the left and Oathsword bit through to the thigh bone of the second. The latter began to tumble down the slope, his life blood pumping away. The former ignored the small cut and raised his sword to take my unprotected head. I raised my shield and as the sword smashed down on it, I rammed Oathsword up between his legs. He screamed so loud it sounded above the din of war.

Gandálfr and Faramir ran to me and hoisted me to my feet. The last of the bodyguards were being slain by Dreng and Snorri who had been joined by Galmr's men as well as Lars, Leif, Diuri and Bodulf. "Hersir, a little advice. Keep your helmet upon your head!"

I nodded and turned to see how the battle was going. Ulfcetel was defeated. He and the last of his men, the Cambridge fyrd, were making a fighting retreat north to Thetford pursued by the rest of our army. I pointed Oathsword to the copse, "Let us see what they have left for us there."

The last of the horses had been taken and much of the baggage that they had brought but there were spare weapons and they were finely made. There were boxes with religious artefacts and some banners. We found a small chest of treasure and we found food. Galmr brought the survivors from his crew and we sat beneath the tree and ate the food. I looked at him and said, "Was the butcher's bill high?"

"Not as high as it should have been. They came for you and that made it easier." He pointed to the east where the slingers and archers were returning. "That was a clever command. It stopped the East Anglian fyrd from reforming." I drank from the ale skin I had found. "That was a hard battle. Will we go home now, do you think?"

"I fear, Galmr, that this will just encourage our leaders to stay. Ulfcetel was the only leader he feared and we have destroyed him. The whole of the land of the East Angles is ours for the taking. We will not return home."

I heard a neigh and turned. I spied Cnut riding a pony up the hill. He had a look of joy upon his face, "You saved the day, Sven Saxon Sword. You have slain two of their great leaders and Thorkell the Tall pursues Ulfcetel to Thetford. He sent me to ask you to hold the field and care for the wounded." The last phrase was more sinister than it sounded. Any who could not be saved would be given a warrior's death. Enemy wounded, no matter how minor the wound, would be killed. There would be few of those. Any who were able to move had already fled.

"Thank you, Prince Cnut, and I am pleased that you obeyed my command. It bodes well for you that you are able to curb your natural instincts and use your head. Galmr, we will use this as our camp. Have your men fetch our wounded here. Gandálfr, take the hearthweru and give warriors' deaths to those that need it."

They both nodded.

"Prince Cnut, I left Saxon Slayer and my helmet somewhere, if you could fetch them for me."

"It will be an honour."

We had lost fewer men from my wing of the army and we had a well made defensive camp although I did not expect us to have to defend it. We had broken the hearts of the men of the land of the East Angles. The archers and slingers returned and were elated. They had stripped the bodies of those they had pursued and some even sported helmets now and good swords. We made two piles of dead. The greater one was the enemy one. We burned them both and it was morning before the flames died down. We ate better than the rest of the army for we had their baggage and that night men sang songs of the battle. I smiled as I listened to their words for none of them were as good as the one that Sweyn One Eye would have made up. I missed my cousins.

Chapter 7

We joined Thorkell at Thetford. He was camped outside and keen to move on. He awaited me for I had a quarter of his army. For the first time since I had come to England, I felt welcomed. Even Hemingr did not have his normal scowl when he viewed me.

"You are well named, Sven Saxon Sword. Your blade held their attack and, I hear, you have slain Oswy as well as Æthelstan." I nodded. "With Æthelstan dead we have sent a message to Æthelred. Ulfcetel and his men are in Thetford. We attack this afternoon. My men are eager for more treasure." He looked as though a thought had struck him, "What did you find at the enemy camp?" I gave him the chests with the artefacts and the banners. He smiled, seemingly satisfied, "They may want these back and will be willing to pay for them. Are your men ready to fight?"

"They are tired, Thorkell the Tall, but we both know that victory makes a warrior eager for more. They will fight but I would not like to have to fight another battle such as that one too often."

"And I do not expect we will have to do so. Like yesterday, you take the right wing. Cut off their escape east."

We had a smaller band this time so I allowed Cnut to accompany us in case I needed to summon help. We marched through fields that had just been ploughed and planted with seeds. Our tramping feet would ensure a smaller crop. The manned walls were just four hundred paces from our left flank but there was no attack from the gates to deter us. When we reached the east gate, it was closed and so I ordered a triple row of warriors with our slingers and archers on the flanks. We waited for Thorkell and the rest to attack. The horn sounded for the attack and we hefted spears and locked shields. We heard the clash of steel and then cheers. After a surprisingly short time, the gates opened and one of Thorkell's hearthweru waved us forward. We had taken the town so easily that all our warband had needed to do was to wait outside the gates.

It had been a token defence of Thetford. Ulfcetel was not there and the thegn who had tried to defend the town had paid with his life. We enjoyed the hospitality of the town for three days. The people were thrown out and we devoured all their food and drank all their ale. Their treasures were divided between us and when we left, we burned the wooden town and headed for Northwic. We took that easily for Ulfcetel and the rest of the senior warriors had fled to Æthelred. We enjoyed three months of raiding and then headed back to Wiht and Sandwic. We did not do so directly but went west to take Northantone. There we took so much treasure that had we not taken many horses we would not have been able to carry it. We raided west until, by Ýlir, we had reached our ships. Galmr's was still at Sandwic and so I went there with him. Thorkell and the bulk of the fleet were at Wiht.

We parted north of Wintan-Caestre, "We are not done here yet, Sven Saxon Sword. I know you wish to return to your family but you must know we are close to claiming this land for King Sweyn. Come the summer we will raid again and extract even more gold from these Saxon sheep. I will send our snekke to keep you informed of our actions and you can be assured that you and the men you lead will have your reward."

My performance at Hringmaraheior had made me an invaluable part of Thorkell's war machine. Perhaps if I had done less well, he might have let me go but, as we headed southeast to our winter home I knew that I was deluding myself. The Norns had spun and you cannot undo the past. For good or ill it shapes our lives. Had I not fought so well then, we might have lost and if we had done so then it might have been our bones left on the hill south of Thetford and not those of the men of Cambridge.

This time we did not have to live like monks. The men I commanded were all my men now. I had led them in battle and we had no drunken incidents. The men behaved well. We had food and while we still took from the surrounding villages, we did not take all that we could. We even managed to make friends with some of those left in Sandwic. Not all had fled. There were fishermen there who could not simply decamp somewhere else. Their boats were here and they soon came to an arrangement with us. We were Vikings and liked our fish. We bought their catch from them and in such a way became allies, of a sort. They were no longer paying Æthelred's Danish tax and the coins we gave them made them better off than they had been under that weak king. We got on with them.

Faramir even found a bride although she did not become so immediately. Seara was the daughter of the fisherman from whom we bought most of our fish. She helped her mother and sisters carry the fish to the hall we used. Over the winter they got to know each other and found mutual attraction and after but a month decided they would be wed. In those days handfasting was all that was needed. They called it a marriage in the Danish style. Her father was happy for he saw that Faramir was a good man and Saxon fathers wanted their daughters to wed as soon as it was practicable. She would stay at Sandwic until Galmr's ship left and she would come with us back to Agerhøne.

Gandálfr was the happiest for his friend. Gandálfr was married and had children. He had often urged his friend to take a wife. For me, the marriage was both good and bad. Good, for I wanted my oathsworn to have a happy life but sad because I missed my wife and my children and the marriage was a reminder that they were growing up without me. By the time I returned it would be more than a year since I had left. In the days when I used to raid for such long periods, I was not married and Mary had my mother for company. I felt I was abandoning her for she would be the one who was running the village. That she would do it well was small compensation. I was hersir and it was my responsibility. My guilt weighed heavily upon me as winter turned to spring. At Easter word came from Thorkell. We were to begin raiding to the west of Sandwic and meet up with the rest of the army that would be heading east.

Cnut had grown over the winter both physically and mentally and was keen to become a warrior. I would not risk his life fighting in a shield wall although it seemed unlikely to me that we would have to fight a major battle. With Ulfcetel finally defeated the Saxons would be reluctant to meet us in the open field. We had taken enough mail and weaponry to equip Cnut with a better fitting byrnie and a helmet. Seara made the prince a padded head protector and a padded undershirt. She was richly rewarded by Cnut. He already had a sword and all we needed to do was to make him a shield. Lodvir and Griotard had taught me well and, under my supervision, Cnut spent a month cutting the planks to size, glueing them to give maximum protection and then fitting a metal boss. We had no weaponsmith but there was a smith's workshop and the five of us helped Cnut to beat the boss into shape. There were plenty of nails and we made a solid shield that he covered with leather and then painted. He found it heavier than he expected but we all reassured him that if he carried it around every day then his left arm would become stronger.

We headed east over the land that had supported us over the winter. My decision might have met with disapproval from Thorkell but we did not start raiding until we reached Haestingas. There was a mint there. Whilst it was not an important mint it did produce coins and that meant that as well as actual coins there would be both silver and copper within its wooden walls. It was not big enough to produce the much rarer gold coins. What we had not managed to do was to take a burh but at Haestingas there was no burh, just a wooden walled port protected by a rock promontory. I went with Galmr and my hearthweru to scout it out.

I saw that the rocky promontory as a defence was an illusion. Because it was rough and could not support a ram or an engine of war then those in the town thought themselves safe from attack. I saw a way to affect an entrance to the town. We viewed the promontory from the shelter of some rocks.

"I can see how we could use that rocky promontory, which is unguarded and, it seems, unwatched, to scale the wooden walls of the town. Galmr, you can command the bulk of the army and place yourself at the main gate to the town. Make out as though you are going to attack. Use a shield wall and as much noise as you can. I will lead my hearthweru and twenty young warriors. We will approach along the beach just as the tide is turning and climb the rocks and then the walls. I will take a horn and when it sounds you attack. I hope to have their attention and the sight of twenty-five Vikings in the heart of their town should draw men from the walls. I will march to the gate and open it for you." I made it sound easy but I knew it would not be. The reason for my confidence was that I had done this before.

Cnut shook his head, "That is very risky, Sven."

"And is the reason that it has every chance of success for they will not expect it. I do not fear men who hide behind walls. We met their best at Hringmaraheior. I am content with my plan and as I will lead volunteers then all is good."

We had more than forty volunteers to follow me and I chose those who had yet to earn mail. It would aid their ascent of the walls. I gave one of them, Eirik, the horn for he had saved me from being wounded at Hringmaraheior and I left Saxon Slayer with Cnut who would join Galmr on the attack. The twenty-five of us left when the night was at its darkest and waded through the sea to scramble up onto the rocks. We then had the most difficult part of our attack; we had to negotiate slick and slippery seaweed-covered rocks so that we could hide below the wooden walls. Once there we waited and our clothes began to dry. My hearthweru and I knew that our mail would need to be cleaned thoroughly but I had no intention of leaving Haestingas too soon. We would spend at least a week there. I would send men to bring Galmr's drekar to take off the treasure. We said nothing as we waited. I knew it would be harder for the twenty volunteers than it was for my hearthweru and me. We had done this before and they had not.

We did not hear any noise until the sun was almost up and then we heard, on the fighting platform above us, the sound of Saxon sentries looking out to sea. They were just thirty feet above us but we were sheltered by a carefully chosen overhang. We could hear every word that they spoke.

"I see no fleet approaching. Perhaps we are safe for a while. They must still be enjoying themselves at Sandwic. So long as they stay there, I am happy. Had we seen a fleet of ships then I would have feared our end had come."

"I hear that the land around Wintan-Caestre has been plundered again. The Vikings are back."

"Aye, and what does our king do? Nothing. He is going to pay them off again. Why does he not do it now and save people losing their lives?"

"We could fight them."

I heard a laugh, "Have you ever faced the Vikings?" I guessed the other must have shaken his head for the sentry continued, "Well I have and let me tell you they are a terrible foe. Even when they wear no mail they fight as though they care not for their own lives. They are pagans and barbarians. How can you fight a man who does not fear death?"

Just then a bell sounded.

"The alarm. They are attacking here. Come, there are no ships in sight and we will need every man we can to repel attackers."

We could hear shouts from within the town and I moved from beneath the shelter of the rock. I risked a look above and saw no one. I waved my arm and with my shield on my back, I began to climb. So long as a man was patient and careful then there was little danger and we reached the bottom of the wooden wall without mishap. They had not made the palisade high enough. I had seen that from our scouting expedition. It was relatively simple to get over the top. Ten of the volunteers held five shields between them. My hearthweru and I stepped onto the shields and we were boosted so that we could grab the top of the wooden wall and pull ourselves over. Snorri and Dreng tied the four ropes we had brought to enable the others to climb while Faramir, Gandálfr and I sought out danger. This part of the defences was deserted. Even the two wooden towers they had were empty. I saw men rushing to the north wall. We waited until ten of the young men had joined us and then Dreng and Snorri led half of them one way along the wall while we led the others along the fighting platform to the wooden tower I could see was manned. Galmr had their attention.

The defenders were already wasting arrows at the serried ranks of shields that Galmr had assembled. His men were banging their shields and there was such a din that when we burst amongst the archers on the tower, we slew them all before anyone even knew. I nodded to Eirik, the young warrior with the horn and, as we left the tower to descend the ladder into the town, he sounded three strident blasts. I was the first to reach the bottom and I saw the surprised faces looking up at the top of the tower. The five of us slew four men before they even realised who we were. The gate lay just forty paces from us and I shouted, as I pulled around my shield, "Behind me!"

We were a small wedge and we had no spears but we were organised while the men we fought were not. They had been on the walls or rushing to reach their positions. A walled town normally had some sort of warning of an attack; our speed had forestalled their preparations. With my shield held before me, we hurried, rather than ran, towards the gate. The inhabitants had allowed too many buildings to be added within the walls and the gap between the wall and the first buildings was narrow. It suited my small number of men. The warriors on the fighting platform turned as we hurried by. I knew that they would be confused for we were dressed in a similar way to themselves. These men were unused to facing Vikings in war and their first view of us might make them think we were defenders hurrying to reinforce the gate. The delay would cost them. I saw, taking out the men in the other tower, Dreng and Snorri with their warriors. We might be just twenty-five warriors but we were inside their defences and I saw the fear on the faces of the men who came toward us. How had we managed to enter? How many of us were there? Was treachery involved?

The mailed warrior who tried to organise his men into some sort of defence stood with his spear poking over the top of his shield and his men tried to counter our wedge with a spear bristling shield wall. I felt a stone hit my shield and it was a warning that although we had surprise unless we opened the gates then all would be lost. We barrelled into the line before the second rank could lock their shields behind them. The spear that was aimed at my head was deflected up by my rising shield. I did not know the warrior who was behind me but his height cost him his life as the spear was driven into his skull. His death saved the rest of us because the spear was held in place and as the defender tried to pull out his spear, I rammed Oathsword up under his chin and into his head. He was dead before he even knew I had stabbed him. Although the young warrior behind me was dead Eirik had reached my small wedge and hurled his body into the back of the last rank. The sudden impetus pushed us forward and as the warrior fell from my sword we had moved through their lines. I almost stumbled but I had fought in enough battles to know how to recover my balance and suddenly we were through.

"Gandálfr, take Eirik and open the gate!"

Gandálfr was on my right and he simply peeled off shouting, "Eirik!" to the last warrior in our wedge.

Faramir warned, "Ware left."

More warriors were coming down the main street of the town to the gate. I turned and said, "Shield wall."

The men who charged at us were not warriors. They were the townsfolk armed and armoured in a variety of ways but they outnumbered my shrinking band of warriors. We locked shields and braced. I saw one of my young warriors pitch forward with a spear in his back. The men on the fighting platform now knew that we were enemies. When one of their missiles hit a defender racing towards us they stopped their assault but my line shrank even more. I blocked the blow from the wood axe with my shield and slashed across the man's unprotected middle. Backhanding Oathsword, I sliced up and through the right arm of the man who was trying to hack his sword into Faramir's head. We were lucky that they came at our line piecemeal so that we could defend those next to us. Even so, we might have lost had not Dreng and Snorri suddenly led an attack on their flank at the same time as the gates were opened and Galmr led our men into the town. I had just raised my sword to slay the Saxon I faced when his eyes took in the warband and, throwing his sword at me, he turned and ran. Others joined him. They had lost and the town with one of Æthelred's mints within its walls was ours.

In all, four of the young warriors who had followed me over the walls died. They had come from different ships and warbands but they died as the warriors who had followed Oathsword. The best mail, weapons and helmets from those who had fallen were given to the survivors and, when we took the mint, I made certain that they were rewarded before the hersirs and my hearthweru. None objected. We sent the townsfolk hence. They left with alacrity for they feared their women being ravaged and abused. I had no intention of doing so but Thorkell wanted confusion and this seemed to be the best way to achieve it. They would all flee far and wide seeking relatives and friends in nearby villages. When we approached the next village, they might have more numbers to face us but those numbers would be the ones who feared us and would run rather than fight. If Cnut's father was to have his kingdom, then people would suffer. I was just trying to ensure that they did not die.

Cnut joined me and Galmr when we emptied the treasury. I cocked an eye at him and said, "Should this be shared with Thorkell the Tall, Galmr Galmrsson?"

He smiled and shook his head, "I am learning Sven Saxon Sword. You have lost few men and you took all the risks. No one can dispute that this is your treasure and how you distribute it is your decision."

After sending the treasure back to Sandwic we spent several days in the town eating all that there was to eat and taking all the treasure that we could find. We took over forty horses and that enabled us to have mounted scouts as well as sumpters to carry supplies. Before we left, we set fire to the town. They would rebuild but I guessed they might choose a different location perhaps further up the valley.

We made our way north to join up with Thorkell's band, the main army. We took a couple of small towns, villages and farms. We did not have to kill more than a handful of people for most fled. The roads would be choked with families fleeing and seeking safety in a burh. We avoided every burh as we had learned it was not worth the cost of taking them. After three weeks our scouts reported the main army was in sight and my independent command ended.

Chapter 8

Thorkell and the others had been as successful as we had. There was no talk of sharing what we had each taken, Hringmaraheior had changed that. We joined him at a large farm he had captured. It had been a sheep farm and the flock had been slaughtered. The sheepskins were valuable and we would eat well. He held a council of war while we enjoyed a mutton stew that had been cooking for six hours. The meat was so tender that even a toothless crone would have managed to eat it. The ale was good too for we were close enough to Cent to benefit from the hops they grew there. Some of the hersirs had been killed and there were now just twenty-two of us. we were seated in the large hall and the thralls who had been taken by Thorkell were serving us.

"We head for Cantwareburh and take all that there is between here and there."

We looked at each other but it was clear from the looks exchanged by Eilifr and Hemingr that they knew of the plan already. Galmr asked, "Did we not accept coins from them to leave them alone?"

Another hersir who had served with me, Eystein, added, "And it is a burh. Why risk losing many men to take it?"

"Let us say that we have a friend within the burh and we shall not have to take it. The archbishop there, Ælfheath, is a rich and powerful man. Æthelred dare not lose him. Already representatives of the king have visited me to ask how much Danegeld we want. This is a way to increase the amount we take."

I wondered who the traitor was. He must be important and powerful for how else could we manage to enter a guarded burh? They would know we were approaching and simply lock and bar their doors as they had the last time.

Cnut was with us and he asked, "And who is this man that aids us, Lord Thorkell? What is in it for him?"

Thorkell smiled, "Prince Cnut, does it really matter what are his motives? The taking of Cantwareburh brings the day your father gains the crown closer. I do not wish to reveal all that I know."

Eystein growled, "Do you not trust us?"

Thorkell shrugged, "Let us just say that the Saxon traitor has made me wonder about the men I lead."

I had not spoken but I did so then, "And what evidence is there that you have a traitor amongst our number? We have all done all that was asked of us and thus far there is no evidence that the enemy knows anything about our plans."

I was watching Thorkell's face and I saw a lie in his eyes. Lodvir had taught me to look for such things. He shrugged, "No evidence yet but it pays to be cautious and so long as I lead King Forkbeard's army then I will be the one to make those decisions."

It was the end of the discussion.

We split up again for if we had all used the same road, we would have been spread out too far along a single road and would have meant we could be ambushed. We had three columns but it was clear where we were heading for and I wondered if the English traitor would still manage to help us gain entry.

I rode at the head of our column with Galmr and Cnut. "Perhaps this is a good thing, Sven. We take Cantwareburh and King Æthelred pays us a fortune. You will get to go home."

"And that, Prince Cnut, is the hope in my heart but I like not this treachery for the bloody sword of treachery is a double-edged weapon. Once it is used then you know not where it will end."

We neared the walls of the burh and, as the last time, they were barred to us. I did not think that our return, so soon after we had taken the last bribe, would result in further money. We camped beyond the range of their bows. Thorkell seemed very calm about the apparent setback. I wondered if the battle at Hringmaraheior had made him overconfident. We had all enjoyed many months of success. He had devastated the lands for many miles around his base at Wiht. I feared he might wish to attack the walls of one of the strongest burhs in England. King Alfred had done his best work to defend his holiest of churches. When on our second night we were asked to arm and be ready to attack I wondered if we would try a night assault. It was the only chance of success we would have but such an undertaking was risky. We had not fully explored the ditches and defences. Had Thorkell and his brother been doing so when they had disappeared for two hours during the late afternoon?

The answer when it came was far simpler. As we waited, just two hundred paces from the wall I spied a small side gate opening and a light was flashed three times. I watched Thorkell, his brother and their hearthweru slip away from the main army and head for it. We had been ordered to remain silent and not to move until a horn was sounded. One good thing about the army, even those I did not like, was that, when it came to war, they all obeyed Thorkell's orders. He had led us well and it would have been foolish to go against them, for a variety of reasons. To my amazement, the main gate was opened and at the sound of the horn, we all poured toward the defenders. There was opposition to our attack but it was perfunctory at best. I did not need to bloody any of my weapons and I do not think above fifteen men died as we took Cantwareburh. We had their holy city and Archbishop Ælfheath and we had an untouched treasury. It was Thorkell the Tall's high point.

The low point came the next day when Thorkell ordered the men of Cantwareburh to be slaughtered and he allowed men to abuse the women. I went to speak with our leader because I did not like the abuse. Prince Cnut came with me. I found him with Abbot Ælfmaer and it became clear to me how we had gained entry to the burh. The abbot crept away guiltily when I was admitted.

"Thorkell, why do we behave like barbarians? We took the town easily. What do we gain from this savagery?"

Archbishop Ælfheath, an old man, had been dragged, shackled, through the streets and was now held a prisoner. He had been forced to pass through streets filled with bloodied corpses hearing the screams of women.

Thorkell narrowed his eyes, "You confuse me, Sven Saxon Sword. In battle, there is none better and your sword is worth a thousand men but then you baulk at the killing of men who are enemies to our plans."

"War is the place for killing and you make war against soldiers and not the people who live simple lives just trying to get enough food to eat."

"This will make Æthelred pay us even more gold and we have an archbishop who we can ransom." He looked over at Cnut. "This will gain your father his kingdom sooner rather than later, Prince Cnut. One day it might be yours."

Shaking his head Cnut said, "And I would not wish to inherit a kingdom that hated me. I would rather not have the kingdom."

I knew that Thorkell was operating under Sweyn's orders. His father would approve of all that Thorkell had done.

"If neither of you can stomach it then raid the lands along the Medway. Bring food and animals."

I did not want to do that either but I knew that if I remained in Cantwareburh then I might come to blows with Thorkell or his men and I did not think that would do anyone any good.

We spent a month raiding and when we returned, just before the Christian festival of Easter I expected to find a burh that was calmer and where peace reigned.

We drove the animals we had collected through the gate towards the market. Some of those who had fought with us at Hringmaraheior greeted us and they were less than happy. As we had driven the animals we had seen that more than half of the men who were in the burh were drunk. There were fights amongst fresh corpses. The slaughter of Cantwareburh had continued, it seemed unabated in our absence.

Sigismund the Swede shook his head as he spoke, "You have arrived back not a moment too soon, Sven Saxon Sword. I know not what our leader is thinking. He was offered three thousand pounds of gold to stop the slaughter and he demanded more. He has since been paid eight thousand pounds but," he spread his arm around the market where the signs of violence were still to be seen, "the unnecessary slaughter continues. We could have made them thralls and made more money from them. A dead body can do nothing for anyone. I am glad that you are back, Sven Saxon Sword and you, Prince Cnut. You might be able to bring some reason back into this camp of men who were once warriors but now...I know not what."

"Where is Thorkell?"

"He and his brother are with the archbishop near the church. He is begging the archbishop to see reason."

I stopped, "See reason?"

"The archbishop is refusing to be ransomed."

"But why?"

"He thinks that we should be punished not rewarded for our barbarity."

Cnut nodded, "Perhaps he is right."

We were still armed and my hearthweru stood protectively around Cnut and me. The scene that greeted us was the most terrifying I had ever seen. There was a mob of drunken men, I recognised the leader as Thrum. They were baiting the archbishop and using bones, presumably from the charnel house, to beat the archbishop. I watched as Thorkell tried to plead with them. He had lost all control of his army in the short time I had been away.

"Thrum, brothers, I beg you, let the archbishop alone. He has said that he will not be ransomed. We have the gold from Æthelred. If you wish more gold then take my share."

That told me much for Thorkell loved gold and if he was willing to give up his share then he truly had no control over his army. I drew Oathsword and said, to the men around me, "When I give the word we take out Thrum and those close to him. We protect Archbishop Ælfheath. Perhaps if we do that then we might help Thorkell regain control over this drunken mob."

The Norns were spinning. Even before I could move four paces Thrum had taken his axe and used the haft to smash open the skull of the archbishop. The drunken men around him then began to beat the corpse to a pulp.

I turned to the prince, "Is this well done, Prince Cnut?"

He shook his head, "No it is not but I am glad that I was here for if you had come back to Heiða-býr to report that which I have just seen I would not have believed you. We must return to Denmark and tell my father. Thorkell has lost control of this army. It is now just a mob."

"Galmr, we shall speak with Thorkell and then I would sail home. Will you take us?"

"Aye, for I feel sick to my stomach. War is one thing but this…"

Eirik, the one who had carried the horn at Haestingas said, "We should do something about this Thrum."

I shook my head, "There are hundreds of drunken men there and while we might be able to kill many of them some of us would die and for what? No matter what Thrum believes he will be punished."

Sigismund gave a wry laugh, "He was baptised yesterday. Until that moment he had the hammer of Thor around his neck. His first act as a follower of the White Christ was to kill the head of the church. *Wyrd*, is it not, Sven Saxon Sword?"

I knew he was right. The sisters had spun. We made our way to Thorkell who was with Eilifr and Hemingr. I had sheathed my sword and saw, before me, a broken man. His eyes pleaded with me when I neared him, "What could I have done, Sven Saxon Sword?"

I had no sympathy for him, "You could have stopped the slaughter before it got this far. You had a duty to keep the people of Cantwareburh safe and you did not do so. Thrum acted as he did because you allowed him to. I come here to tell you that Galmr and I will be sailing home. I tell you this to your face rather than sneaking away in the night. I do not do this out of fear but disgust."

Thorkell nodded, "Aye, you have honour and I can see that I have none. And you, Prince Cnut, what will you tell your father?"

"The truth, Thorkell the Tall; I will tell him what I saw with my own eyes. And you?"

He shook his head. I could see that he, too, had drunk too much and could hardly think straight. Too much wine can do that to a man. Vikings were not used to it and Cantwareburh had been a sea of wine they had tried to consume. "I know not."

His head sank and I said, "Then farewell."

It was not a long march to Sandwic but the news of the murder of the archbishop had inflamed the people of Cent. Had we been as Thrum and his men, a drunken mob, then we might have been murdered on our way south but we marched armed and rather than missiles we had to endure curses, boos and jeers as we and another ten drekar crews headed back to our ships.

Sandwic was still a Danish port and the rest of Thorkell's fleet lay there. Faramir went to fetch his bride, Seara. There would be tears when she left her family but they had expected that. My other three hearthweru would have to shoulder the burden until we reached our home. As we began to load the drekars and while Galmr ensured that the boat was sea-worthy, we told the men who had guarded the fleet what had happened. Some could not believe it and I saw what Cnut had meant about the reporting of the atrocity; even by our standards, it was shocking. In the end, we worked out that it would take three days to ready the drekar that had been damaged slightly in the spring storms. It was on the second day that Hemingr and Eilifr arrived with the crews of Thorkell's one hundred ships. I went to their camp to speak with them.

"Are you sailing home with us, Hemingr?"

The warrior who had looked down on me from the king's table at Heiða-býr now had a different view of me. He had seen me fight and he shook his head, "My brother and I... we did not mean the archbishop to die." He pulled a cross from around his neck. "We are Christians." He looked into my eyes, "Sven, I tell you this because we have fought together and I know your worth. My brother and I have taken King Æthelred's gold. Our drekar will now fight to protect this land."

I heard the sharp intake of breath from Cnut and I held up my hand to prevent him from speaking. He did not know it but this was a dangerous situation. We were outnumbered by Hemingr and his men. "And are you here to prevent us from leaving?"

Shaking his head he said, "No, but I know that one day we may have to fight. I cannot see the prince's father forgiving this betrayal. Go in peace, Sven."

I was not certain that I believed him but I nodded and we hurried back to Galmr. I told him the news and saw the shock on his face. "I think we leave as soon as we can. I do not trust Hemingr."

Galmr nodded. He turned to his sailing master, "Prepare the ship. I will go and tell the other captains. I agree with you Sven and I do not trust this Hemingr. If he can betray his king then a lie to us is as nothing."

We helped Faramir to make a nest for Seara at the prow. I could see that the girl was terrified for she was aboard a warship filled with men she had been told were savages. "Seara, these are good men and you are safer here than you would be in any burh for they have fought with your husband. You can sleep easy as we sail to your new home."

She gave a thin smile, "I know but I go from what I know and into the unknown."

Gandálfr said, "Then view it as an adventure, eh? Fear not, for when we reach Agerhøne my wife will make you welcome and you know that the hersir's wife comes from this island too and is a Saxon." Her eyes widened and Gandálfr added, "Aye, she is a fine lady and you will like her."

In the end, we left, in the early morning, with another thirty-two drekars. It proved to be a wise move. We had lost men in the campaign and no longer had a double crew. We sailed without any real order except that Galmr, perhaps because he carried Prince Cnut, was seen as the senior ship. We all had to take a turn at the oars, even Cnut. Galmr did not think that I ought to row but, if the truth were told, it helped me for the physical effort of rowing our ship home expunged the memory of what had been done at Cantwareburh. The need for oars was necessitated by a wind from the south and east. We were forced to sail almost due east to avoid being driven onto the Centish shore.

The voice from the ship's boy perched precariously on the cross tree came as a shock, "Sails, captain, to the south."

We could see nothing but I watched as Galmr clambered up on the gunwale and steadied himself with the backstay. He peered at the horizon.

Cnut was next to me and his hands were already showing the effect of half a day of rowing, "Ships? What does that mean, Sven?"

"It means danger for if the ships come from the south, then they represent a threat of some sort. If they come from the south and west then they may be Normans. They are not averse to taking a Danish ship, especially one that they think is filled with treasure. If it is from the south and east then, unlikely though it is, this could be the fleet built by Eadric Streona."

"But there are thirty-three of us. Surely we are too big a mouthful for them."

"You would think so but if they trailed us then they could pick off stragglers. With the wind in their favour, it would be easy to do."

Galmr went to the steering board and began to turn to the north. We would have to risk the shore. "Let fly the sail." We had no other way of signalling and letting fly would be an instruction for everyone else. While there was still a chance that the encounter might prove to be innocent, we could take no chances and as the wind bit, Galmr shouted, "In oars. Arm yourselves!"

The ship's boy shouted, "There are more than forty sails, captain, and they look to be Saxon." Many of the ship's boys had spent the winter with the drekar and had seen, at first hand, many Saxon ships as the Saxon fleet patrolled along the coast. They had not risked a battle there for the ships were well guarded but here at sea, it was a different story. Saxon ships meant that we would have to fight. I did not don my mail. I still remembered the many warriors who had drowned at Svolder. I took my shield from the gunwale and Saxon Slayer from the prow. Once I had strapped on Oathsword all I needed was my helmet and I would leave that until the last moment for I wanted to be able to see the enemy.

I strode to the stern and Galmr said, "We have some ships that are too small to withstand an attack. There are ten of us who are large enough to defend ourselves." I nodded. He knew ships better than I did. "I will order the other nine to form a line with us and let the smaller ships flee. They should be able to outrun this fleet if we can slow them down."

"I agree." I saw Cnut taking all this in. he had been a child when we had fought at Svolder and only heard of the horrors of a seas battle. I wondered if he was regretting coming along with us.

It took time but Galmr passed his commands to the ships around us and the orders were passed. The Saxon fleet gained inexorably on us for we had to maintain a relatively slow speed to enable the orders to be given. We could see when they had been given for the smaller ships let fly their full sails and began to speed away. Most of them had their oars manned to increase their speed. As they moved north so the other nine large drekar formed a long line with us.

While Faramir made a small fort of barrels and sacks around his wife to prevent her from being injured by arrows or stones I studied the ships following. Unlike us, they were in an arrow formation with a large ship leading the way. The Saxons did not know how to build sleek ships like our drekar and they were tubbier. The leading ship looked to be half as long again as us. An idea came to me, "Captain, if we can tempt the big ship at the front to nudge closer we could take it out before the others can react. I think we could then outrun them."

Although we had repaired the damage from the spring storms what we had not done was to clear the hulls of weed. The Saxon fleet was less than two years old and weed would not be a problem.

"And how do we do that?"

"We and *'Kraken'* are the largest ships." I pointed to the drekar next to us. She had forty oars, as many as we had and I knew she had a good crew. "We leave a tempting gap between us and then ask the other eight to increase sail and begin to pull away. The Saxons may see us as stragglers who can be plucked. We let her come between us and the two of us close on her like the claws of a crab. We board her, disable her and get back aboard before they have time to bring the rest of their fleet."

The Saxons had rarely defeated Viking ships and the only ones in which they had were the ones where they had superior numbers. I hoped that whoever commanded the large Saxon ship was confident.

"It seems a good plan and they are gaining in any case." Once again, the orders were passed and the gap between us and *'Kraken'* widened as the others spread out and drew away from us. I did not take my eyes from the Saxons and I saw that our plan was working. The leading ship was gaining and using her oars to close with us. The ships behind were smaller and they were struggling to catch up with their leader. I gathered the warriors around me at the mast fish.

"Those who have bows I want you to line the gunwale. Your job will be to rain death upon them. Once we board you will have to keep any other ship from coming to her aid. The rest of you will join my hearthweru and me. We will jump aboard. I will eliminate their captain and disable the ship while you kill as many as you can. I want every sheet severing. If we can find fire then good but whatever we do when I shout, 'back' then all must obey. If you are left aboard her after that you will enjoy a warrior's death. I would rather you heeded my words and have a warrior's life."

I saw some of the faces of the men who had come with me at Haestingas. They were now dressed as warriors and it was they who cheered and shouted, "Oathsword!"

I held my hands up, "We want them to think we are defeated. Save your cheers for the moment we board."

It took a full hour for the Saxon ship to be close enough for an attack. She had a white horse upon her sail and I could see that she was new. She had the figurehead of what looked like, to me, the Virgin Mary. It explained her speed but with a more rounded bow than us she was far less manoeuvrable. It was clear that she was coming for us. The captain of *'Kraken'* would wait until she neared our steerboard side before he turned his steering board. We would have to hold off a full crew until they joined us. We would be aided by the fact that to close with us, she had her oars manned to catch us. The ships behind were two lengths away.

Galmr was the one who would make the decision when to turn into her. We needed to do so while her oars were manned. Once they decided to attack us then they would simply take them in. As the Virgin Mary came close to our steerboard I watch Galmr push the steering board over. The drekar was nimble and headed for the oars outboard of the Saxon ship even as they were beginning to withdraw them. Galmr and his sailing master were clever men. As our bows touched and jarred together, our hull rose to crush and crash into the larboard oars. We were so close, as we waited by the gunwale, that I heard the cries and screams of men hurt as their oars were destroyed. Shards of oars flew up into the air like arrows.

I grabbed the steerboard backstay and drew Oathsword. I hoped that the Saxons would not be expecting us to attack and so I did not shout a command, instead, I leapt into a ship with more than twenty men wounded already. I trusted that my hearthweru would follow me and as I landed on the chest of a wounded man I saw *'Kraken'* looming closer. I bent my knees slightly to brace myself for the collision. Three Saxons, making their way down the centre of the ship, did not anticipate the coming together and they fell to their knees. I used the dead and the dying as human steppingstones as I raced towards the steering board. As I passed two of the three Saxons who had fallen, I hacked one across the neck and drove my sword into the chest of the other. Three warriors guarded the helmsman. Drawing Norse Gutter I ran at them. Close to the stern, there were just four bodies and they had been slain by our archers and slingers. Blocking the first sword with Oathsword, I used Norse Gutter to rip open the middle of the first defender of the helmsman.

Gandálfr and Faramir were with me and the other two defenders fell as quickly. The helmsman was no hero and he threw himself overboard. Knowing other Saxons were following he must have thought he stood more chance of surviving the sea than our swords. I hacked through the steering withy while my hearthweru slashed at the backstays. Behind me was a cacophony of noise as our two crews slaughtered the Saxons. Having cut all the ropes holding the steering board I picked up an axe that was lying by the helmsman and chopped through the steering board, throwing the pieces overboard. I saw that three more Saxon ships were closing with us and I shouted, "Back!"

With my hearthweru before me, we made our way back to Galmr's ship. Some of our crew had been wounded but none so far as I could see were dead. Waiting until all were safely off the ship, I clambered over the two gunwales to cheers from the crew. As the stricken Saxon was fended off, Galmr turned our steering board as the ship's boys let the last reef out of the sail.

"Do you need us to row, Galmr?"

He shook his head, "No, they are trying to save their ship and the rest of our fleet has escaped."

Prince Cnut, his face aglow, joined me as I began to clean my sword and dagger, "That was heroically done, Sven. Sweyn One Eye could make a saga of that."

I laughed, "I would just as soon he did not. We did what we could do to save our comrades and we have done so. The Saxons have learned that even a wounded Viking is a most dangerous beast."

Chapter 9

We caught up with the rest of the fleet. They had waited for us and that touched me for they need not have and it showed me that our battles had bonded us. We sailed north to our home. Had we not had Prince Cnut aboard then I would have disembarked at Agerhøne but I was responsible for the prince and I had to deliver him safely to his father. As we passed my home, a grey, indistinct line to the east I closed my eyes and said a silent prayer to the Allfather to continue to watch over my family. It took some time to reach Heiða-být and the empty anchorage told us that we were the first ship to reach King Sweyn's home. We would have to be the ones to deliver the bad news and I did not relish it. Saying farewell to the crew was also hard. We had fought together and while we were all much richer in terms of weapons, mail and treasure, the greatest riches we had gained came in the form of friendship. We were now brothers in arms and that would never change. Galmr Galmrsson was a warrior who would never let another warrior down and I appreciated such men.

Karl Three Fingers greeted us and his face showed surprise, "You come with just a handful of ships? Where is the rest of the fleet and Thorkell the Tall?"

Just five other ships from Heiða-být had returned with us.

I looked at the prince. It was time he began to take responsibility, "Prince Cnut."

He nodded and began to tell Karl what had led to the abandonment of the raid. Karl shook his head when the full message was delivered, "The king will be mightily displeased at that. And the gold that Æthelred paid. The Danegeld?"

"We have a share of it for the king but the bulk of it was kept by Thorkell and the one hundred ships that followed him."

"It gets worse." He turned to lead us in and then said, "Your brother is here."

I had often spoken with Cnut about his elder brother, Harald. They did not get on and that was no surprise. One of them would inherit Denmark when their father died and it was likely the one who did not inherit would be banished at best or executed at worse.

Leaving Seara and my hearthweru outside, Cnut and I entered the hall and the king and his eldest son were seated with scribes and were surrounded by maps. I recognised them as being maps of England. The king was already planning his invasion. He beamed, "So my warriors are returned. Æthelred has paid us?"

Cnut stepped forward. To me it was the bravest thing I had ever seen anyone do for this was far harder than facing a Saxon shield wall. "Thorkell the Tall and one hundred of your crews have hired themselves out to fight for King Æthelred. The money he would have paid us he now pays Thorkell to fight against us."

Silence filled the hall and I saw anger creep up the king's face. He suddenly jabbed a finger at me, "And you, Sven Saxon Sword, what have you to do with all of this? Why are you returned here?"

I understood what he was doing. He was venting his anger on me. I bowed my head, "When you sent me to accompany Thorkell the Tall I did so reluctantly, King Sweyn. You asked me to watch over your son, Prince Cnut, and I have done so. I would have returned directly to my home had I not promised you to deliver Prince Cnut safely here. I have done so and now I will return to Agerhøne."

The king's eyes narrowed. Cnut said, "Father, Sven Saxon Sword was the reason we defeated Ulfcetel at the Battle of Hringmaraheior. He is the reason that the Saxons have no leader to fight us."

"Except Thorkell the Tall."

Was the king blaming me for the hiring of Thorkell?

Silence descended like an executioner's axe. It was only broken when Karl Three Fingers said, "All that this does, King Sweyn, is delay your invasion until next year. In many ways, it helps us for we now know the army that will face us. I do not fear Thorkell the Tall nor his brother."

"He will pay for his treachery. You may return home, Sven Saxon Sword but tell your foster father that I will need all the men he commands next year when we invade England. Tell him to prepare. I will send Karl with the details closer to the time." I was dismissed.

I backed out and I saw Cnut turn to follow me but he was halted by his father's voice that commanded, "No, Cnut, I need to speak with you. You have information about this land and I would pick it from your mind."

I did not get the chance to say goodbye to the prince whom I now viewed as a friend. Karl led me outside, "Do not be annoyed by your treatment, Sven, it is the king's way."

I shook my head, "And such treatment is more likely to make any man choose a different king. Perhaps Thorkell had the right idea. He will be well rewarded for his treachery."

"Peace, Sven, you are angry. You had best keep such thoughts within your head. Speak with Sweyn Skull Taker and he will put all of this into perspective."

We went to the stables and I used my authority to commandeer six horses. I had no intention of walking back to Agerhøne and we had Seara with us. It was one thing to ask a warrior to walk but Seara had endured much already and I wanted her to have as easy a journey to her new home as possible. The journey home was necessary as I managed to expunge from my body all my anger. Karl was right. Kings are not like ordinary men, how could they be? They followed different rules and any warrior who expected anything different was a fool. I was going home much richer and I had not lost a man. That was rare. I knew that I would be needed to help Sweyn Skull Taker follow King Sweyn but I would have almost a year at home with my family first. Who knew what might happen in a year?

Faramir, Seara and I talked as we headed west to Agerhøne. "You will need a home. Old Olaf's farm is empty. It is not a large one but there is a house and it is not far from Gandálfr."

Old Olaf had outlived his wife and their sons had died at Svolder before they could father children of their own. He had died just a month before we had left and I hoped that Mary had not decided to give it to another.

Faramir must have had the same thoughts for he nodded, "If Lady Mary has not given it to another, hersir, then it would be perfect. Gandálfr's land is also small but that suits as neither of us have the time to tend to fields."

As hersir, I paid my hearthweru so that they did not need to spend every moment of daylight tending to fields and animals. "Then it is settled and Seara will be close enough to our wives so that when we go to war she will not be lonely."

"Go to war?"

Seara's face filled with fear. I nodded, "Sadly we have to obey our king and when he asks us to fight for him we have to do as he says. We will have a year, at least, before the call comes. You shall have a year with your husband." Saying the words made me feel guilty already. Mary hated the idea of war and especially a war to take the place of her birth. I knew I would have a difficult discussion when I reached my hall.

I almost wept when I spied the wooden wall around Agerhøne. We had been away for more than a year and I resented every moment that I had spent away not only from my family but my friends and comrades. War is not just about fighting it is about comradeship and I knew that when we sat in the mead hall and feasted, I would enjoy hearing the tales of what we did together as warriors.

Six riders on the road from the east were easily spotted and some sharp-eyed boy must have seen us for by the time we reached the east gate to our home there was a crowd to greet us. Sweyn One Eye stood with a grin on his face as wide as the hull of a fat knarr. "The hero returns and he seems to be whole. Does that mean there are no tales for me?"

We dismounted and I hugged my foster brother. Gandálfr laughed, "There are enough tales, Sweyn One Eye, to keep you busy for a month or more."

"Good and I see another tale here. You have brought something else from the land of the Angles, Faramir?"

"Aye, this is my wife Seara. Seara, this is the son of the Jarl, Sweyn One Eye."

Sweyn made a dramatic gesture as though he had been struck by an arrow. "This is how you describe me Faramir? The son of the jarl? I would have expected the title, the greatest singer of songs that Denmark, nay, the world, has ever seen."

I laughed, "You will become used to this modest man, Seara."

"And I would like to get used to my husband again."

I turned and saw Mary with my children. I rushed to her and picked her bodily up. I kissed her and squeezed her tightly, "I have missed you."

She kissed me back, "And I have missed you but I can see that you have not bathed since you left. Gunhild, go with your brothers and have the thralls heat water for a bath. Have the cooks prepare food."

I said, "First, come and give your pungent father a hug. I hope that you do not mind the smell." I picked the three of them up. I was strong but I barely managed it. They had all grown so much in the time I had been away.

Gunhild's arms were around my neck and she squeezed, "I like your smell, father. It is your smell and I have missed it."

I lowered them quickly before my back broke. It was as they ran to the hall that I realised that Gunhild was twelve and would soon be able to bear children and Steana was old enough to be a ship's boy... if his mother allowed.

"And from what I heard as I approached you must be Faramir's wife, Seara."

"Yes, my lady."

"None of that, it is Mary. Do not fear these men. They look like uncouth savages but most of them are pleasant enough."

89

She had a tongue like an adder at times. "My love, is the farm of Old Olaf still empty?"

"It is. Why?"

"I thought to give it to Seara and Faramir."

"It is not fit yet." She pointed to my hearthweru, "Come, you shall help me clean and you, husband, can bathe."

She was not one to be argued with and after unloading my horse Sweyn and I carried my war gear and my chests to my hall. "I know there is much to tell me, Sven, but the most important is how went the raid?"

"We had the land in our grasp and then Thorkell the Tall and most of the men joined King Æthelred and his army. We will have to start again and King Sweyn wishes the jarl to be ready to raid next year."

We entered my hall and we placed the chests and war gear on the floor. "My father will not like that." He nodded to the chest. "You have brought back gold?"

"Aye, that is one good thing that has come from the time we spent n England but I know I was lucky and lost not one of my hearthweru. When we take the men of Ribe and Agerhøne to war then we will make widows and for what? To give King Sweyn more power."

"I will go and speak with my father. Today you shall eat with your family but your return means that my father will wish to honour you and your hearthweru. There will be a feast in the mead hall." I nodded and he grinned, "Let us see if I can manage to tease out some stories from Snorri before then."

My heart sank. Snorri had no family and Sweyn knew his liking for mead. He would ask my hearthweru about the raid and there would be a song at the feast. My cousin meant well but I liked not the attention. In that respect, I was more like my mother than my father. Bersi Faramirson would have loved the accolades and the attention. I preferred to be anonymous.

The thralls we had were more like servants than slaves. Mary saw to that. She had been a thrall, albeit for a short time and she had not enjoyed the experience. The thralls smiled and greeted me when I entered. Mary believed that cleanliness was next to godliness and I confess that it was one aspect of her religion of which I approved. She had employed a builder to line a sunken piece of earth with clay and tiles. Aksel had raised his eyebrows when she had asked him to buy her tiles. They were not cheap. The bath would be filled with hot water and infused with vinegar and rosemary. All the wildlife that had grown attached to me would disappear. Of course, the hard part was emptying it. Buckets made the first part easy but when there was just a thumb's depth then cloths had to be used. As I began to undress, I realised that Gunhild was becoming a woman for she blushed and left the bathing chamber. The two thralls who were filling the bath laughed.

Mathilde, the older of the two Frisians laughed, "Aye, hersir, your daughter will soon enjoy her first moon. You had best look out for a husband for her. She is going to be as beautiful as her mother."

I had not thought of that. I looked on Gunhild as a child still but I knew that some girls were already mothers at the age of twelve summers.

Steana and Bersi were waiting for me to take off my baldric so that they could handle my weapons. I unfastened the strap and handed it to Steana, "Be careful, boys. Remember what I said about blades."

"Aye, father, a blade that is dull is not a sword but an expensive iron bar. We will be careful. Heed our father, Bersi. I know you are still a child but you will need to learn how to handle a weapon if you are to become," he looked around and I smiled, for I knew he feared his mother would overhear, "a warrior, like Father."

"I am not a child. I have seen six summers."

Steana laughed, "Then you are no longer a baby but the next time father sails to sea then I shall be with him. Is that not right, father?"

I fended off the question as deftly as I would a badly wielded sword, "As that will not happen for some time it is not something we need to worry about, is it? Besides I need to see if you have trained well in the time I was away."

I took off my shift and stepped into the water. I winced at the heat and Mathilde asked, a little nervously, "Is it too hot, my lord?"

I shook my head and waited until my feet and calves were accustomed to the water, "It will kill the wildlife and I like a hot bath." I sat down, somewhat gingerly. I could not help an involuntary gasp as I sat in the water and Steana and Bersi laughed. "Instead of mocking your father, save Mathilde the task of bringing soap, combs and a cloth. Hurry."

My wife knew how to make good soap and kept it in the kitchen. Mathilde smiled, "They are good boys, my lord. You should be proud of them."

I nodded absentmindedly. I knew she was right but I barely knew them. My body now accustomed to the water, I sank down so that I was immersed completely in the steaming water. All sound seemed to cease. I wondered if drowning was an easy death. Svolder had seen many men die as their mail sank them to the bottom of the Østersøen. I stayed there for as long as I could. I enjoyed the peace. When I emerged, I saw Bersi and Steana scooping up the lice, fleas and nits that had hidden in the hairs of my body and were now floating on the surface of the water. When we had been on campaign, we had regularly checked each other's bodies and hair for wildlife but some always remained.

"Soap."

Bersi handed me the soap and I rubbed it all over my body and hair. It was fragranced. I stood and did the parts that had been beneath the water. I sat again and dropped below the water. When I rose I saw a dirty, soapy scum. Mary had been right; I did need a bath.

"Cloth."

I stood and took the cloth Steana handed me. I wiped the scum from my body and Mathilde handed me a fresh pail of warm water and I doused myself in that while Anya, the other thrall, scooped the scum from the surface. I sat again and held my hand out for the combs. I had made them myself when I had first gone to sea. The bone had taken many months to carve and I had carved the handle so that it looked like a dragon. I was proud of that first comb for the teeth were fine. I carefully dragged it through my beard. The last of the lice came with each stroke and I crushed them between my fingers. That done I said to Steana, "Use the other comb on my hair and you, Bersi, can use the dragon comb to finish off."

My words pleased both of them and it was soothing to lie with my eyes closed as my hair was groomed.

"You need your hair cutting." I looked up and saw that Mary had entered. Anya and Mathilde had been dismissed. "Long hair breeds creatures. Bersi, fetch my shears. Steana, go and fetch clean clothes for your father."

Mary had instructed our weaponsmith to make her a pair of shears that she used to keep our hair in some sort of order. Most just used a sharp blade but Mary had been well brought up and that was not good enough for her. I had learned not to argue and I just lay with my head out of the water and she began to cut. The regular click-clack of the blades made me drowsy and, allied to the warm water would have sent me to sleep had not Steana burst in with my clean clothes.

Mary dried me and I dressed myself. The thralls began the laborious task of emptying and cleaning out the bath.

When we were in the main hall of my home, I was brought ale and my family sat around me. It was time for me to tell them of my adventures. Just as the water and soap had cleansed me of dirt and lice so I cleansed my account of the time in England. I knew that when Steana went with me, next year, then he would have a rude awakening to the reality of war. I told them of the taking of Sandwic and Haestingas as well as the battle of Hringmaraheior but it was when I spoke of Cantwareburh and the treachery of Abbot Ælfmaer and the murder of the archbishop that my wife reacted. She was not angry with me. I told her the truth about all the events and she knew I had nothing to do with either event. She was angry for, her father having been a priest, she held all such men in high regard. That one could behave in such a fashion appalled her.

"And now this Thorkell the Tall serves King Æthelred. The men who rule my homeland have changed since King Alfred ruled."

I drank my beer and sat in silence having learned that it was better to say nothing for whatever I said might be misconstrued.

"What does King Sweyn say about this treachery?"

I had known I would have to tell her but had hoped for a period of grace. It was not meant to be, "He intends to wrest the crown from Æthelred's hands."

"He wants to invade?" I knew that my words had lit a fire in her that would make her angry.

I nodded, "And that means every warrior will be needed."

She shook her head, "Men's greed never fails to amaze me. Why cannot King Sweyn enjoy the life ruling this land which is at peace? Why does he need to make war? Men will die."

"Cnut will be a better king than his father."

My wife was a clever woman. She understood politics. "But his brother will be the next king, will he not? Is he a good man?"

I shrugged, "I know not the elder son but I believe Cnut gives us hope." I had calmed her anger a little for she knew Cnut and liked him.

It was good to eat in my own home for the first time in over a year. My children chattered like magpies as they recounted every incident that had happened since I had left. It was wonderfully mundane and so simple that I prayed I would never have to go to war again for I wanted to be there to witness the loss of a tooth or the birth of a new piglet. Each event seemed to be as important to my children as the capture of a crown was to King Sweyn.

I spoke with Edward who acted as reeve for me. His father, Egbert, had been a thrall who had taught me much. When my mother had died, I had given him and his wife their freedom and a farm. Edward was his son. He was young but he was keen to learn and he ran the farm well for me. We discussed what was needed and I left him, secure in the knowledge that all would be well with my farm. The gold I had taken would be well used to build and to restock with new fowl. I wandered my land to visit with the people. I went first to Faramir to ensure that he and Seara were happy. They were. My wife and my hearthweru had ensured that their new home was clean and had all that they needed. I even recognised some of the furniture I had bought from Aksel the Swede. My wife had given it to the couple. I went to see Gandálfr. His children were growing although it would be another year or two before his sons could go to war. Gandálfr still enjoyed the life of a warrior. I knew that Oathsword had changed my life. I might wish for a life of peace but so long as the Dragon sword was in my scabbard then I would never be able to enjoy it.

I trekked with my sons to see Siggi the Pig. He had been my oar brother on my first voyage. He had managed to make a life of peace. He had not enjoyed war and the jarl and I allowed him the luxury of being a farmer. He was successful. His sons and daughters helped on the farm and he had but one thrall. He lived a different life from the rest of us and I admired him for his choices. When we had sat at the prow of the ship, we had grown close and even though I rarely saw him, the moment I did it was as though we had never been apart. His sons took Bersi and Steana to see the new piglets. I had ensured that when we brought back the new pigs Siggi had been given a good boar and sound sows.

We sat at his table and his wife poured us ale and served us crisp roasted crackling smothered in salt. "I have a gift for you, hersir. The animals you gave us were fecund and I have two piglets you can have. They are weaned and are to thank you for remembering your old oar brother."

I smiled, "When you have fought together, Siggi, you are brothers for life."

"They are not just to thank you, there is a favour I would ask of you."

"Anything."

"Siggi, my eldest and Snorri, his brother, would go a-Viking. They see the other boys and their fathers go to sea and they wonder why I do not." There were unsaid words but I knew that Siggi's choices had not sat well with his boys. "I would have them sail with you. I pray that they will realise that the life they enjoy here is better than one on a drekar but the Norns have spun and I have to let them learn for themselves. I know that you will take care of them and while they might not return, they have more chance of doing so with you than anyone else."

"You know that I will but, at the same time, I cannot guarantee their return."

"I know. Thus far my other son, Sven, shows no signs of wishing to do anything but be a farmer. He is still young. The Allfather gave me three and Sven will be a farmer like me."

Blood Sword

"The king has asked for us to be ready to sail next year. You can tell them that I will happily take them with me when we sail to England."

Siggi looked relieved, "Thank you, Sven, you have made my life easier already."

As we walked back to my hall, the two piglets grasped firmly by my sons, they asked me about Siggi and why he was not a warrior. His sons must have spoken of it to them. I tried to explain the choices that men make. "Without men like Siggi and Aksel the Swede then we would not enjoy the life we do."

"Yes, father, but without you and the men who raid we would not have all that we do have."

"In a perfect world, we would not need to raid."

"You could not be a farmer for you have the Dragon sword, Oathsword. It is a magical blade."

I shook my head, "Steana, do not use the word magic around your mother. It is a special blade and when it was forged King Alfred had it made to make for peace. It was a gift to the king of the Danes to mark his conversion to Christianity."

Steana was persistent, "But is that not magical, father, for it brought peace for a time anyway?"

I could see that Steana would be good at Hnefatafl. "Just be careful what you say around your mother." I suddenly stopped, "You are both Christian!"

Steana gave me a sly look, "We say our prayers and attend church but is not the White Christ the same as the Allfather?" I said nothing. "Christians have nothing to explain the Norns, father, and even Bersi here can see that they do exist."

"I am cleverer than you know, brother."

Steana laughed, as we continued to our home, "That may be true but remember this, Bersi Svensson, you will always be my little brother and nothing can ever change that."

"We will see."

I had been the youngest of my father's sons and being much younger than they were I had envied them. I understood Bersi.

The feast held by the jarl was magnificent and as I had dreaded, was all about me. It was a celebration of my deeds. My hearthweru had spent the last two days with Sweyn One Eye and he had revelled in the chance to sing songs about me. The mead and the ale flowed and the food, fish, fowl and salted beef were delicious. However, each time I began to enjoy myself Sweyn would sing another verse about the Battle of Hringmaraheior and when that was done, he would sing the song of the storming of Haestingas. Mary smiled throughout the night at my discomfort. We were unusual amongst the clans for we often allowed women to attend our feasts. That had always been true but since Agnetha and Mary had taken the reins of the clan it happened more frequently and all male feasts occurred rarely. I did not mind for having women present kept some of the wilder warriors under control.

During a lull in the songs, when Sweyn was busy drinking mead, his father spoke to me about the king and his sons. "You know, Sven, that many of the Danish nobles do not like the way that King Sweyn uses his warriors." I was not drunk by any means but his words sobered me up. My foster father said, "I am discreet and know that you, of all warriors, can be trusted. I have spoken to Karl Three Fingers and he has told me that there is a great deal of unrest in the land. The Battle of Svolder seemed to fan the flames of his ambition. This news about Thorkell the Tall can only encourage more nobles to think of refusing to follow his commands." He drank from his horn. "What do you think of his desire to wrest the crown of England from Æthelred?"

"Æthelred is a poor king. There is no doubt about that and the strongest warriors we met were of Danish stock. I think that he could take it but he would need to ally either with Thurbrand the Hold or Uhtred of Bebbanburgh."

"And is that a problem?"

"Thorkell did not even go close to the Humber. He knows nothing of that land and yet it is half of the country. Uhtred and Thurbrand hate each other. Both have large armies and if they ever joined up then they would be powerful."

"How do you know this if you did not venture north?"

"I spoke with the people. When we were in Gippeswic I found those of Danish stock who were happy to tell me that they wanted a stronger king. Some favoured Uhtred and some favoured Thurbrand. None knew King Sweyn and therein lies his problem. The people of England will want a leader that they know. Those who live in the south and the north will not aid King Sweyn. They may not like their king but, thanks to the way we have raided they are fearful of Vikings of any sort."

He nodded, "A messenger came today." He smiled, "King Sweyn wasted no time once you spoke with him. He is holding a husting with every noble in his land. It is to be held at Mörsugur on the day the White Christ was born." A husting was like a Thing but of a more specific nature. It normally focussed every voice on some important decision.

I smiled, "The shortest day."

He smiled back, "The shortest day. He thinks to hold a feast and get us all so drunk that we will agree to anything. We shall see."

Sweyn One Eye had been listening to the last part and he said, "One thing is for sure, the men of the clan, especially the young, untested warriors, will be desperate to raid England. Your sword is seen as a beacon. You never lose when you use it and even when you sail with just four men you bring back riches that a drekar crew would envy. You are a good luck charm, Sven. You may not wish to go to war but the clan do."

Just at that moment Gandálfr, who was happily drunk, stood and shouted, "Oathsword!" Suddenly the hall erupted as every man, youth and boy stood and emulated him. Sweyn was right and the Norns had been spinning.

Chapter 10

Although I settled back into the life of a hersir I had four boys to prepare for war. Steana, Siggi and Snorri would all be part of the crew of *'Sea Serpent'*. Bersi would not be sailing with us but he needed to be trained. Once a week they joined me and my hearthweru as we practised. They already had skills with a sling and even a bow but they needed to be trained in the discipline of choosing a target and sending either a stone or an arrow on command. We would spend an hour on that activity and then when their arms burned, I would give them a wooden sword each and a small shield and we took them through the art of fighting with a sword. My hearthweru ensured that none were hurt too seriously but there were bruises and even cuts. The tears they shed were masked by shouts of rage. The last part of each training day was spent using a short version of the ash spear and their shields. This healed any rifts that might have occurred when they were training with swords for they saw that in a shield wall every man was dependent on every other. We taught them the simple chants and how to march in step. It was almost too much for Bersi who was much smaller than the other three but he never gave in. I saw the effect on both of my sons when as soon as we had finished the evening meal, they both took to their beds without a word of complaint.

Mary was never happy about the training or the bruises. "Bersi should concentrate on his reading. He neglects it."

Mary had taught all the children to read but swordplay was preferable to the reading of dry and dusty religious tracts. They preferred the stories about King David, Goliath, and the Egyptians to the stories about miracles.

"And if I told him he could not join his brother what then? Would he not resent the reading even more? This way we can use the threat of withholding weapons to encourage him to read."

That she did not like the threat was clear but she was clever enough to realise the practicality of such a strategy. Gunhild began to feel neglected. I was surprised that my wife did not notice but she was busy with matters of the clan. Seara was new and having been such a stranger, Mary understood her problems. It was kind but in that kindness, she became a little blind to our daughter's own problems. I had just returned from the port where I had been supervising the repairs to my drekar when I saw her approaching from our hall. The boys were busy with the two new pigs and my clever daughter saw an opportunity to have time alone with me.

"Well, my little princess, what brings you wandering down to the sea?"

She linked my arm and squeezed it, "Is there something wrong with wanting to be with your father?"

I put my hand on her two and held them, "Of course not. You have made my day."

"I am pleased for I think you prefer my brothers to me."

I stopped and I felt my heart sink down to my sealskin boots. She was right and I did spend more time with the boys than her, "No, my sweet! That is as far from the truth as is possible. You were my firstborn and for the first year of your life you were everything."

She said, quietly, "And then the boys came along and the daughter was dismissed from your mind."

I could almost hear Mary in her choice of words and the logic she had applied. She was right again and showed that she was perceptive.

"Should I become a shield maiden so that you will spend time with me?"

There were women who fought; we had few in our clan but it was not unheard of. "Do you wish to wield a sword?" I looked down at her.

Looking up she shook her head, "No, not really, but if it would bring me closer to you then I would."

My heart was breaking. I squeezed her hand, "And I am glad that you have spoken to me of this. It does not do to hide words that should be said." A sudden memory came back to me, "I was the youngest of my family and I thought that my father did not like me as much as my brothers. I never spoke to him and it was only after he was killed that I knew he loved me more than the others. I had never asked him the questions I should." We stopped because we were close to the hall. "I was about your age when he died."

"That is sad and he died never knowing what you thought?"

"He did, but," I patted the hilt of my sword, "he set me on the path to finding Oathsword so perhaps it was *wyrd*."

We passed into the outer yard close to the stables.

"Mother does not like us to speak of the Three Sisters."

"I know but I have seen evidence of their spinning too often for me not to. It is one of those things on which we have different opinions."

Her eyes told me that there was more she wished to say and if we went into the hall there would be others there. We needed privacy.

An idea sprang into my mind, "Shall we ride?"

Her eyes lit up. She loved horses but Mary thought it unladylike to go riding. "Oh, please."

We went into the stable and I saddled a pony for her and my horse for me. There were a couple of cloaks hanging from a hook and I took them in case the weather changed. She sat astride the pony and if Mary had seen that she would have chastised us both. I would risk her ire. I ensured that she was secure and then mounted. I dug my heels into my horse and we clattered across the yard. Edward, Egbert's son looked up as we passed.

"Tell my wife, if she asks, that we have gone riding and I am not sure when we will be back."

"Yes, hersir."

She would be cross and I would suffer her scold's tongue but I felt it was worth it. We did not ride through the village but took the track that led to the woods and the hill that afforded a good view of my land, Agerhøne and the sea. Gunhild was a good rider. I had taught them all to ride but Gunhild was the most natural of riders and she was at ease, even when cantering. Bersi tended to cling on for dear life. After we had passed through the gate from the farm there was a large patch of open land for grazing and Gunhild dug her heels in so that her pony took off. Mary would have screamed in fear but I knew that my daughter had her mount under control. She squealed with joy and her hair flew behind her. I soon caught her up in case she had miscalculated but, as we neared a rise she reined in and slowed.

"You feel such power when your pony rides like that. I would do this every day if Mother would allow it."

"She prevents you?"

She nodded, "Not something a young lady should be doing, are her words." I smiled for she was a good mimic and had her mother's tone perfectly. She carried on, "If you are to marry a priest then you must conduct yourself in a manner that befits that status."

"Do you wish to marry a priest?"

I knew why Mary wished that. Her father had been a priest and he had been the most important man in her life until I came along. I knew that Mary loved me and we were meant to be together, that was the work of the Norns, but she did not like my going to war. She wanted Gunhild to have a husband who did not go to war.

"I do not think so but I know not whom I would marry. You are the hersir and a great warrior. Mother is aware of that and thinks that the man I marry should be as important." She jerked her pony's head to the side as it tried to eat from some bushes we were passing. "But not a warrior. I can see me being an old woman living alone until such a man comes along."

I stopped our animals for we had come to a clearing and had a good view of the village and the sea, "That will not happen. You are still young and not yet a woman, is that right?"

She blushed and shook her head.

"Then enjoy life. I will speak to your mother and you can ride any time you like; however, you cannot ride alone. If I am away then Bersi or Edward can accompany you."

"Bersi? He is a poor rider."

"Then you can teach him to be a better one. As for a husband... I did not seek to take your mother back here as my bride. That came in time. There is a whole world out there and many young men. I know not if the Norns have spun but they may have and one day you might see a young man whom you like and he feels the same way."

"Really?"

"Really." I grinned, "Of course, he has to meet with my approval and I have such high standards."

She laughed, "If you were the only one who would have a say I would not be worried for you are the fairest man in Denmark. Everyone says that. Sweyn One Eye says that you are the noblest Dane and as he has met the king and his sons that is saying something."

"I think my cousin is exaggerating."

She ignored my words and continued, "But Mother is something different. You and she will have words. Of that, I am sure."

I nodded for she was right. "Well, I have faced many fierce enemies in battle. I am sure that I can face your mother." I winked at her, "If I drink enough ale!"

She laughed and dug her heels in. We galloped through the woods with our animals jinking from side to side. It was a good day. We stopped on the way back at Siggi the Pig's farm. We watered our horses and were offered food. Siggi's sons could not take their eyes off Gunhild and she loved the attention. As we rode back to my hall I said, "See, Siggi and Snorri see you as a beauty and there will be others but you will need to use good judgement. I trust in you."

She beamed. I had said the right thing, "And I will use good judgement but it will be mine and not my mother's."

I knew then that the battle with me would not be the only one coming Mary's way.

When we reached home Mary was waiting with arms folded across her chest. I saw anger as well as worry on her face. "And where have you been gadding?"

I saw Steana and Bersi. Their faces were watching us knowing that there might be words between us. "Our daughter wished to ride and as she is a good rider, I rode with her. We had a fine day and we shall do it again, soon." I looked at Steana and Bersi, "And if you wish to ride with your sister then that is no bad thing. Of course, it will be when you are not needed for your studies or when you practise with my hearthweru and me." I looked at my wife and cocked my head to one side. I saw the slightest nod and knew that I had given her a way out. "Now, Gunhild, go and wash up. You need to help in the kitchen."

She rushed up to me and throwing her arms around my neck kissed me on the cheek, "Of course, father."

Mary said, "And you boys can do the same."

When we were alone, she said, "What was all that about?"

Sometimes it paid to be honest, "Gunhild thought I gave the boys more attention and she was right. You should have told me, Mary. You know what I am like."

"I thought that you had enough matters on your mind without worrying about a silly girl."

"That silly girl is our daughter. I expect you to help me in such matters."

She took my arm and said, "And now that you have spoken, I will do so."

Pulling her around so that she faced me I decided to push my luck, "And when it comes to choosing a husband, that will be Gunhild's choice. It may be a warrior." I saw the guilt on her face. "Or it may be a priest, or a fisherman or a merchant but whoever it is, it will be Gunhild's decision." She nodded and I pushed my luck too far, "Or the Norn's."

She detached herself from my arm, "You are a barbarian!"

She scurried off into the kitchen. I shook my head. When would I learn to keep my mouth shut?

Gunhild's words made the next months different than they might have been, had she remained silent. I threw myself into family life and ensured that I spent time with all four of them. I listened and I was kind. I was still the father and that also meant applying discipline when it was needed such as when Steana was cruel to his brother. Bersi had not grown as quickly as Steana and when Bersi was mocked I punished Steana. He did not like it and sulked. I took him outside. It was a wintery day and wind and rain came down. I faced him and saw him knuckling his fists and glowering at me. We both stood there getting wetter and colder.

"Steana, I am not only your father but your hersir. When we go to sea on the drekar I will command you not as Steana, my son, but Steana, the ship's boy. My voice will not always be gentle and you may not like the commands that you are given. Do you understand me?"

He did not say anything but he unclenched his fists.

"You will soon be a man. Already I see you broadening out and growing the muscles that will help you to pull on an oar." I saw the glower leave his face. "A man has to behave like a man. That means protecting those that are weaker than you. Bersi is smaller than you. How do you think he feels about that? He can do nothing about it for he trains as hard as you do and eats all that you do but the Norns have spun and he is not growing. Is it kind to mock him?"

He shook his head, "I did not think I…"

"Then here is a lesson for you, Steana, think before you act or speak. It is a sign that you are becoming a man."

"I will, father, and I am sorry."

"It is not me who is owed the apology."

We headed back indoors and I had to endure my wife's tongue for we were both soaked to the skin. It was worth it because Steana changed that day. He became his brother's keeper. The Norns had been spinning for a month or so later Bersi had what my wife called a growth spurt and became a whole head taller.

When the nights were drawing shorter we headed for Heiða-býr. None of us wished to leave our homes but the king had demanded that every hersir and jarl attend. Alf stayed in Ribe but Lodvir, the jarl, my cousin Sweyn and our hearthweru rode through black skies and snow-flecked sleety rain to King Sweyn Forkbeard's hall. Steana had asked to come but this was not the moment and I refused. He accepted my decision knowing that within months he might be part of a drekar crew and orders had to be obeyed.

We rode huddled beneath our oiled cloaks and there was surprisingly little conversation as we rode. Even the normally garrulous One Eye was quieter than unusual. For my part, it was the conversations I had with Steana and Gunhild that prompted my reflection. I was Sven Saxon Sword, the owner of the Dragon sword that was Oathsword but I was also a father and a husband. I had to find a balance between those roles. There were Norse, I had heard, who had such balance that they could run along oars held out of a drekar by its crew. I would need as much balance as that if I was to pull off this trick.

It was as we neared Heiða-býr that the jarl spoke, "We need to act as one in this hall. I beg you to trust my judgement and agree with whatever I say. Denmark has too many factions for my liking. We are the clan of Ribe and Agerhøne. Let us act as one."

Lodvir laughed, "Sweyn, you know before you speak that we trust you and will back you no matter where you go. The men who ride with you are not wild young men who have mouths that they cannot control. We will enjoy the king's hospitality and listen to his words and whatever you agree to then so shall we."

I think Lodvir was the most loyal warrior I ever knew. He was Sweyn's oathsworn and that oath would be to the death.

We were not the first to arrive nor the last and so we were able to find sleeping places in the warrior hall that were close together. It was a good omen for the rest of the time we would spend at Heiða-býr. Karl Three Fingers greeted us warmly when we entered the mead hall. The feast would not begin until the evening but already mead and ale were being consumed in great quantities. King Forkbeard was anxious to gather support and men with too much ale inside them would agree, in most cases, to anything.

"It is good to see you Sweyn. The king will need counsel such as yours."

My foster father looked at his old friend, "And your counsel?"

"I am seen as old and younger voices think I should be put out to pasture like an old bull." His eyes flickered to the head of the table where the king was flanked by his sons.

"Harald and Cnut."

Karl looked at me, "Sven here did a good job with Prince Cnut and he is a fine young man. You are to be commended."

That told us whence came the criticism, Harald.

As we sat at a table some distance from the king and thralls fetched us delicately carved horns of ale and mead, Sweyn asked, "And Thorkell the Tall?"

"He and his brother have kept King Æthelred's kingdom safe. The people of that land still pay the same taxes, the Danegeld, but they are not plundered at the same time." I shook my head and Karl asked, "There is more, Sven?"

I nodded, "The ones who plundered, raped, abused and murdered are the ones who stayed with Thorkell. That is not to say that all of his men were like that but the ones who returned with us, like Galmr, were the ones who obeyed orders and did not behave like animals. Thrum the murderer lives still and serves Thorkell."

Karl nodded, "He is now one of the leaders of a warband. We will have to fight them."

My foster father asked, "And you Sven, you who have served with our former brothers in arms, can we beat them?"

"Aye, but it will be bloody for we are evenly matched. The difference will be in the quality of our leaders," I spread my arm, "our hersirs and jarls."

The door opened as the last of the hersirs arrived. I saw Galmr who waved to me. Our table was now full and he and the others went to the table that had empty benches. I would speak to him later.

King Sweyn made a formal start to the feast by having his bishop bless the food and the king and his family. The queen was absent. It might have been a decision made by the king but, equally, the queen might have decided that if ale and mead were flowing freely then she was better in her chambers with her ladies. The king did not make a speech at the start of the feast but allowed men to eat to their hearts' content and to drink as much as they wished. As I ate and, like my foster father and his son, drank sparingly, I noticed how Cnut was a lonely, isolated figure. I did not watch them all the time but whenever I looked across at them the king was speaking to Harald. The bishop, who was next to Cnut was greedily consuming as much food as he could. When he caught my attention Cnut smiled. I also noticed that Ulf, Eilifr's brother and King Sweyn's son in law was not present. Eilifr was still in England with Thorkell and King Sweyn did not want to draw attention to his son in law.

It was when the first hersir fell face down onto his wooden platter that the king spoke. The vacant expressions on some of the faces of the hersirs on our table told me that they had drunk to excess. The king was a calculating man.

"My hersirs and jarls, you all know why you are here. Treachery has occurred and one we thought we could trust, Thorkell the Tall and some of the traitors who followed him now serve King Æthelred. They will be punished. At the end of Einmánuður, we will gather off Ribe and sail east across the Danish Sea to bring these traitors to battle and I will lead the army that will conquer England." The drunks cheered and banged their hands upon the table. I wondered if the king would acknowledge that Cnut had not followed Thorkell. His next words showed he would not. "My eldest son and heir, Prince Harald has shown that he is ready to become one who can lead our people. While I am in England, he shall rule Denmark in my stead." That brought more cheers and Prince Harald stood to acknowledge them. "Between now and then you will all prepare your men and ships. I do not expect to be kept waiting for tardy ships. Any who are late will be deemed to be traitors and punished accordingly. My son shall see to that." I saw that

Harald had gathered around him some of the more ruthless hersirs. Sigiberht the Fierce, Hrolf Long Nose and Bergil Black Helmet. He was preparing to hold on to the crown should it come his way. The supporters of Cnut were just the men of Ribe and Agerhøne, and me.

My foster father looked at Karl who shrugged. The king intended to scour his land of any who failed to obey his every order. Gathering at Ribe meant that Sweyn Skull Taker would have to be at the fore of the fleet when we sailed. He would not have any chance to leave men at home. Every warrior would have to be aboard the drekar when we sailed.

The king, Harald and the bishop left with the king's hearthweru and the three hersirs. Some hersirs also left and the mead hall gradually emptied. The sleeping drunks apart, the men who remained were, generally, the ones I would call good leaders. They were men like the jarl and Galmr. Galmr came to our table.

"Galmr, this is Sweyn Skull Taker."

Galmr nodded, "I recognised you from the songs sung about you. Your foster son is a credit to you. He is a leader I would follow."

There was an implied criticism of both the king and his son but none would speak it openly.

I saw Cnut, a lonely figure, stand and look over at us, "Prince Cnut, come and join us. We have an old friend for you to see." His smile showed his delight.

Karl Three Fingers said, "Sven, you are a thoughtful man but be careful. This is not the place to play politics."

"Karl, I respect you as much as any man but you do not know me if you think I play politics. I was asked twice to watch over Prince Cnut. He is as close to me as my cousins. I just want him to know that he has at least one friend in this hall, me."

I saw Karl wince at the harshness of the words. The others all nodded and my cousin said, "Aye, I like the boy and we know from Sven that this son has courage."

Karl stood, "I fear that as the king's counsellor I cannot stay here to hear such veiled criticism."

My foster father nodded, "That may be for the best, Karl, for you are not the warrior alongside whom I fought all those years ago."

Karl had a sad smile on his face. "I should have had a warrior's death but now I am too old. You may be right, Sweyn. You, at least, have never changed but I counsel care." He waved a hand around the hall. "There are ears everywhere. Be guarded in what you speak."

After he left us, Lodvir shook his head, "I would never have thought a man could change so much, Jarl."

When he had gone I wondered how many of the men who were lying face down on the tables were asleep or drunk and how many were listening.

Cnut joined us. I said to Galmr, "Do not forget the treasure that Aksel holds for you, my friend. It is not a small amount."

He smiled back at me, "Sven Saxon Sword, I am going to bet that you have yet to collect your share, too."

I grinned, "Aye, well, I have not needed it yet."

Sweyn One Eye laughed, "I know you, cuz. It may well be that you fear the lady of the house will spend it the moment you take it back to Agerhøne."

"Perhaps."

An awkward silence descended until Cnut said, "I am to be with my father on this raid."

Sweyn Skull Taker said, "It is not a raid, Prince Cnut, this is an invasion. Why else leave your brother to rule Denmark in his stead? We go, not just to punish Thorkell, but to take England."

Galmr nodded, "And we have to fight men alongside whom we fought Ulfcetel. It will not be easy." He smiled, "However, at least I will take a crew who own mail and that is thanks to you, Sven. Eirik and the other wall jumpers are all keen to fight alongside you again. With your permission, Jarl, my clan would fight with the men of Ribe and Agerhøne."

"And for my part you are welcome but the king may decide otherwise."

Cnut smiled and said, quietly, "My father knows your worth, Jarl Sweyn, and he will use you and the Dragon Sword as the tip of his army. You will be able to choose the men with whom you fight."

"But the king will fight, will he not, Prince Cnut?"

The prince frowned, "Of course, why would he not?"

Lodvir the Long said, "At Svolder he was the last to reach the Norse." He shrugged, "It may have been bad luck or the Norns but it was us who took the last Norseman."

Cnut nodded, "Then this member of the royal family will fight, you shall all see me for I will be as close to you as I can manage, Sweyn Skull Taker."

My foster father smiled, "And you will be protected as though you were of our clan."

The pact was made and I believe I heard the Norns as they spun.

Chapter 11

The year was passing rapidly. Seara was with child and Gandálfr would be a father again. I knew that would affect both of my hearthweru. Sweyn Skull Taker began to organise the training of the crews for he knew that we might have to bear the brunt of any fighting. I also spent at least two days a week, as winter gripped the land, practising with my men, the crew that I would lead. The four boys joined the other youngsters who, once we were ashore, would act as slingers. Bersi trained with us although he would not be coming. I taught the men I would lead the signals to change formation. Although the jarl would give the overall command I knew, from the battles in which I had fought, that often the hersirs would be called upon to adapt. I intended my men to be the most efficient on the battlefield.

Galmr arrived at Agerhøne just a month after the feast. He came with his hearthweru and animals. "I thought I would visit Aksel the Swede and collect our money. I hear they have good weapons for sale. If we are to go to war then we should have the best of weapons."

Mary was never happy about unexpected visitors and she kept out of Galmr's way. He and his men only stayed one night. I ate with them in my warrior hall. Four of the young men who had been with me at Haestingas were now his hearthweru and I was pleased that Eirik, who had carried my horn, was one of them. He was keen to fight Thorkell and the others. "When we were with them at Hringmaraheior, they looked down on us for we had leather byrnies, old helmets, and poor swords. I want them to see what we can do with a mail byrnie, good helmets and a fine sword."

I shook my head, "You and the others showed your mettle when you followed me over the wall of Haestingas and faced ten times our number. That you did so with just a leather byrnie makes you more courageous than any who stayed with Thorkell. A good warrior does not judge himself against other men but himself."

Galmr's hearthweru looked at me in surprise and Eirik said, "Even you, Sven Saxon Sword?"

"Even me. I strive to be the best warrior I can be for that way may mean I survive. I never believe that I am the best warrior on any battlefield for the day I do is the day I will die."

When we reached Ribe Galmr met Alf, my cousin. Hawk was no longer a warrior. He had lived apart for too long and I saw that Galmr was surprised when he met the man who looked like a merchant. We had told him of Alf at the Battle of Svolder and I think he was a little disappointed. I was not for a man did not choose his life, the Norns did. Alf was happy. His wife was pretty but like Alf, had become a little plumper. Their four children were all happy and, like Siggi the Pig, Alf had a perfect life.

"Ah, you have come for your treasure, we have kept it safe. My father-in-law is in Sweden at the moment but I run the day-to-day business. Come, we will go to the room we use to hold gold." He led us through the hall to a door guarded by a huge Rus Viking. Alf grinned, "Olaf is the first guard." After the door was unlocked, we descended some stairs and I saw a light. There was a second guard who stood and drew a sword as our feet made the stairs creak. "And this is Ulf our second. These are friends, Ulf."

There were chests and boxes stacked neatly around the room. My cousin went unerringly to two that were placed apart. "We put the coins from the four boxes you sent into these two. There are equal amounts in each one but I do not know how you will divide it."

I smiled, "And we have not decided either. Let us take them upstairs for I would not like to be Ulf. It is like a tomb down here."

Alf nodded, "We have four such guards and each one has one day in four down here. They do not seem to mind."

Once upstairs we were served good ale and we counted out the coins. Alf had been right, the treasure was equally divided and Galmr said, "I am quite happy with this division, Sven."

"Good, then our business here is done, Alf."

My cousin said, "And if you wish to invest any of your gold then I can promise that we shall double it in a year."

"Aye, but in a couple of months, we shall be in England. The gold will be well invested in arms and then when we return, we may have even more money for you to plant."

I bought a good cloak for each of the three boys. Siggi and Snorri were not my sons but I felt I owed it to my friend to equip his children. I showed Steana how to oil one side to make it waterproof. I had bought cloaks with hoods. At the same time, I bought some sealskin for both Steana and Bersi. I knew that I could have taken the boys to the sands close to Herterpol and hunted for them but we had the coins and we would be sailing across the sea soon enough. We would make the sealskin into boots. I also invested in some beaver pelts. Mary and her women made them into hats for Steana and me. While they worked on those I helped my son to make the boots that would keep their feet dry when at sea. I knew I did not need to make Bersi's yet but by doing so I included him in the plans for the trip.

The closer the date for the embarkation came the more fraught were the relations between Mary and the rest of us. Mary was short-tempered with even Bersi and he was not even going. It came about whenever he spoke of the voyage. Even Gunhild was not immune from the tongue of my wife. Whenever Gunhild offered to help Steana or me in our preparations my daughter was snapped at. I had endured enough and a month before we left, as we lay in our chamber I bearded her about it.

"You are being unfair to our children and it is not right. I am happy for your savage words to tear and claw at me. It is to be expected for I am your husband but our children do not. They did not ask to be born, we chose life for them. They have done nothing wrong and you should not take your anger out on them. It is not Christian."

We lay in the dark and I waited for the response. None came and then she snuggled into me and I felt her tears on my arm, "You are right and I am sorry. I am just fearful that neither my husband nor my son will return or if they do then Steana will wish to go again and take Bersi with him. I do not want to be left alone."

I kissed her forehead, "And I will not lie. All those things could happen. The drekar is well made but if a storm blows up then we could die that way. There are many ways for us to die. All we can do is pray to our own god to watch out for us and to live as good a life as we can and hope that we are spared. You know that I would not go on this invasion if I could avoid it but the king has made it clear that all those who do not take part will be severely punished. It is not right but that is the way of the world and we have to live as best we can."

The day we had to leave to prepare our drekar came too quickly. There were three tearful ones at my hall on the day my men gathered outside my walls to await me. Bersi, wept because he wished to go to war while Mary wept because we were going to war. Gunhild wept because we had grown close and she enjoyed the rides we had shared and the freedom it gave her. I sighed as I turned to lead my men up the road to Ribe. We did not have enough horses for us to ride and so we led the ones we did and they were laden with our chests and war gear.

It was as we talked that I noticed that Steana was taller and broader than many of the other boys who were going to war at the same time. Siggi Siggison was the only one who was the same size and even his brother, Snorri, was a handspan smaller. The three of them had practised together for almost half a year and they were easy in each other's company. It boded well. Apart from Siggi the Pig I had been largely alone on my first voyage and I had not enjoyed it. I walked with my hearthweru. Seara had moved in with Gandálfr's family for Seara would give birth within a month or two. The two women, like their husbands, were close and that was also good. The walk helped us to do two things; we bonded as a crew for there were at least ten boys and men who had not been to war before and it helped us to get into a rhythm. We sang songs and marched in time with each other. When we were aboard our ships that could only help.

We would be rowing *'Sea Serpent'*. She was getting old and had been the largest ship of the clan but Sweyn Skull Taker had asked Bolli the shipwright to build a newer one with more oars. I had not seen *'Falcon'* since she had been a keel and strakes on the beach at Ribe. The jarl had taken her on her sea trials when I had been in England with Thorkell the Tall. That seemed a lifetime ago. It meant that *'Sea Serpent'* would have a new sailing master. Lars Thorsteinsson was Thorstein the Lucky's eldest and this would be his first voyage. He had served as an apprentice to his father and Thorstein the Lucky thought that this son was ready. That was good enough for me. We would all sail as a fleet and I knew that Lars would be able to follow his father and speak to him often. Lars had been a ship's boy on *'Sea Serpent'*; indeed he had been at Svolder. He knew the drekar but this would be the first time he had held the steering board without his father's hawk-like gaze upon him. It would also be a new experience for me. I would not be taking an oar. It was now my ship to command. I confess I might have been more worried had I not been instrumental in Galmr's ship fighting off the Saxons.

We had a week to await the king but that week would be a busy one. We had not sailed to England since we had sought the animals and food. We had ships to prepare. *'Falcon'* apart, the rest needed weed to be cleaned from the hulls and then covered with the liquid that killed the worm. Sheets, stays and ropes would need to be replaced and a spare mast and crosstree placed in the hold. It would be a busy week. While we had the ship on the beach the crew would camp on the shore. I had been offered a bed at Hawk's home but I had told my cousin that I would endure the same conditions as my men. He would not be coming with us. He commanded one of his father-in-law's knarrs, a large one with a crew of twenty and he plied the seas fetching goods for them to sell. Aksel the Swede had done well since he had chosen Ribe as his home.

It was dark when we reached the ship and the men lit large fires both to cook the food and give warmth. There was an old sail we used to make tents. The new sail would be one of the last things we fitted and we were all excited. A new sail was fresh, clean and had sharp colours. Over the years the colour would fade and the sail darken. This first voyage was important. My son and Siggi's had their own tent. Although

Steana was the son of the hersir that would garner him no favours and I knew that Mary would be appalled at that thought. She had ideas about what she called our place in the village. She expected special treatment for our son.

The next day we stripped to the waist and worked barefoot as we all used flint and metal scrapers to clean off the weed and wildlife from the hull. The ship lay on logs that acted as rollers. We canted her over so that we could work on one side. It took a whole day. We would do the other side the next day. It was dirty work for the weed stank. We piled the weed close to the fires to dry out and we would use the dried weed to feed the fires. We wasted nothing. I worked with my men for most of the first day and half of the second and then I went with Lars and his father to prepare the worm killing potion we would paint on the hull. I did not know the ingredients and Thorstein was passing his recipe to his son. I was honoured to be there. We also prepared pine tar for we would cover the hull with that first and then the solution. One task for the ship's boys would be to keep the pine tree roots burning all night. It would be good preparation for the times they had to keep watch all night when at sea.

After three days we had finished what Thorstein had warned us would be dirty work. Our hands were still sticky and stiff from the pine tar we had failed to clean from our hands. Our clothes stank of the worm killer but the drekar was ready to be launched. I clambered aboard with Lars. The rest of the crew waded into the water with ropes held to pull us into the rising tide. They were spread out in a half-circle so that the ship did not cant over while they pulled. The crew chanted as they heaved on the ropes. It was the Agerhøne chant and helped them all to pull at the same time, at the end of each line.

We are the bird you cannot find
With feathers grey and black behind
Seek us if you can my friend
Our clan will beat you in the end.
Where is the bird? In the snake.
The serpent comes your gold to take.
We are the bird you cannot find
With feathers grey and black behind
Seek us if you can my friend
Our clan will beat you in the end.
Where is the bird? In the snake.
The serpent comes your gold to take.

We had sung the song when we had headed to Ribe but now, the ship's boys, who were also helping to pull the drekar, realized the real purpose of such songs. It did not take long to pull the drekar so that the bows were in the sea and the rising tide did the rest. With the ropes trailing from the side the crew hauled themselves aboard. The ones who did not manage it, and there were not many, would have to endure cruel banter from the rest. Steana, Siggi and Snorri all managed it easily. The first ones aboard took oars from the mast fish and under Lars' direction began to turn us. We would finish the work in Ribe harbour. We rowed the mastless ship down to join the other ships. That we were the last to join our fleet was down to me. I had wanted our work to be meticulous and, perhaps, I was too careful. Only time would tell.

The rest of the fleet cheered as we entered the harbour and tied up next to the quay. Sweyn Skull Taker and Lodvir the Long had ensured that the best berth was reserved for the king when he arrived. Ours was not the best but it suited and we began to fit the mast and crosstree. My heart was in my mouth as Steana scrambled up the mast to help fit the stays but I knew it was necessary and doing so in the calm waters of the harbour was much easier than it would be in a stormy sea. By the end of the day, the drekar looked more like a warship.

It was as we hauled aboard the ale barrels and barrels of salted herring and pork that the first of the invasion fleet arrived. Galmr was one of the early arrivals and I waved him over so that he could tie up next to us and use our ship as a bridge to the quay. It was a courtesy not every ship would enjoy. We had no time to chat as the loading of the stores was vital and Lars was keen to have the ship as balanced as he could. The larger barrels would be the last to be loaded for they would occupy the deck, but the smaller barrels were placed in the hold along with spares such as the steering withy, crosstree, mast and spare sail. The last three items were at the bottom of the hold, close to the ballast and we all hoped that we would not have to fetch them for it would mean that disaster had overtaken us. There were spare oars stacked there too. When Lars was satisfied, then the deck was refitted and we brought aboard our chests. They had been stacked on the quay since we had tied up and now, they were placed where the men would row. Their place was determined by me. My hearthweru occupied the two oars closest to the steering board. The nearer to the prow the less experience the rower had. I had learned much when I had been at the furthest end of the drekar. It was a good system. As I walked down the drekar, with Steana in close attendance, he asked me, "Is this it? Are we ready for sea?" I looked at him sternly. He grinned, "Hersir."

"Almost. Tomorrow, we fit the figurehead and that tells the world that we are ready for sea. If this voyage was longer than a few days, we might have some fowl at the prow to give us eggs, but England is not far away and we will not need it." We had reached the prow and we turned to look down the length of the drekar, "You know, Steana, that from the moment we set sail I cannot watch over you. I have a duty to the king and that means I neglect my son." I pointed to the quay. "I leave my son there and Steana the ship's boy takes his place. You will learn much and endure more. Some things that will happen to you may be unpleasant." I remembered my two tormentors, Erik and Ulf, long dead, they had made my life a misery.

He nodded, "I know, hersir, Gandálfr told me. I will make you proud of me."

I shook my head, "You need do nothing for that to happen. I would rather you just stay safe for this voyage."

The ceremony of fitting the figurehead was an important event. Sweyn Skull Taker had commanded the ship for many years, and he came with his hearthweru to observe the ceremony. All our warriors were dressed for battle and stood with their oars in the air as Thorstein and Lars carefully fitted the figurehead which had been carved many years earlier by Bolli's father, Bergil. The crew banged their oars on the deck and the jarl and I emptied our horns of ale over the figureheads. There had been a time when blood would have been split over it, but those days were gone.

As the crew replaced the oars I stood with my foster father and my cousin to watch the ale drip from the serpent and into the sea. "The ship looks good Sven and you have made her as new. I shall miss her."

I nodded, "Yet your new one *'Falcon'*, is bigger and faster, you will have more crew. As Lodvir discovered when he first sailed *'Hyrrokkin'*, sometimes an older slower ship seemed better somehow."

Sweyn One Eye said, "Aye, and we shall have a new crew to whip into shape."

"That is true of all the ships. Death does not just come in battle but old age and disease."

We had lost four warriors over the winter. Perhaps they might not have sailed with us but we would never know.

"And the king's plan, has he told more?"

I knew that Karl Three Fingers had visited the jarl but I had not seen him. I had assumed that it was to tell him more about the invasion. Sweyn shook his head, "Karl came to speak to me. He thought that when we had parted there was ill-feeling. There was not but it was as

114

well to clear the air. Karl and I are no longer young men. As far as I know, the king intends to land, as he told us, at Sandwic."

I nodded, "That is because he hopes that Thorkell will meet him there. He will not. Thorkell is not foolish enough to fight us there. He will choose his moment and his battles. Lundenwic is a fortress and Thorkell will squat there knowing that he is safe. He will have mooring for his fleet and he will hope that the men of Wessex wear us down."

The jarl turned to walk back down the drekar, "All is well then. I will have one last night with my daughter-in-law and grandchildren for the king will be here within a day or two and he will expect us to jump when he barks."

After they left, I thought about their words. I had only ever heard King Sweyn bark. He had never, to my knowledge, praised anyone. It did not seem, to me, to be a good way to encourage men to follow you. I wondered if this time he would lead. It would be a test.

The king arrived the next day and I wondered if he had awaited his moment for he sailed in, at the head of forty drekar, just as the sun was setting and his drekar was flared by the red and yellow sky of dusk. It was effective and I heard those on the quay gasp. The fact that the ships at the rear might foul a rock in the dark appeared immaterial. His sails lowered, he docked at his berth just as the sun dipped below the horizon and darkness enveloped us all. He waved to the onlookers and then headed, with Cnut, Karl Three Fingers and his hearthweru to Lodvir's hall. By rights, it was Jarl Sweyn's hall but my foster father preferred to stay and live in Agerhøne.

I turned to the crew, "If you wish one more night ashore then this is it but there will be no excuses for thick heads. When we sail, and it will be on the morrow, we will show the other ships that 'Sea Serpent' is the best ship with the best crew."

They all cheered and a voice shouted, from the dark, "Do not worry hersir, the Dragon Sword will not be ashamed of any of us."

Chapter 12

The problem with such a large fleet, there were two hundred or more ships, was that it took some organising. The king led the way from our harbour. The ships that had waited outside, in the sea, had an easier task than those who had moored in the harbour for the ones outside the harbour merely had to turn and find sea room. The rest of us had to manoeuvre and navigate around captains who were unfamiliar with these waters. It took some hours for us to get into formation and then follow the king. The king's ship, *'Sky Dragon'* was the largest ship I had seen since we had sunk *'Long Serpent'* at Svolder. Double crewed she would be faster than any other of our fleet and already she was establishing a long lead. The jarl led twelve drekar, most of them had been with us on the Trent. In addition, Galmr and four more drekars joined our smaller fleet and we formed up in an arrow behind *'Falcon'*. We gradually caught up with the king as he was forced to reef sails and allow the rest to catch up with him. We managed barely thirty miles that first day and we all reefed our sails, as darkness fell, to keep us together. With lights hung from our sterns, we edged our way south.

We had not yet needed to row but the ship's boys had worked hard as they raced to obey Lars' orders. He was as nervous as they were and, to speak the truth, he gave too many orders. It was better, however, for him to make his mistakes now rather than later when it might have mattered. Here, it just tired out the boys so that when the sail was reefed for the night, they grabbed food and then collapsed in heaps along the deck. I took the cloaks of Steana, Siggi and Snorri. I covered their bodies in case it rained. Rain it did and the whole crew of boys learned a lesson. My three charges suffered the least and they had dry clothes. Most of the boys would have to endure chafed skin from damp clothes until their rain-soaked clothes dried out. There was nowhere to dry them.

The next morning some ships were missing and it took time to get going again. The pattern for the next four days and nights was set. The only difference was that the crew, most of whom had been a ship's boy at one time, threw lines over the side to catch fish. It was normally a task for the ship's boys but Lars kept them too busy. I decided I would intervene but only if Lars kept up the same routine. Gandálfr and my hearthweru caught many of the shiny fish that appear, to me, to be the most stupid fish on the sea. They would bite at anything shiny. Their deep red flesh, however, was tasty and, like the rest of the crew, I ate two raw straight away. We brined the rest for we wasted nothing.

As we ate them Faramir said, "Hersir, I have heard we sail for Sandwic." I nodded. "My wife's family live there."

I knew what he meant and I shook my head, "We can do nothing about that, Faramir. If you can reach them first then you may be able to save them, if not…" His face was downcast. "If you and the hearthweru wish to seek them as soon as we land then you have my permission. There are enough others to do all that the king commands."

Gandálfr growled, "I like not this leaving of you, hersir."

I laughed, "This will not be the first time I have raided Sandwic and thus far I have not suffered a scratch. All is well." Even though I believed what I said I still kept hold of Thor's Hammer.

The Saxons would know that we were coming. We saw ships' sails in the distance and knew that they would see us. They would sail back to England with the news and soon be raising the fyrd. Enough warning had been given that King Sweyn Forkbeard was coming and the sight of so many ships would raise men to face us. As we neared the coast of Cent and Cantwareburh we saw that they had an army to meet us. Shields backed by spears lined the coast and when it was clear that we were heading for Sandwic then riders left to fetch more men. King Æthelred was now paying for an army, Thorkell the Tall's, and they would be used at some time to fight us. As we drew closer to the shore, I saw that there were no Vikings amongst the men awaiting us. Thorkell the Tall was elsewhere. The jewel in the English crown was Lundenwic and they would be desperate to keep us from it.

King Sweyn signalled for all the ships to land at the same time. It was a risky strategy as it meant one ship's crew might well be outnumbered and destroyed but it gave the advantage to the king in that thousands would be ashore at the same time. We obeyed and we found ourselves landing with the men of Ribe and Agerhøne to the east of Sandwic and closer to Remisgat. We would not be able to use the ship's boys as slingers for they would have to remain aboard the ships and so we just had a few archers who would try to thin out the enemy. Our one advantage was that we were landing in a place with few buildings.

I stood with my hearthweru at the prow. I had my shield over my back and Saxon Slayer was in my two hands. A few desultory arrows came at me and my hearthweru but we were mailed and had good helmets. The arrows would do little harm. The beach and the dunes were just three hundred paces from the sea and I had to be the one to gauge when to jump. I had my hand on the prow and when I saw stones beneath the keel I leapt into the water. Thankfully, I landed well and while the water came above my knees the surf was not strong enough to sweep me from my feet. Holding Saxon Slayer in two hands, I forced my way up the sloping beach to reach the dry sand. It was only then that I swung my shield around and waited for others to join me.

One Saxon, braver or, perhaps, more foolish ran directly at me. He wore no mail and held a shorter spear than me and a smaller shield. As I prepared a blow I wondered if he thought my mail and war gear would slow me down. He ran as close to me as he could and when he was just three paces from me hurled his spear at me. It was laughable for I just blocked the spear and then took three strides to plunge my spear into his middle. He looked in shock as the ash shaft entered his soft middle. I struck well and there were no bones to block the blow and it was only when the tip touched his spine that I twisted and pulled back. His body fell from my spear as my hearthweru flanked me. My men all cheered at this first victory. I looked down the beach and saw the jarl. Between us was the warband of Lodvir the Long. On my left were Galmr Galmrsson and his crew.

While we waited, I began to bang my spear against my shield and I chanted, "Ribe! Ribe!"

Others took up the chant. The Saxons began a half-hearted version of their own but as our numbers were swollen by more men joining us so Viking voices drowned out the Saxons. I looked down the line and when Sweyn Skull Taker pointed his spear at the enemy I did the same and stepped forward. Although our men acted quickly the leaders of our line were always a step ahead and we had a spiked formation, often called boar's snout. The sand sucked at our feet and there was a temptation to move faster. I did not because I knew that would be a mistake. Slow and steady would win the race.

The Saxon line was at the top of the beach and they had the slight advantage of height. The advantage was an illusion for we would be striking up at their middles with our superior spears. Had they taken the initiative and charged down at us then they might have enjoyed more success but they did not and it was we who drove our spears up at them. Some of the Saxons blocked the blows with their shields and their spears stabbed at heads. Our heads were well protected by helmets while less than two out of every five of the Saxons wore mail. Those who failed to block with their shields were struck and men began to fall. A spear scratched and scraped along my helmet. Another smacked hard into my shield but the three men before my hearthweru and me died and I pulled back my arm to drive Saxon Slayer at the man in the second rank. The battles of Svolder and Hringmaraheior had been fought against men like we. Warriors who knew how to fight and were prepared to die. The English we fought that day were already demoralised having never won a battle in living memory. There was no Ulfcetel Snillingr to lead them. When I saw the fear in the eyes of the next warrior I faced, I knew I had won before I struck my blow for he turned and ran. Had I so minded I could have run after him, caught him and skewered him in the back but there was no need. He would never face a Dane in battle again.

I raised my spear in the air and shouted, "Ribe and Agerhøne!" The shout echoed down the beach and as much as the deaths that they had endured, broke the will of the defenders and they fled.

The battle had been spread out over a large area and we had no idea how the others had fared but when we saw smoke coming from Sandwic then we knew that the king had taken Sandwic. I caught Faramir looking in that direction.

"If you wish to go and see if your family lives or dies, Faramir, then go." He hesitated, "Tell the king that the enemy in the east is defeated." I gave him a reason and the king would not be angry.

He nodded and ran.

The aftermath of any battle is never pleasant. Saxon Slayer and the other spears we used inflicted a terrible wound and none would survive. We went among the English to end their misery. Some cried for a priest. All that we could do was to put the cross of the White Christ in their hands and then end their suffering as they mumbled his name. It had been easy for us and we had lost none. Once the battlefield was cleared and our wounded tended to, we headed inland. We sought food and treasure. Knowing the area as I did, I led the jarl and our men towards Remisgat. There we found wagons, carts and refugees on the road. The laden wagons and carts were abandoned and the people fled. We did not pursue them. We took what they had tried to save and headed into the port. Animals like cattle and oxen had been left. We slaughtered them. We would eat well. What we did not eat we would salt.

We returned to the beach and our drekar. Lars had anchored the drekar and sent the ship's boys ashore to light fires for our food by the time we returned. A short while later a despondent Faramir returned. He went first to the jarl. "The king wishes to speak with you jarl."

"And the hersirs?"

"They are not needed."

Once he was told Sweyn Skull Taker and his hearthweru headed along the beach. We had taken horses from the leaders of the army. The leaders were dead.

Faramir shook his head, "Seara's father is dead. He was a fisherman and he was butchered along with the other fishermen. They had neither helmets nor mail."

I nodded, "And the rest of the family?"

"Therein lies hope for I saw only dead men. The women must have fled. The king burned their ships."

"As we would have done, Faramir."

"I know."

Although my hearthweru understood the actions it would not help him when he told his wife of the death of her father.

To keep all my men busy we loaded the treasure we had taken aboard the drekar. I was not sure how long we would stay and it was always better to keep men busy. I was on the beach supervising the loading, never an easy task up a precarious gangplank, when Lodvir strode over. He nodded to Steana, "I see you have brought your son to war. How did he fare?"

"I confess, Lodvir, that I do not know. I had too much else on my mind. He did not fall from the crosstree and he appears to be unhurt. I will speak with him this night."

"And those two with him, who are they? They look like handy fellows."

"They are the sons of Siggi the Pig." He frowned, "He shared an oar with me on my first voyage."

He looked shocked, "That is *wyrd*. I never thought Siggi the Pig would be a warrior but those two look like your son." He took some dried venison from his satchel. Lodvir was fond of it and offered some to me. I chewed as he continued, "If all the opposition is like this then Sweyn will have his kingdom. Will he stay here as a ruler or milk it dry and return home?"

I think because I was so close to Cnut that men, even those that knew me well thought I was better informed than I was. "I know not but Harald rules Denmark for his father and there is no need for the king to rush home. Besides, this is a big country. The further north one travels the better are the warriors. I hope to be home soon but I do not expect it."

By the time darkness had fallen, we had all loaded our treasure on our ships but we remained on the beach feasting on the animals we had butchered. Warriors are always concerned to have a full belly when you can for you know not whence the next meal will come. Lars ate on the ship alone. We had sea anchors out and were close enough to swim out if there was a problem. It meant my son, along with Siggi and Snorri were ashore and all three were full of excitement. They had not been ashore when the brief battle had taken place but they had a fine view of it from the drekar. They were excited and bubbled out their observations as we ate.

"The Saxons just buckled like a badly made sword. Are they all like that, hersir?"

"Most are, Steana, but make no mistake, there will be sterner tests the further north that we go."

"Hersir, do we not march on Lundenwic and take that city?"

"I doubt it, Siggi. The city has a good Roman wall and excellent defences. There is but one bridge and the river has many twists and turns. We will have to go there but it will not be any time soon. The next time the clan fights your bows and slings may well be needed." I pointed along the beach. "A good warrior takes when he can. There are many perfect stones here. I would spend time gathering bags of them."

They jumped up and soon every ship's boy was scouring the beach for stones.

Sweyn Skull Taker returned while the boys were still occupied. The hersirs all rose and went to see him. He pointed to the north, "We sail on the morning tide to the land of the East Angles. We now have a plan. We subjugate that part of the land for there are the better warriors and then sail to the Humber." He smiled, "It seems our raid there, that was once so heavily criticised by the king and Thorkell, is now seen as a most useful raid for we know the land. Once the north is in our hands then we will move south."

Lodvir nodded, "So this time he intends to stay until the crown is upon his head."

"It seems likely." He turned to Galmr, "As your drekar raided Gippeswic the king wants your ship to lead the attack on the town. Do not worry Galmr, the men of Ribe and Agerhøne will be at your back."

"I am not worried, Jarl Sweyn, for I have served with Sven Saxon Sword and know that your hearts are brave hearts."

Lodvir said, "It is a good plan for when we leave here, they will expect us either to sail to Wiht or to Lundenwic. We may have to row but we will be there before a messenger can warn them what we have done." It was grudging praise from Lodvir who did not like King Sweyn.

The king's decision to use us as the vanguard was also wise for we were to the east of the rest of the fleet and our natural position was at the fore. Galmr and his handful of drekars led us but it was *'Falcon'* that followed.

Lodvir was right and sailing first east then north meant that we had to row more than we had on the way south. If the ship's boys thought that they would have an easier task they were wrong for they were kept busy fetching ale to the rowers. We sang a song of Jarl Sweyn. The saga of Svolder would be kept for another time. We needed a chant about beating the Angles and Saxons.

Sweyn Skull Taker was a great lord
Sailing from Agerhøne with his sons aboard
Sea Serpent sailed and ruled the waves
Taking Franks and Saxons slaves
When King Sweyn took him west
He had with him the men that were best
Griotard the Grim Lodvir the Long
Made the crew whole and strong
From Frankia where the clan took gold
To Wessex where they were strong and bold
The clan obeyed the wishes of the king
But it was of Skull Taker that they sing
With the dragon sword to fight for the clan
All sailed to war, every man
The cunning king who faced our blades
Showed us he was not afraid
Trapped by the sea and by walls of stone
Sweyn Skull Taker fought as if alone
The clan prevailed Skull Taker hit
Saved by the sword which slashed and slit
From Frankia where the clan took gold
To Wessex where they were strong and bold
The clan obeyed the wishes of the king
But it was of Skull Taker that they sing
And when they returned to Agerhøne
The clan was stronger through the wounds they had borne
With higher walls and home much stronger
They are ready to fight for Sweyn Skull Taker
From Frankia where the clan took gold
To Wessex where they were strong and bold
The clan obeyed the wishes of the king
But it was of Skull Taker that they sing

It was almost fifty miles we had to row. Galmr, who led us, managed to find some wind to afford some relief but it took most of the day to make the voyage. Galmr had been placed in command by the king and he took advantage of that authority. He took the fleet further out to sea so that when we reefed our sails and headed into the shore it was coming on to dusk and the fleet appeared from the darkness of an eastern sky. The king had not said to wait for him and Galmr knew the town, as did I. The last time we had raided from the west and we knew the paucity of their eastern defences. He hove to a mile offshore and spoke with the jarl. King Sweyn and the rest of the fleet followed our lights.

"We have the chance to take this port easily while they sleep. You spoke with the king; will he approve?"

Sweyn Skull Taker had placed *'Falcon'* close to Galmr's drekar and I had gone to the prow of *'Sea Serpent'* so that I could hear their words.

I could not see his face but I heard the smile on his voice, "I was told to lead the fleet so that we could take Gippeswic. Let us obey that order. I would sleep under a roof this night."

Placing archers at the prows of our ships we rowed in under reefed sails. The men were armed and ready for war. The cloudy night made us invisible but I knew that they had watchmen on the moles that protected their harbour. We would be seen but by then it would be too late.

The shout when it came was a strangulated one as the closest watchman was struck by an arrow but others took up the call and the beacon flared into light at the same time as a bell sounded. It was not a large bell but it would awaken the inhabitants. Even as we turned inside the harbour, I saw Galmr lead his men from his drekar to secure the quay before his boys had even tied up the ship. I had been there and I pointed to a place Lars could land us.

"Larboard side, up oars!" As half of the crew raised their oars, we crabbed next to the quay and with Oathsword in my hand and my shield around my back I jumped the narrow gap to the wooden quay along with the ship's boys as they sought to secure us to the land. Until the crew had stacked their oars, I would be alone. I would not just be protecting myself but my son and the other boys. This was the first time they had done this. I ran down the quay towards the four sentries armed with shields and spears who ran to try to skewer the boys. I do not think that they expected an armed warrior to have landed so quickly. Leaving my shield on my back I drew Norse Gutter.

The four men each had a helmet and a leather byrnie in addition to their weapons. As was usually the case one was always more eager or perhaps braver and he was the one who reached me the first. I flicked aside his spear with Norse Gutter and swung Oathsword at his neck. The blood spurted and sprayed but I did not falter and ran past him. Behind me, I heard the sound of boots landing on the quay. My men would be hurrying to join me. I was mailed and the three men I fought were not. It meant I was heavier and I was certainly bigger. Using my sword and dagger to deflect their spears I simply ran at the next two men. They were knocked apart and the fourth man was suddenly faced by a warrior who was before him before he could bring his spear around. Norse Gutter gave him a swift death as I dragged it across his throat. I heard two cries behind me and saw Gandálfr and Dreng stab the two men I had knocked from their feet.

Gandálfr snapped, "How can we protect you, hersir if you go charging off?"

"Learn to run faster. Have the men form up behind me." Already the rest of our ships had tied up and I could hear from further along the quay, the sounds of clashing steel. Galmr was engaged closely with their defenders.

The men had landed quickly and Gandálfr said, "They are here, hersir."

Swinging my shield around I said, "Agerhøne!"

We ran along the quay and all our training and work was demonstrated as we ran in perfect time. Galmr and his crews were hemmed in next to their drekars. In the darkness his slingers and archers cold do little but when we ploughed into the side of the defenders it was like the breaking of a dam. They were not expecting an attack from their right and they died.

After slaying the man before him, Galmr saluted me with his sword, "Thank you, Sven Saxon Sword, that was timely."

Sweyn Skull Taker did not know the anchorage and he had only just placed his drekars next to the quay. Fortunately, it was on the far side of Galmr and so we had enough men to take the town.

"The king can use our drekars as a longphort. Follow me."

We poured through the roads that led from the sea. There were warehouses and houses as we passed the first ones, I shouted for men to search them. We knew that as the vanguard we would have to clear the town of warriors but we were owed a reward for being the first.

The men we fought were hard men. They had suffered at the hands of Thorkell the Tall and were willing to die, this time to save their homes. It took all night and most of the morning to completely eliminate the warriors. By that time the women and children had fled. They would join other families and warn them of the threat from the east. Sweyn Skull Taker called a halt when we reached the palisade that surrounded the port.

"Pile kindling against it and set it alight. With the wind from the east, it will not harm the port then we return to enjoy the food and houses of Gippeswic. Bring our wounded and dead with us."

Once again, the wisdom of investing in good mail and helmets had paid off. We had lost not a man. Galmr's band had lost three but even that was lower than we had expected. King Sweyn had an easy landing and was at the mint in Gippeswic. It was not the largest mint in the land but it was big enough to yield silver and copper coins. He nodded his thanks to Jarl Sweyn Skull Taker. "Tomorrow take your warband north and raid the land for a week. By that time we should have taken all that there is to take."

There were no thanks although Prince Cnut came with us to the warehouse our men had commandeered. He wished to talk with me and the jarl although I think I was the main reason he came with us. "I wish I had been with you, Sven. I heard warriors also saying that they would follow Oathsword. You have a powerful weapon."

I shook my head, "Thus far I could have used any sword. We have yet to have a real challenge, Prince Cnut."

"When we reach the Humber, I am to be given the responsibility of guarding the fleet. It is an honour."

"And one you will do well."

The jarl nodded too and said, "I will find a room for you and your hearthweru, Sven. Prince Cnut, I hope you learned well from my foster son."

He did not wait for a reply and Cnut frowned, "What did he mean by that, Sven?" I did not answer. Cnut was clever and he worked it out for himself. He lowered his voice and replied, "You mean do not be like my father?" I said nothing. "Come, Sven, for I would talk with you."

As much as I wished to be with my men and enjoy some rest, I knew that the Norns had spun and my thread and that of Cnut were entwined and could not be broken. I followed him. The bodies from the quay had been stripped and then hurled into the harbour. The crabs would feast well.

"My father has told me that I am to marry Lady Ælfgifu. He has sent a ship for her and when we take Lundenwic we shall be married."

"The moment is important?"

"I think so. My brother will rule Denmark and I hope that I shall be allowed to rule this land for my father. Lady Ælfgifu has royal connections and gives us a legitimate claim to the crown."

I knew, from speaking to Galmr, that King Sweyn also wished to complete the conquest of Norway. There King Olaf was also a weak king and there were factions who wanted a strong King Forkbeard as their king.

"I hope you will achieve all that you wish."

"What I want, Sven Saxon Sword, is for you to be at my side. I would have you as my Karl Three Fingers."

"I have not seen any evidence of his influence so far, Prince Cnut."

Karl Three Fingers was a remnant of the past. The king largely ignored him.

"It will be different with us, Sven. Now is not the time for you to make a decision but I would have you think about it. I have planted the seed and I hope that it will grow within you. I know that I am young and that it will take a long time to conquer this isle but I am patient. Just think about your answer, eh?" He hesitated, "Keep this to yourself. If others know I seek the crown of England, then…" I knew what he meant.

As I went back to my men my mind was a maelstrom. The decision I would have to make would change my life even more than the sword that had called to me. I wished I had Mary close to hand so that I could speak to her. She was not only the wisest woman I knew but the wisest person.

King Sweyn himself led one warband as we took treasure and supplies. By the end of the week, the land of the East Angles had been scoured of all that there was to take and we boarded our ships to head north to the Humber. Once again we led the fleet for we had hunted here. Before we left Gippeswic King Sweyn consulted the jarl and we learned that we were to sail the Trent once more. We were heading for Gegnesburh. It was upstream from where we had camped and raided. We had not even attempted to take it for it was a burh and had been built by King Alfred himself. The plan was to land the army there and to bring the English to battle.

We sailed along the Humber and there was no sign of Thurbrand the Hold nor his ships. He would have been foolish to attempt to prevent our passage for we had two hundred ships but I had expected him to be an interested spectator. He was noticeable by his absence. Such a huge fleet took time to navigate even a wide river like the Humber but the Trent was much narrower. We all took down our masts at its mouth and it was King Sweyn who led the stately procession of drekars down the Trent to Gegnesburh. It made sense for him to lead us as he had the longest drekar. We would stop when we came to the last place, he could turn his ship around and then we would all moor next to the east bank. We would only make a longphort when we needed to cross the river.

I had done Karl Three Fingers a disservice for he had been the one who had advised the landing site. The drekar bringing Lady Ælfgifu would come directly to Gegnesburh and the king intended to have his son married in the church there. It would be a symbolic act for King Alfred had married Ealhswith, a Mercian princess in the town and had thereby gained Mercia as he had united the kingdoms of England. There was also symbolism as he and his son marched into the town and took it with just one crew of warriors. I later learned that the king had bribed the warriors in the town to admit him but it was a dramatic gesture and meant we lost not a single man taking the burh that had a wooden castle within its walls. We were amongst the first to invest the town and the king was restrained. No blood was shed and the men of Gegnesburh were invited to support the man who would be king.

We camped in the verdant fields around the town. Emissaries were sent to the five important towns in the area. All of them were ruled by the people descended from Viking raiders, Deoraby, Ligera caestre, Lincylene, Snotingaham and Stanford. We did not raid until the emissaries returned. It was not only the emissaries that returned but also the leaders of the five towns. They came to offer their support to King Sweyn and to swear allegiance to him. It was the first major defection from the ranks of those who supported King Æthelred. Their visit coincided with the arrival of the drekar bringing Lady Ælfgifu. King Sweyn wasted no time and the couple were married so that his new allies could see that he was allying Denmark to the house of Wessex. He was laying claim to the throne. We were in England to stay.

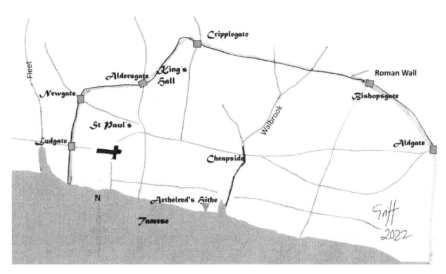

11th Century London

Chapter 13

I had not seen Lady Ælfgifu since we had rescued her. Then she had been a fearful, fey young woman. The woman who married Cnut was confident and happy with the marriage and she had grown into a beautiful one too. Of course, she had been groomed to marry Cnut by Queen Sigrid the Haughty. The queen's recent death might have been the reason for the hasty marriage. Whatever the reason Sigrid the Haughty had done a good job and Lady Ælfgifu won over the new allies of King Sweyn with her charm and her smiles. I saw beneath the smile a woman in the mould of Sigrid the Haughty. I was not sure that Cnut would have a happy marriage but then he was a man who would be king and such men do not have the luxury of marrying for love as I had done.

Leaving Cnut and his new bride in what was now referred to as the capital city of King Sweyn's new kingdom, we marched south and crossed the old Roman road of Watling Street. King Guthrum and King Alfred had made this the border between what was England and Danelaw. The moment we crossed it into the land that had been Mercia then it was as though King Sweyn unleashed his dogs of war. Men were sent to raid, plunder and burn. The message was clear. Submit or die. By the time we reached Oxnaford the army had devastated so much of the land that the city submitted without a fight and hostages were offered up to the king. The same happened at Wintan-Caestre and so we turned and headed up the valley of the Temese to Lundenwic. King Æthelred and Thorkell the Tall were there and with Thorkell's ships guarding the river and the bridge, there would only be two ways we would take the city, trickery or assault.

We had a much larger army now that the army of the Danelaw had joined us and we pitched our camps around the walls of the city so that, the river apart, it was completely surrounded. Thorkell's influence could be seen for he had improved the defences. The walls had been repaired and the ditches deepened and seeded with traps. They had used the time we had raided well. A council of war was held and this time the hersirs, as well as the jarls, were invited. It was the first time I had seen Karl Three Fingers for a long time and he looked gaunt. In addition he had not been, since Svolder, at the forefront of a campaign and he was no longer a young man but he sat at the king's right hand and I saw his influence as he guided the king through the different choices available to us.

Many ideas were thrown at the king. Some wanted to return for our ships and fight the drekar of Thorkell the Tall. Others suggested using the river to get to the bridge but then those who had been with Thorkell when we had raided spoke of my sneak attack on the walls. My success at Haestingas now came back to haunt me. Some of those who had been with us said that it would work on the Roman walls of Lundenwic. I did not think so but to have said so would have made it seem as though I was afraid.

I pointed out that the walls we had scaled had been made of wood and were not as high as those of Lundenwic. It was the king who put me in my place, "Sven Saxon Sword is it that you will not be taking a treasury that causes you such fear? Here you are serving your king. Perhaps you sailed too often with Thorkell the Tall, or should we now call him Thorkell the Traitor." He was trying to make a comparison with me and Thorkell.

It was unfair and I heard the murmur of disapproval that ran around the hall we were using. Karl Three Fingers leaned in and spoke to the frowning Forkbeard. He shook his head and then, after Karl had spoken again he smiled and nodded. "Perhaps I am being unfair, Sven Saxon Sword. Karl here has reminded me of your many skills and your clever mind. Have you a solution to our problem? Can you see a way for us to get inside the walls of Lundenwic?"

The simple answer was that I could not and I needed thinking time, "Perhaps if the king would give me a day and a night to scout out the walls then a solution might present itself."

The king had no choice but to accede to my demand and he grudgingly nodded. He also gave orders for warbands to build rams and ladders. As we left the hall, I was not confident that such war machines would work but I knew why the king ordered them built, it kept the warbands busy.

Once outside I was assailed by many warriors offering to come with me. I shook my head, "My hearthweru are all that I will need."

Lodvir the Long smiled and said, "I think, my young warrior, that you will allow me, your old teacher, to come with you. My eyes are not yet rheumy and may see something that you do not."

He was right and I nodded.

Eirik, the standard-bearer said, "And I would beg you to allow me to come, if for no other reason than I bring you good luck, Sven Saxon Sword, and even a great warrior like you cannot have too much good luck."

He was right and so there were seven of us who left the camp. I was pleased because seven is a lucky number and I was happy with each of them.

We began our walk by the river. We saw Thorkell's fleet and they were moored close to Æthelred's Hithe, the quay the king used. We were close enough to be seen and I recognised Thrum on the wooden quay. We were too far for their arrows to be effective and I knew that they would not waste them.

However, he saw me and could not resist a taunt or two, "Ha, it is the one with the so-called magic sword. You will blunt it on these walls."

Normally I would have remained silent but I did not like Thrum and knew he was instrumental in the defeat we had suffered. "Killer of old bishops, let you and I step before the walls and I will show you how sharp is my Dragon Sword."

It was a clear challenge and I saw his companions look at him anticipating that he would fight. Thrum was a bully and a coward. I had met enough in my life to recognise the type and he shook his head, "I will not waste my time with the likes of you. Loose arrows at them!"

It was pathetic. The arrows flew and we raised our shields. They were badly made, not one even penetrated the leather. Laughing we left. It was a small victory but Thrum had lost so much face that when we attacked, I knew that he would recklessly try to reclaim his lost honour. It took all morning for us to march around the walls and I spied just one piece of hope. When we came back, we stopped at a spot halfway between Cripplegate and Bishopsgate. There was a twin branched stream, the Walbrook, that passed beneath the walls. There was a Roman tower guarding it but there were no metal bars to prevent access.

Lodvir nodded with approval when I pointed it out to him. "You have sharp eyes, Sven, but it will still be a difficult undertaking for there are sentries in the tower and on the wall."

I nodded and pointed to the ditch, "Aye, but crossing the ditch at nighttime and trying to scale the walls would be even harder. It is the only weakness that I can see. The Romans built their walls well."

The king liked the plan but he would not let me lead the men who would attempt to gain entry, "We shall let another try that. Galmr and his crew have shown themselves to be worthy warriors. I want you, Sven Saxon Sword, to lead an attack on the western wall, close to the Danish ships. Your notoriety and sword will draw the attention of the defenders to that part of the wall and give Galmr the greatest chance of success. We will wait with our army to the north to enter the Cripplegate and Bishopsgate as soon as they are opened."

Sadly Galmr was all too keen to do as he had been asked and was confident enough in my ability to draw the defenders that he agreed quickly. His crew were also as eager, especially Eirik. I determined to make our attack as strong as possible.

The attack was planned for the next night. There would be no moon and enough ladders had been built to enable us to cross the ditch. As the king had given me the task I would lead and I would plan. Jarl Sweyn Skull Taker and Lodvir the Long would follow my orders. I met with my tiny group of counsellors and told them my plan.

"The king wants a diversion and I will give him one but we will not assault the walls." I saw my foster father frown and I smiled, "Do not worry, the diversion will do all that is expected." I then laid out my plan. When they all smiled and nodded, I felt proud that I had concocted such a good one. We spent the rest of the day collecting kindling and building bridges. Only our clan knew what we planned.

At dusk on the day of the attack I visited with Galmr, "I am sorry that I came up with this plan, Galmr Galmrsson, for you will be in danger."

He laughed, "It is a good plan and you will be in as much danger, perhaps more. You gave my clan pride, Sven Saxon Sword, and so long as we fight alongside you then we will go from strength to strength." He nodded to his son, Haldi, and to Eirik. "These two warriors will follow me in and it will be my son who sounds the horn to tell the king that we have the gates."

I nodded and clasped his arm, "May the Allfather be with you."

"And you."

The Norns were spinning and I could not shake off this feeling that one or both attacks would end in failure.

As we were attacking at night, we blackened our faces and hands with soot and charcoal. We wore cloaks for we could discard them when we had to but it would allow us to close with the walls and, hopefully, remain hidden. The majority of the men I led were mailed. The ones who had no mail byrnie were to cover us with arrows and slings. With our shields across our backs, we moved into position just two hundred paces from the walls. There was a wooden bridge across the Fleet but most of the men, me included, would wade across the shallow river. The sound of too many boots tramping on wood would alert the defenders in the towers and along the walls. We wanted them to know we were there but we wanted it to be at the last moment. Dreng carried the precious pot with the fire within. All eyes, including the jarl's, were on me for I was the leader. I had made the plan and if it failed it would be upon my head.

Blood Sword

Drawing Oathsword I raised it above my head. As soon as I pointed it at the walls, we crossed the river and headed for the Ludgate. Two out of every five men carried ladders, wooden bridges, or kindling. The men with bridges were at the fore and they dropped them across the ditch. We were unlucky for it was the dropping of the wood that alerted the defenders and a horn sounded. The men with the ladders and the kindling followed me across the river. I ran with the chosen men carrying the kindling, towards the drekar we had seen moored close to Æthelred's Hithe. There were five guards there and as soon as they saw us, they drew their weapons. We ran and struck them even as they were summoning help. They did not have a true longphort but they had tied three drekar together. There were men aboard each of the ships and they began to dress, arm and race toward us. Arrows flew from the walls. With our backs facing the walls, they struck the shields across our backs. My plan was to make them think we would assault the walls and that was why ladders were being placed against the walls but it was a feint. Our archers and slingers would try to clear the walls while half of the men stood with shields held above them. The real attack was on their ships. We ran up the gangplank of the first drekar. I recognised it as the one I had sailed in, it was Hemingr's. The deck watch ran at us but they had not had time to don mail. It was pitifully easy to slash swords across unprotected bodies and heads. The first ship being taken, we crossed to the next and after disposing of their watch took the third ship. Here men had donned helmets and taken shields. They faced us with determination for they thought we intended to cut out their ships and none wished to be stranded in this land.

I had to draw Norse Gutter to block the blow of a sword and I hacked beneath the shield to bite deep into the thigh of the warrior who tried to kill me. I dragged the blade back across the bone and when blood sprayed, I knew he was dead. The others died as bravely.

"The kindling quick!"

We knew where to place the wood, close to the mast fish where the fire would soon take hold very quickly. As the bundles of faggots were laid around the mast so Dreng dropped burning coals. The bone-dry kindling flared and ships that had laid at anchor for months were dry enough for the fire to begin to bite and to race up the masts towards the crosstree. We headed back to the next ship. I could see that the walls of Lundenwic were manned and the small gate to Æthelred's Hithe was opening; it would allow men to come and attempt to stop the fire. With the wind from the west I hoped that we could destroy, perhaps ten ships but whatever damage we did was immaterial. The attack had drawn the enemy.

As the last fire was started, we jumped ashore and Sweyn Skull Taker shouted, "Shield wall!" He and the bulk of the men formed a single line facing both the walls and the Danes heading towards us. I saw that Hemingr led them. After swinging around my shield, I joined the warriors forming the second rank. We had no spears but we would fill the gaps when men fell.

Hemingr and his men were trying to save his drekar. I knew he would fail for I could feel the heat as the flames of the inferno we had started were fanned by the western wind and raced up the mast to set fire to the sail and crosstrees of the three stricken ships. If they were quick then they might save some of the drekar downstream, but they seemed intent on having vengeance on us. It was a mistake. They hurled themselves at our line. They did not know that we had already planned to move back towards the River Fleet and that our purpose had been fulfilled. We had drawn their best warriors to us and that would allow Galmr and his men to gain entry. Oleg the Strong fell to an axe wielded by Hemingr. It was a quick death for he had his helmet and skull split open. I stepped into the gap he left. I stood next to Sweyn One Eye and Haaken Hairy Mouth. I blocked the spear that came for my cousin and rammed Oathsword into the Jomsviking's ear. His round helmet afforded him little protection.

Hemingr roared a challenge, "Treacherous snake, face me!"

I laughed as I turned, "I was not the one who changed allegiance, Hemingr the Unfaithful."

He held his war axe high and I knew he would try to end my life as he had Oleg the Strong. Lodvir who stood on the other side of the jarl had taught me well and I angled the shield so that when he struck although it hurt my arm the blade slid down my shield to lodge under the edge of my boss. As he tried to pull out his axe head he was distracted and I lunged up and across his shield with my sword. His shield slightly deflected the strike but I still sliced across his cheek and through his leather straps. The helmet flew from his head. He pulled back the axe head and tried to punch with it. I punched at the same time with my shield and our arms jarred together.

"Back!"

The jarl's command had to be obeyed and I stepped back. Hemingr saw it as weakness and lifted his arm for what he thought would be the final strike. I stabbed as he came forward. It left me slightly isolated as the rest of our line had stepped back but it allowed me to sink the tip into his throat. I tore my sword to the side and Thorkell the Tall's brother died.

Before I could step back Thrum saw his chance. He had been humiliated by me and was probably drunk. He roared a challenge and as I stood before our line with my hearthweru trying to get to my side he ran at me almost like a berserker. Once again, my training with Lodvir came to my aid. He had pretended, during one training session, to be a berserker and with two swords had rained blow after blow at me. I had survived and learned that using weapons so wildly meant your blows were inaccurate. I would use Thrum's own recklessness to defeat him. He had not yet used his sword and it would be sharp. He screamed and while punching the boss of his shield at me he tried to end my life with a wicked swing of his sword. He was travelling too quickly and I turned so that his shield struck fresh air and his sword headed not for my head but the wood of the quay. I punched him in the side of the head with my shield and as Gandálfr and Faramir reached my side I hit his neck so hard that I almost severed his head.

"Enough, my lord! Back! This is your plan enjoy the fruits of victory."

Gandálfr was right and, after taking Hemingr's short sword and scabbard, I stepped back into the line. The death of their leader and the killer of the archbishop allied to the fact that two of the drekars we had fired were hissing into the Temese as they sank, demoralised them. The horn from the north wall drew them back within their fortress and we were able to back away without losing another man. We even had the luxury of fetching back our dead and wounded. I wondered if we had done enough for King Sweyn to take Lundenwic. My worries before the attack appeared to be groundless. Seven of their drekar were already destroyed and they would be lucky to save another five. We headed back to our camp in high spirits. We would mourn Oleg the Strong but he had died well and Sweyn One Eye would remember him with a song.

We drank and ate back at the camp and awaited the order from Karl Three Fingers to join the king once he had breached the walls. Daylight came and still, there was no order. Worse, we saw other men whom we had thought would be already over the walls wearily making their way back to us.

The jarl called over Harald the Swede and Urse the Hairy, "What went wrong?"

Urse the Hairy was a huge warrior whose name was as accurate as any, "They did not even make it through the river. There were guards on the inside. Galmr and his hearthweru were slain. They fetched their bodies out but we could not manage to take the gates." He nodded towards the blackened masts rising from the river, "I see that you did your part." He shrugged, "*Wyrd*, the Norns have spun. Perhaps we will have to try an old-fashioned assault."

Sweyn One Eye and Lodvir tried to console me but I could not help thinking that the deaths of Galmr and his men were down to me.

Galmr's son and the rest of their crew joined us later that day. They did not blame me but the Three Sisters. "My father died well, Sven Saxon Sword. There was a smile on his face when we fetched his body. We will now go home. I have spoken to the king and he has given us permission to return to Gegnesburh, collect our ship and sail home."

"I am so sorry, Haldi, tell your mother…" I knew there were no words. What could I say that would ease the pain?

He shook his head, "She knew that this would happen one day. But I have a favour to ask."

"Anything."

"Eirik would join your clan. He did all that he could to save Galmr but failed. I have told him he was wrong but he thinks he let down my father. He wishes to atone and he says that your threads are entwined."

I looked at the young warrior who had blown the horn at Haestingas and then saved my life in battle. As much as I did not want to be responsible for another death I knew that I was bound to take him on. If I did not then…*wyrd*. "Very well, Eirik, you are welcome. Fetch your war gear and Gandálfr will show you to our camp."

"I swear, hersir, that I will serve you unto death."

His words were like a lead weight for me to bear. "I would rather you served me in life."

Chapter 14

Little happened for a week and then I was summoned to King Sweyn. The jarl was not sent for and I wondered if I was to be punished for the failure of Galmr's attack. When I reached the house he was using Karl Three Fingers was not there and that, to me, was ominous. The king was alone and that also surprised me for the king was careful not to lay himself open to assassination. He saw the surprise on my face and smiled, "Sven Saxon Sword, of all the men in my army you are one I know I can trust. Karl Three Fingers is the greatest judge of men that I know. I would not allow your foster father to be alone with me for I would fear he might try to take my life and my crown. You are not a threat. Sit."

I sat and he gestured for me to help myself to the ale. I did so and waited. He was watching me carefully as though he was weighing me up and making some sort of decision.

"I did not thank you properly for helping to secure the release of Lady Ælfgifu. You did all that was asked of you. You have also shown yourself to be resourceful for the attack on Hemingr's ships was surprisingly successful. My son also seems to hold you in high regard and he has asked me if you can be his adviser when…" he waved a hand, "that can wait. So, Sven Saxon Sword, I wonder if you have diplomatic skills too?"

"Diplomacy, King Sweyn?"

He leaned closer to me and I could smell his breath; it was foul and seemed to me to be a sign of ill health, "I need you to take your ship and sail to Jorvik. You will go in peace and seek out Styr the merchant. He is a rich and powerful man and of Danish blood. He is my man." He smiled, "He is like your Aksel the Swede. These are men who survive wars and changes of rulers as easily as a housewife changes the sheets on a bed. He is my man in Jorvik. You are to use him to get to Uhtred the Bold, the ruler of Northumbria. I wish Uhtred to submit to me as King of England and I want to offer him a bride."

I frowned. Since we had been in this land, I had heard of many of the nobles and their wives. I had heard of Uhtred, "Is he not already married already?"

"He is but the marriage has broken down and Styr has a daughter, Sige. It is said she is the most beautiful woman in this land. If Uhtred marries her then he will have the support of the Danes in Jorvik and I know, from Styr, that they support my claim to the crown."

It made sense. "And what of Thurbrand the Hold?" I knew that I would have to pass through his lands to reach Uhtred and I also knew that the two men did not like each other.

"Do not worry about Thurbrand. He will wait to see what Uhtred will do. The south of Northumbria supports Thurbrand. When Uhtred marries Sige then Thurbrand will have lost for Jorvik is the most important settlement in Northumbria. You are tasked with bringing Uhtred to Gegnesburh. It is now Gormánuður. You have until the start of Ýlir to bring him to the new capital of this land. By then I hope to have the crown in my hands. Whatever happens I shall not spend Christmas here in this pestilential hole but at Gegnesburh." I hesitated for the task seemed simple enough and I could not see the danger to me. The king took a different meaning from it. He smiled that silky smile of his, "You married a Saxon, I believe?" I nodded. "When I am king then you shall have the manor where she was born. Norton?"

"But that is in the land of the Northumbrians, King Sweyn." Even as I raised the objection, I knew that the Norns were spinning. Mary wanted a return there and that impossibility might be realised by the very man she despised.

"When I am king then all the land shall be mine, you shall be the lord of Norton, the thegn. When I reach Gegnesburh I will have it so written. As soon as Uhtred submits to me then he can witness the document. I want men like you here, in this land when I become king. It is one thing to take a crown but another matter entirely to hold on to it."

"I will do as you ask. What do I tell my foster father and the other warriors? They might see my act as cowardice."

He laughed, "They would not do that, Sven Saxon Sword, but the story you can tell is that my son wishes you to return to Gegnesburh. He seeks your advice. They will all understand that."

I left and headed back to our camp. I felt guilty as I told the lie to the others. My crew, I would tell the truth but only when we reached our ship at Gegnesburh. The guilt was offset by the knowledge that I would be reunited with my son. I knew that Lars would watch out for him but I would be happier when I could keep an eye on him.

We had taken horses on our campaign and the king was happy for us to take them. Our battles with Hemingr had resulted in mail and treasure and, allied to that which we had already taken, our animals were laden as we headed north. It was almost two hundred miles north but we rode along a Roman Road that made the journey quicker. We travelled quickly and in just four and a half days reached the ships still anchored along the Trent. Cnut had been left with a sizeable army of two hundred men and he had improved the castle. I saw, in him, a leader. Marriage looked to have changed him and he had more confidence. The king had told me that I could confide in his son and even before I was reunited with my son I sat closeted with the prince. We were alone and I told him everything that his father had told me.

"I have not been idle here. I knew that Thurbrand the Hold might harbour resentment against me but the presence of the ships I sent to the Humber have seen no sign of him. You should be able to sail safely to Jorvik. Now that it is winter the rivers are high and the city is almost like an island. Did my father ask me to go with you?"

The blunt question came from nowhere. I looked at the young prince and saw that he had deliberately used the question to catch me off guard. "No, Prince Cnut. He will return here at Christmas. I am supposed to return with Uhtred. The leaders of the five boroughs will also be here to submit and I think he wants you at his side."

"He sees me as his heir?"

"Do not put words into my mouth, my prince. You are here and your brother is in Denmark. The king will have Æthelred's crown." I shrugged, "I confess that I cannot see it being the actual crown for King Æthelred appears to stay elusively hidden." That was a real fear for me. Until we brought the English to battle and not only defeated them but took their king then the crown would never sit securely on the head of King Sweyn Forkbeard. I cursed the king for planting the idea that I would have land in England. He had tempted me and I could not shake it off. Before he had offered me Norton I had not worried or even thought about my future in this land. I knew that Mary would wish to return to the place I had torn her from. Once an idea is planted it will grow and consume a man from within. I could feel it already.

Prince Cnut nodded, "You are wise, Sven, but we take it one step at a time. Thanks to my wife and her murdered father, Ælfhelm, my children have a claim to the crown. None can take that away from me now and I have you to thank for that. Have a safe voyage, Sven Saxon Sword."

I did not see his wife while in the castle that Cnut had improved. I guessed that he had ensured his wife had the best of quarters. I headed for my ship. My crew had gone directly to it and had already unloaded our treasure. By the time I arrived, the deck was being replaced over the hold. Steana beamed when he saw me.

"Have you a weapon for me, hersir?"

I glared at Gandálfr who shrugged, "Hersir, your son has missed you and we told him that you had taken Hemingr's sword. You need not such a weapon…"

"And I should have been the one to surprise him, not you Gandálfr. He is my son."

My hearthweru looked contrite, "I am sorry, hersir. I have failed you."

I relented and gave him a half-smile, "In the things that matter, Gandálfr, you have never let me down." I reached down into the warbag that lay on the deck and retrieved the weapon. "Here, Steana, this is your first sword."

His face lit up. I remembered my first sword. I had not used it often for the Dragon Sword found me but I could still remember the joy of holding my first weapon.

I turned to Lars, "We will be sailing north, to Jorvik. Make the ship ready for I would leave as soon as we can. We have to be back by the start of Ýlir and we both know that the weather can be unpredictable at this time of year."

"Aye, we will be ready. The boys have worked hard since you left us and the ship will fly." He gave a wry smile, "I have learned to trust them, hersir, and I will not be the tyrant who merely tires them out." Lars had learned too.

We had the shields fastened inboard as we rowed up the Trent. It was a harder trip than I had anticipated for there was a double row of drekars moored along the east bank. As we had the first time when we left the smaller river to enter the Humber we were thrown forward as though a god had hold of us. We also had difficulty finding the mouth of the Ouse for the rivers had burst their banks and the swamp and mud were covered by the waters. We had to use the ship's boys to lean over the prow and try to see through the silt and mud while the rowers sculled as slowly as possible. As soon as they found clearer water then we were able to make faster progress but it was still a voyage fraught with more difficulties than I had imagined. When we neared the city then it became easier for while there were few ships on the river at this time of year there were enough to show us the safe channel and when we neared the quays there were plenty of empty berths to make it relatively easy for us to be close to the centre. The port master pounced upon us as we tied up and demanded his payment.

Leaving Lars in command of the ship I went with just Gandálfr and Faramir to seek Styr. I had been told he had the largest house in Jorvik and the description was not wrong. Men directed us to it and we found a building with a second floor. He had armed guards and strong gates. The home was attached to a warehouse and while the house faced the better part of the city the warehouse was so large that it ended at the quayside. I realised it was a clever design. If trouble came then the merchant could leave by the river without having to venture into the streets.

"I am here to see Styr."

The scarred Dane snorted, "Aye, but does he wish to see you, boy?"

I had learned long ago to ignore such insults. Some men reacted to them but there was no point, in my view. I knew my skills as a warrior and did not need to boast about them, especially to a pot-bellied warrior who had not fought in a real battle for many years. His knuckles might be scarred but his blade looked to be old and I doubted he would be able to draw from his scabbard.

"If you will not admit me then tell him that I bring a message from Sweyn Forkbeard." He looked confused so I added, "King Sweyn Forkbeard. Surely you have heard of him?"

The guard's companions laughed and the man snapped, angrily, "Let them enter but if our master disapproves of them then they will feed the fishes in the Ouse."

Gandálfr laughed, "You know I almost hope that he does dismiss us just so that I can see how you attempt to do that." My two hearthweru had the measure of the bully.

The two men who escorted us made sure that they entered the hall first. There was another warrior there. They spoke to him and he nodded. "Wait here."

The hall was unlike any other hall I had ever seen. We were left in what looked like a small room, almost an antechamber. The two doors would hinder anyone trying to gain entry and the doors were solidly made. When the guard had disappeared through the inner door, we had felt a waft of heat but one that appeared perfumed. I could not quite detect the exact aroma but it was pleasant.

I turned to the two men who had escorted us, "Does Styr pay well?"

The taller of the two laughed, "Why, are you looking for a job?"

I laughed back at him, "No, for I am a warrior." I patted the sword.

The shorter of the two took umbrage at that, "We are warriors too. None can get close to our master and it is known that there are tough men in Jorvik. We are the best!" He said it defensively as though challenging me to question its veracity.

I held up my hands, "I meant no offence, friend, it is just that we take our money from those we fight and we are paid well. I just wondered if the pay was worth being away from war."

The taller one said, "Aye, Ulf, do not be so prickly." He leaned over to me, "His brother, the one at the door, Olaf, is even more prickly. It must be in the blood. Their mother was a Scotswoman. To answer your question we do get to fight enemies. Sometimes we sail aboard one of our master's knarrs. Occasionally there are pirates foolish enough to try to take our cargo. They pay with their lives and we line our purses with the proceeds."

The men chatted amiably. I realised that they were keeping us occupied and I studied the door leading to the inner chamber. There was a hole and we were being watched. Styr was a careful man. We must have passed scrutiny for the door opened and the warrior came out.

"You may enter." As Gandálfr and Faramir made to follow me, the warrior held up his hand, "Your master only."

"We are his hearthweru. Where he goes so go we."

I put my hand on Gandálfr's for he was reaching for his sword. "Peace, Gandálfr. I think I will be safe." I stared at the warrior, "And I know that you two will be safe. Is that not true?"

The guard nodded, "No harm will come to those who behave themselves."

I knew there would be words spoken for the five I left outside were all tough men. Styr was alone in the small room. It reminded me of the room Mary's father had in Norton but while her father had been interested in the pursuit of knowledge, the parchments I saw lying around were filled with numbers and inventories. Money drove Styr. He half stood, "Welcome, Sven Saxon Sword. My house is honoured to have you as a guest."

"You know my name?"

"There is not a ship lands on the Ouse but I do not know its purpose and cargo within half an hour of its arrival. *'Sea Serpent'* was recognised." It begged the question as to why we had been made to wait but I just smiled. "Sit and take some ale."

He poured me a horn of ale. It was not just the simple horn we might have used but was decorated with jet and silver. It was a striking looking piece.

"You say you come from King Sweyn." I nodded and tasted the ale. It was good. "Have you any proof of that?"

I shrugged, "None save that there is no reason for me to make up such a thing." I put the horn in the beautifully carved holder and placed my hands on the table, "I have little time to complete my task. Already you have wasted time by keeping me waiting unnecessarily." There was an edge to my voice and I saw a flicker of fear in his eyes. "You have a daughter Sige and King Sweyn would have you offer her to Uhtred the Bold in exchange for his support to his claim for the throne. He would have Uhtred return with me to Gegnesburh by Christmas so that Uhtred can publicly show his support and to bend the knee." The merchant's eyes widened. "I believe that you and the other Danes of Jorvik also support the idea of a Danish king rather than Æthelred. It seems to me, a simple warrior, that if you are related by marriage to the ruler of Northumbria and have the support of the new king then that can only bode well for you. Am I wrong?"

He smiled, "No, and I can see that you are far from a simple warrior. The king chose well. I had taken you for a wild warrior who could fight but not think. I can see that I was wrong. Your idea has merit."

"The king's idea."

"Just so, the king. Sige is an obedient girl and Uhtred is also a rich man. It would mean, of course, that he rids himself of Ecgfrida, his current wife, but from what I have heard Uhtred is less than happy with her and they have lived apart for the last six years. She has served her purpose for she was the daughter of the Bishop of Durham." He studied his fingers and then said, "You have to return by Christmas?"

"Aye, and time is passing."

"Then we cannot delay. Do you wish to stay here in my hall? It will be more comfortable than your drekar."

"Thank you, Styr, but we will remain aboard my ship." I was in a place I did not know and with people who might wish to cause harm to me. We were safer in my drekar.

He nodded, "Then wait for my summons. I will speak with Uhtred and if he is in agreement, we shall send for you and confirm all."

I did not relish the prospect of returning to the king with bad news. The seed of land in Norton had grown and I was already envisaging a life there with Mary.

Gandálfr and Faramir were more than happy to spend time on the ship rather than in the sumptuous hall. "Those guards are not warriors, hersir. They would last but a moment in a shield wall. I would not trust them to keep out a Saxon priest."

I smiled. Gandálfr was a true warrior and had contempt for those who played at being one. "We may be here for a week or more. We have food aplenty but we need ale. Let us call at an inn close to the river and see what they can provide."

We found one just a hundred paces from the ship. It was called *'The Saddle'* and must have been here when the Romans called the town Eboracum, for the saddle that hung outside to market was an ancient Roman saddle with four protruding horns. The owner, Edgar, was a pleasant Saxon who saw the opportunity to make coin while not having to risk wild Danes in his inn.

"Aye, my lord, we can supply ale to you on your drekar and we can do so at a fair price. If you want hot food then we can provide that too."

He sensed my hesitation and said, "They do not allow men to light fires on the quayside. There is too much danger of igniting the wooden buildings."

"Then, Edgar we shall have one hot meal a day and a firkin of ale each day too."

I gathered the crew around the mastfish and told them of the arrangements. "I am happy for men to visit the markets here but I want no one to travel alone. At the same time, I want no groups of more than four for it might cause trouble. We serve King Sweyn Forkbeard and what we do, we do for Denmark."

The lie almost stuck in my throat. This was all for the king but I had to explain our purpose in terms that they might understand. I saw Steana, Siggi and Snorri put their heads together. I went over to them, "And if you think I will allow you three to wander this town alone then you are mistaken. When I am summoned to meet with Styr again then you can come with me and either Faramir or Gandálfr will be your nursemaid." I saw the disappointment on their faces. "And Steana, your new sword stays aboard the drekar." I smiled as his face fell even further.

Both the food and the ale were good and my men behaved themselves. It was rare for us to be able to buy. Usually, we raided and the goods that my men bought were the sort of things that were taken away before we could get them when we attacked. There were jewellery makers in the town and with Hwitebi not far away there were fine pieces of jet as well as gold and silver. My men had full purses and were anticipating a return to Agerhøne. They spent well and their treasures were placed in their chests. We had to wait longer than I had expected for the reply from Uhtred. It was five days before the taller warrior who had spoken pleasantly to me, Ebbe, came to fetch us. The three boys had been sulking for the last days and when I waved them over their faces lit up.

As we headed towards the merchant's house I said, "I will break my own rule, Gandálfr. The five of you can visit the market. Today, you boys shall have the finest hearthweru as your bodyguards."

"Are you certain, hersir?" Gandálfr was a worrier.

"I do not think I will be in any danger." That was not quite true. When Lady Ælfgifu's father Ælfhelm had been murdered on the orders of the king, Uhtred had been made an eorledman of Jorvik by the king. Had Uhtred colluded with the king? The result had been to give Uhtred the ancient Kingdom of Bernicia as well as Deira and explained the feud with Thurbrand the Hold.

My hearthweru took the boys off once I was admitted to the hall. This time I was not taken to the small chamber filled with parchments but to a small dining hall. It was not the one used for feasting and looked to me like the one Styr might use each day when he dined with his family. As yet I had not seen either his wife or the beauty that was Sige. All that I had seen were the guards and servants.

There were three warriors with Styr and two of them were clearly bodyguards. The third I took to be Eorledman Uhtred. He was a warrior and his arms and face showed the scars of battle. His sword was as long as Oathsword and, like me, he wore a byrnie. That told me much about him. He feared that if he walked abroad then an enemy might try to stick a knife into his back. His two bodyguards looked to be good at what they did and the contrast between Styr's Ulf and Olaf could not have been clearer. Uhtred's men could have dealt with Ulf and Olaf without even using a weapon.

Styr said nothing but Uhtred strode over to me and held out his right arm for me to clasp. I did so and he said, "King Sweyn does me a great honour by sending the warrior with the Dragon Sword to seek my help."

I gripped his arm as firmly as he gripped mine. Closer to him I saw that he was as old as Lodvir the Long.

"I serve my king, my lord."

"And that king would be my king, eh, Sven Saxon Sword?"

I was now in uncharted waters for the king needed a diplomat and I was a warrior. "And would he be a worse king than the one you have at present, my lord?"

He waved a hand around the room as though it was Northumbria, "If King Sweyn brought his armies north then he would find us a harder morsel to swallow."

"Perhaps."

He laughed and turned to his bodyguards, "What do you think, how would we fare against these Danes?"

They smiled, "I think that fewer of them would board their ships when they fled back to Denmark."

Was I being tested? I nodded, "Then it is just as well that King Sweyn seeks to attain the crown without fighting the men of Northumbria."

He sat and gestured for me to sit too. One of the bodyguards filled two horns with ale. He handed them to us. It was to show that the ale was not poisoned. Styr looked very uncomfortable for this was his home and yet he was being ignored.

"Let me understand the King of Denmark's offer. He wishes me to come with you and bend the knee and in return, I get this merchant's daughter. Is that correct?"

Said like that it sounded pathetic but I nodded. "And you will provide hostages from your family as surety against treachery."

He waved a hand and nodded, "That is understood. Now Sige may be a beauty but I can have any woman I wish." He smiled at Styr, "No offence, my friend."

Nervously Styr said, "And none taken. There would, of course, be a dowry."

Uhtred's words flew from his mouth like barbed arrows, "Of course, there would, that is to be expected. I am no fool, Styr, and I know that the Danes of Jorvik wish me to embrace the Danish king but I need to know what is in it for Northumbria." Styr shrank back into his chair. Uhtred turned his attention back to me. "Now, Sven Saxon Sword, let me give you, my proposal. You were the warrior that managed to take Lady Ælfgifu from under the nose of Thurbrand the Hold." There was no point in denying it and I nodded. He chuckled, "She was a pretty young thing and I confess I thought that she might make me a bride. I hear that the king's son has bedded her?"

"They are married, aye."

"A clever move on King Sweyn's part. Here is my offer. King Malcolm who lives north of my land has been an irritant and I have heard that he and the King of Strathclyde, Owen the Bald, are thinking of attacking my new fortress of Durham. I will bend the knee to your king but only if he gives to me, you, Sven Saxon Sword, and ten drekar crews to help defeat King Malcolm." He turned to Styr, "I will still marry Sige and take the dowry but I will not bend the knee without warriors fighting for me."

Mary had told me how the White Christ had been tempted by the devil. I now saw that my devil was twofold; King Sweyn and Uhtred. Norton was the lure and I knew that King Sweyn would not be happy if I returned empty handed. I nodded, "Aye, I will lead the men if King Sweyn agrees, but once the Scots are defeated then I return home."

He laughed, "Of course and I admire your confidence."

I smiled, "And if nothing else it will show your bodyguards what real warriors can do."

Chapter 15

Earl Uhtred did not travel on my ship. He had four ships of his own in Jorvik and he took two of them, filled with his men and his hostages. It was a statement of his power. He intended to visit the king on his own terms. The men he took were the best-armed warriors I had ever seen and they were all mailed in the best mail byrnies. He would be telling King Forkbeard that the men he led would be a harder proposition than the men of Wessex. You could see the influence of the Vikings on the design of the ships but they were still not as sleek nor as swift as our ship. We had to reef the sails as we sailed south or else we would have left them in our wake such was the difference in the ships. My son along with Snorri and Siggi had bought presents for their mothers and sisters. They had no chests of their own and their treasures were safely buried in mine. Poor Bersi would have nothing as a present except for the seax I had taken from a dead Saxon for I had not had the time to visit the markets. The wind was with us and we did not have to row. It allowed me to speak with Lars and my hearthweru. While the crew had a relatively easy time the ship's boys were kept busy and raced up and down the rigging to adjust the sails to Lars' satisfaction. My chest was at the stern and I sat on it so that I could glance astern to ensure that Uhtred and his ships were still there and keeping up with us.

"So, Lars when we do this service for Earl Uhtred, we will have to sail north to the Tinea. Do you know the waters?"

"No, hersir, but I am sure that my father does. When we reach Gegnesburh I will seek his advice. Perhaps Jarl Sweyn will take his ship too."

I shook my head, "My foster father will sail home just as soon as he is able. This will be a mission for volunteers."

Dreng asked, "And will there be treasure at the end of the fight?"

I shook my head, "There is a reason we rarely raid the Scots, they are poor people and even their slaves are not worth taking. Speaking with Uhtred I gather that they see Northumbria as a place they can raid for riches."

"And we do this for the king?"

"Aye, Faramir. I felt guilty again for I was really doing it for Mary's dream of a home in her birthplace. I had brought up the matter with Uhtred who did not seem to mind that my king had promised land that was his to give by right. When I spoke with Ebbe he gave me the real reason. "You may have to fight for it. The land is held by Egbert who was one of Thurbrand the Hold's oathsworn. Lord Uhtred would rather someone he does not trust was removed from such an important manor."

"And I am trustworthy?"

He had nodded, seriously, "You may be a Dane, Sven Saxon Sword, but you have a reputation for honour and doing the right thing. Not all warriors are like that."

"How do you know all this, Ebbe? You work for Styr."

"And he has become rich by knowing who is important and what every lord does. When we escort his goods, we are paid to listen and bring back the information. There is no such thing as useless knowledge, Sven Saxon Sword, just that which you have not yet used. I know you think we are piss poor warriors and we may well be compared with you and Uhtred's bodyguards but we earn our coins." He smiled, "Even the prickly Ulf and his brother."

We saw the smoke from the fires ringing Gegnesburh long before we saw the drekar moored along the length of the Trent. The king had returned. We had heard a rumour in Jorvik from a Norse trader that King Æthelred and his family, along with Thorkell, had fled to Normandy and that the continuation of a siege of Lundewic would yield little. He had given up the crown to King Sweyn. We sailed past the other drekar until we reached Gegnesburh and tied up next to the king's drekar. We used the ships there as a longphort. I knew that King Sweyn would not wish to alienate his putative ally by making him trudge through muddy, swampy fields. An army the size of ours soon reduced good pasture to mud wallows. I waited on the shore for Earl Uhtred. King Sweyn would be in the palisaded castle. Prince Cnut had improved it dramatically in the king's absence. When we had first seen it there had been nothing to prevent us from taking it. Now it had a deep ditch and a good bridge. There were two extra towers over the gatehouse and the walls bristled with archers.

We had been seen from the walls and the king was ready to greet us. Earl Uhtred was determined to make an imposing impression on the Danish king and he and his men positively shone in their gleaming armour and the gold and silver ornaments that they hung from their hair. Even the four hostages; two sons and two daughters, all of them illegitimate and, as I had learned from Styr, disposable. The hours I had spent with the earl made me wonder at the strength of this alliance. He would know that King Sweyn would not relish an invasion to take Northumbria and the earl could continue to rule without reference to King Sweyn. That was not my problem for I had done all that was demanded of me and I had even brought the earl to Gegnesburh earlier than I had been asked.

We were taken by Karl Three Fingers to the hall where King Sweyn, on a raised dais and flanked by his son, awaited us. As we bowed and then entered Karl Three Fingers said quietly in my ear, "You have done well, Sven. The king is pleased."

"And my foster father?"

He said nothing and I had no chance for a further question as the king spoke and it would not do to speak while King Sweyn held court. I noticed that there were fewer jarls and hersirs in the room and more Vikings who lived in Danelaw. I could not see my foster father or Lodvir. In fact, the only warriors from Ribe and Agerhøne I spied were mine. I saw enmity from the eyes of some of the English lords as Uhtred boldly strode up to the dais. His look showed contempt for these other warriors. I had learned much about Uhtred during the time I had spent in Jorvik and whilst he had some Viking blood in him, he was a true Northumbrian and that made him an enemy to those in the south.

"Welcome, Uhtred the Bold, we have long waited for this visit." The king looked meaningfully at Uhtred who took the hint and dropped to one knee.

"And I take you, King Sweyn Forkbeard, as the rightful ruler of Danelaw and Wessex, the land that men now call England."

The king frowned for this was not the promise he wanted. He wished Uhtred to accept him as his overlord and he had not done so. There had been no mention of Northumbria. Uhtred was clever. I saw his eyes working and then a sly smile made his mouth turn up, "Come forward, Sven Saxon Sword." I stepped forward and knelt. I was aware that every eye was upon me. The king had not given Uhtred permission to rise and I knew that his knees would be aching and he would be hating every moment of the obeisance. "Lord Uhtred, Sven Saxon Sword brought you here as a favour to me and I promised him, in return, that he could have the land of the settlement called Norton."

I held my breath. If Uhtred accepted the king's decision, then he was agreeing that Northumbria was subservient to Denmark. Would he do? I hoped that Ebbe's judgement was a sound one and that there was another reason for Uhtred to agree.

He glanced sideways at me and nodded, "I like this young warrior and having the Dragon Sword fight for Northumbria is no bad thing. Of course, young Sven, you may have to fight for the land but I shall help you there." He returned King Sweyn's gaze, "And as part of this new accommodation, King Sweyn, I shall have the need for some Danish warriors."

This was like the game I played with Cnut, Hnefatafl. Uhtred had managed to say that I would no longer be King Sweyn's man but would become when it was necessary, Uhtred's. I was becoming dizzy with the wordplay.

"Good. We will speak about that later. Now, Lord Uhtred, I would have you join my council of nobles so that we may discuss my coronation here at Gegnesburh. For the rest, occupy yourselves."

I hurried from the hall and after leaving the castle, made my way back to the camp close to my ship. I was almost mobbed by my men. Their words came in a torrent and it seemed that they had much to tell me. After silencing the babble I waved forward Diuri Thorstenson, "Speak, calmly and slowly so that I may understand all."

"The jarl and the rest of our men have left to return home. The jarl had words with the king and he left."

My plans lay in shreds. I was now bound to sail north and help Uhtred fight his enemies but I would not be doing it with warriors I knew. I had hoped that some Ribe crews would volunteer to come with me. Lars could not consult his father. The Norns had spun. The one constant was Karl Three Fingers and I would speak with him. I put on a brave face and smiled, "This does not change what we have to do. We have until Einmánuður to prepare for our return north. This is not a bad place to spend the short days of Mörsugur and we can prepare for two wars. One for Lord Uhtred and one for us as we take a new home on the Dunum."

They left and seemed happier than they had been. My oathsworn and the one who had become almost a fifth member, Eirik joined me, along with Steana, Snorri, and Siggi. "Is this a good thing, hersir?"

"I know not Gandálfr but I also know that I am powerless to do anything about it. The Norns have spun."

Faramir said, quietly, "We could just go home, hersir, and follow your foster father."

"We could but if we did that then what would the word of Sven Saxon Sword mean? We all know that our destiny is bound with the sword. You four all swore an oath upon it. A warrior cannot undo an oath, Once made it is sacred and to do so would end in disaster. I am not saying that we remain here in this land but we will stay here until all the promises that I have made have been fulfilled."

Steana hung back as the others left to organise our beds for the night, "Hersir, I never thought I would say this but I am ready to return home. Does that make me less of a warrior?"

"No, Steana, for I too wish I was back at home with your mother, Gunhild and Bersi. As you will learn, once you leave your home and cross the sea then you are like a piece of wood floating on the ocean. You do not decide when and where you will land. The Norns spin and events can change your course for good or for ill."

He nodded. My son was growing. It was not just that he was taller and now had the first wisps of man's hair, he was changing within. I remembered that change in me. I had put it down to the Dragon Sword but it might have been an inevitable change.

I did not get the chance to see Karl Three Fingers for a few days. He was busy organising the swearing of oaths from the lords of the five boroughs. In the absence of a crown to be placed on the king's head, this would have to pass for a coronation of sorts. Cnut was also similarly occupied. I was just an interested observer. It seemed to me that so long as the real king lived in Normandy and the crown that would be placed on King Sweyn's head was a copy made by a weaponsmith, then the taking of the throne was hollow. When I did see Karl, it was the day after the makeshift crown had been placed on King Sweyn's head and he had been anointed. The bishops who were there had chosen Christmas Day as the date the crown was placed upon his head. All were doing everything in their power to ensure that the omens were good. I did not think that they were.

The two of us were walking along a frozen riverbank. Many of the Danish ships were preparing to leave. Uhtred and his ships were also almost ready to embark. They had moved closer to the Humber and now had a berth next to the riverbank. It was as far away from the lords of the five boroughs as he could manage. I had come to think that Uhtred was still looking out for himself and that all his words were false. Would his promise of Norton also prove to be false?

"Why did my foster father leave, Karl?"

The old warrior sighed, "He saw no reason to stay here. King Sweyn ordered him to stay and your foster father refused. This will echo long into the future, Sven. You had better to stay out of this and do not come between your king and your foster father."

I began to become angry, "And that is the only advice you have? To do as you do and accept things as inevitable. I have more loyalty to my foster father than I have to a king who just uses me."

I had raised my voice and as we were nearing Uhtred's two ships, Karl said, "Peace, peace!"

I laughed, "You speak of peace to a man who is used as a weapon and not considered as a man?"

Just then Cnut descended from the gangplank of Uhtred's ship and the Northumbrian earl smiled at me from the gunwale, "Angry words, Sven Saxon Sword, what has upset you?"

I gave a false smile back, "Too much ale last night I think."

Uhtred shook his head, "I watched you and you drank sparingly." His eyes tried to see into my head and failed for I had learned to mask my thoughts. "No matter. I have spoken with the king and Cnut. You will lead eight drekar when you come to the Tinea at the start of Lent. I will have my camp at the old Roman fort of Corebricg. From there we shall have a short march north. When that is done and Malcolm is chastised then I will sail with you to Norton on the Tinea and there we shall take your weregeld. Farewell, and keep the Dragon Sword honed. You will need it when we teach the Scots a lesson." He turned to his ship's boys, "Cast off!"

We waited until they had begun to row downstream before we turned to head down the path to the town. Karl was deep in his own thoughts. Cnut said, "Sven, you should be happy. You have won the north for my father and he holds you in high regard."

Shaking my head I said, "And my foster father will be punished for his action. I do not think the esteem can make up for what is likely to happen to my clan."

"My father will soon forget it. He has won a kingdom."

I had learned much from my time in Jorvik. I might not have had the time to buy presents but I had used my time well and spoken with the merchant, his bodyguards, and the innkeeper of the *'The Saddle'*. I was now well versed in Northumbrian politics. "It is an illusion, Prince Cnut." I stopped for we were at an empty part of the river. Other drekars had been leaving all morning. Soon there would just be the fifty ships that the king had brought and the eight I would be leading north for most ships would return to Denmark with their treasure. The war was over. "Uhtred does not want your father as his king. I have spent time with him and I have seen beneath the mask he wears. Northumbria is too far away from your father and Uhtred will continue to do what he wants. He is Æthelred's man. King Æthelred lets him do as he wishes in the north. He has two fortresses, Durham and Bebbanburgh. I cannot see either falling to an attack if they should rebel. You and your father have the support of the lords of Danelaw but that could change, Cnut. As for the rest? They are disorganised but Æthelred has sons and who knows if one of them might be the figurehead that the English need."

Cnut looked at Karl, "Is this true, Karl? You have always told me the truth."

"I fear it is, Prince Cnut. What we have not done is to defeat the English in an open battle. Thorkell and Sven here won the Battle of Hringmaraheior but Thorkell is now in Normandy. Sven will soon be sent to fight the Scots." Waving a hand along the river he added, "And more than half our fleet has gone. We must rely on the men of the Danelaw. I fear that your father has too few men left to fight a battle against the English. Sven is right, we do not know the quality of the sons of the English king. A bold move in winter might shift the balance. We need to be vigilant."

Cnut shook his head, "I will speak with my father."

I did not think it would do any good. When next I spoke to the king it was two weeks after the departure of Uhtred. He had five hersirs waiting for me, "These, Sven Saxon Sword, are the men you will lead when you aid Lord Uhtred. I have decided that six ships are all that is needed to help Earl Uhtred teach King Malcolm a lesson." They all nodded and he said, "Wait without. Sven Saxon Sword will speak with you when I am done with him." They all left and we were alone. "You should know that my son asked to sail with you for he seems to think that Lord Uhtred cannot be trusted. He is right and I have made plans to rid myself of him should he become a problem. It is the other reason I have retained ships here. My son spoke to me as has Karl. You are both right and with so many desertions we are vulnerable."

"He has fortresses where he can hide my lord."

He smiled, "Thurbrand the Hold knows the land and he hates Uhtred. He is my leashed dog and if I unfasten it then Uhtred will die."

"Then why do I have to lead men to help him, King Sweyn?"

"Because I command here and besides your presence will keep him constrained until my son, Harald, sends more men to strengthen my forces. When they arrive and you are with Uhtred, as his guard dog, I intend to head for Lundenwic in a month's time. You will be in the north by then and Uhtred will be not only occupied but also kept in check."

The king was thinking several moves ahead. He was a clever man.

I went to speak to my five captains. All had volunteered and I was flattered that it was my name that had drawn them to the enterprise. One had even raided along the Tinea and would be our guide. Another was Urse the Hairy and I knew him to be a good warrior with a crew the equal of mine. I had not been given the leavings of the fleet. When I went with them to inspect their ships and crews, I saw the other reason they wished to come. Few had mail and they saw the opportunity to follow the Dragon Sword and return better equipped to fight.

It was Sigiberht the Fierce who led the four drekars sent by Harald up the Trent. I know that King Sweyn was disappointed at the paucity of numbers because Cnut told me. The king would have fewer men than he had expected. Cnut gave me the information when he invited me to the castle. The king was holding a feast and needed me to attend. It would be without my hearthweru. I was less than happy mainly because I did not enjoy such feasts and, more importantly, because we were due to sail in a week and there were a hundred and one things I needed to do to prepare. However, the king commanded and I did as I was bid. Karl Three Fingers had a bed prepared for me close to his for I would have to sleep in the main hall while my hearthweru were with the rest of the warriors outside the castle. I wore my finest clothes for the feast. I had not had many opportunities to wear them and a royal feast seemed the right time. Prince Cnut sat on one side of his father and Sigiberht on the other. I sat next to Karl who was also next to Cnut. It allowed the three of us to talk. We spoke of the fight against the Scots. Cnut had genuinely wished to come but his father had different ideas.

Sigiberht had brought some of his warriors with him and they sat at the bottom end of the table. One, who had a scarred nose looked familiar and I kept glancing up at him while we ate. I have learned that your memory works in a strange way. I kept staring at him and then eating and I could not remember him. Then, when I was not thinking of him at all his name came to me, Eystein the Thief. He had been at the Battle of Hringmaraheior and been on the other side of the field from where I had fought. I had not liked him and I had learned that he had his scarred nose, not through battle, but because he had been caught stealing from an oar brother on his first voyage. Prince Harald had clearly not sent his best warriors if Eystein the Thief was one of them. When the king retired the tables were moved to one side of the hall and we moved our beds into the hall. It was a common enough practice but I did not like it. At home, Sweyn Skull Taker had a warrior hall where men slept. Here we slept with the smell of spilt ale and food. I knew I would not sleep well.

The king had a bed-chamber just off the main hall. Karl, as the king's chamberlain, slept close to the door to the chamber and that meant I did too. Karl had enjoyed the drink and Prince Cnut and I had to help him to undress. The prince went to his own bedchamber that was also off the main hall and after making sure that Karl's head faced to the side, I placed the Dragon Sword next to me and covered myself with just a thin sheet. The hall was hot for they had kept feeding the fire.

A warrior gets used to sleeping close to other men. I knew my crew and their snores and other noises did not keep me awake but, for some reason, the noise from the hall did and when my bladder demanded to be emptied, I rose and left the hall. The young sentry on the double doors who prevented us from being disturbed smiled as I passed. He nodded to a pot, "There is a pot here for you, hersir."

I shook my head, "I am hot and the cold night air is what I need. I will piss outside." I went to the wooden palisade and the ditch. There were just ten men on duty and they were at the gate and in the towers. It was an eerily deserted courtyard that I crossed. I emptied my bladder and found that I suddenly felt sleepier. I contemplated, for a brief moment, sleeping outside and then realised the foolishness of such a thought. The sentry nodded to me as I entered the chamber and he closed the door when I entered the hot room. I picked my way carefully through sleeping bodies that looked like the remains of some bloodless battle. It was as I neared Karl that I realised the door to the king's chamber was open. The door was supposed to be kept closed and I sensed danger. I shook Karl awake as I slipped the Dragon Sword from its sheath and Norse Gutter from my belt.

"Karl, there is danger."

The old man was still a little drunk but a lifetime of protecting the king made him grab his sword and stand albeit a little groggily. I pushed the door open and saw the four hearthweru lying dead on the floor. Their throats were slit. Before I could even think about shouting for help, I saw that the king was also dead, his body lay at an unnatural angle and Eystein the Thief and three others were standing there with bloody blades. It was Eystein who shouted, "Treachery! Murder! The king has been slain."

There were cries from the main hall as men awoke. The four ran at us and, as I was at the fore, I bore the brunt of the attack. The four were clearly killers and knew their business. I blocked the two swords with my weapons and then hooked my right leg around Eystein's. As he fell to the floor I hacked across his neck. A second sword scored a red bloody line across my right arm. I ducked my head beneath a sword and drove Norse Gutter up into the belly of another of the assassins. I heard a cry and as I blocked another sword strike saw Karl fall to the ground. I wondered if help would reach me before I succumbed to one of the remaining killers. The Norns had been spinning and the one who raised his sword to bring it down on my head slipped on the widening pool of Karl's blood. Oathsword ended his life and the other warrior, who saw his chance, did not see Norse Gutter and although his sword sliced across my left arm and my ribs, the dagger drove deep into his chest.

The room flooded with light and I stood there with my bloody sword surrounded by bodies. Sigiberht and his hearthweru had drawn weapons and I saw Cnut appear behind them.

Sigiberht pointed at me and said, "Treason and treachery! Cnut's tame killer, Sven Saxon Sword, has killed the king and his hearthweru!"

There was a murmur of anger from the watching warriors.

"That is not true. It was Eystein the Thief and his three men who did the deed and they lie dead as does Karl Three Fingers. He died protecting the king."

One of Sigiberht's men shouted, "Another lie. It was Eystein who shouted the warning." He drew his sword.

I suddenly saw it all. This had been planned to eliminate a threat to Prince Harald. They had waited for me to leave the hall to make water and then slipped inside. They had planned on making me take the blame. I held up Oathsword, "This is the Dragon Sword and I swear by the blade of Guthrum, that I speak the truth."

"And I believe him too." Cnut stood behind me.

Sigiberht laughed, "Of course you do for you put him up to it. We will end their lives now." Cnut had sealed his own fate. Sigiberht had been sent by Harald to kill the king and make Cnut bear the blame.

Cnut drew his sword and we were stood back to back ready to sell our lives dearly when Karl Three Fingers' voice came from the floor, "Sven Saxon Sword speaks the truth and my bleeding body is the proof. The killers of the king lie dead and it was Sven who killed them." His words tumbled out and spilt like his pooling blood. He died.

There were more men who had served with Karl, the prince and me than the ones brought by Sigiberht. I am not sure who struck the first blow but even as Karl's spirit left his body there was a clash of steel on steel and, in the half-light of the king's bedchamber a battle took place. It was a vicious brutal affair for I had no idea who was a friend or a foe but I knew I was defending a future king and any warriors who came close to Cnut would be an enemy. It was clear that Cnut's death had been planned along with his father. The clever plot to implicate me gave them a perfect chance to eliminate Prince Cnut. Harald was behind it and when Sigiberht lunged, not at me but Cnut's back I had it confirmed.

As I smashed Oathsword down on the blade I snapped, "So Harald cannot do his own dirty work. He sends the scum that hides in his dark places to do his work. Are they all thieves like Eystein?"

I had angered him and he tried to launch himself at me. I ripped Norse Gutter across his flying body. None of us wore mail and the blade tore through his kyrtle leaving a bloody line there. As he fell to the side another lunged at me. I was aware that both my arms and my ribs were bleeding and that I would weaken as time went on. Although I pulled my stomach back the Danish sword cut me. Even as the Dane cried out in triumph my bloody sword hacked into his neck and he gurgled his life away at my feet. Sigiberht had risen to his feet and he lumbered towards me. He was the type of warrior who uses brute force to win his battles. Lodvir had taught me to use skill. Sigiberht held his sword in two hands. His wound had weakened him too. Roaring a curse he swung his sword sideways to take my head. I put Oathsword across my body and closed the gap to him. Our blades clashed and sparks flew. He tried to headbutt me and I saw the light leave his eyes as I drove Norse Gutter under his ribs and into his body. The hilt ground against his ribs. His mouth tried to form some sort of curse which I forestalled by my dagger tearing across his throat. He died.

I looked around and saw that Prince Cnut still stood. The blood dripping from his sword told me that he had killed, too. I hacked off Sigiberht's head and holding it aloft I shouted, "Are there any left who wish to harm Prince Cnut, the next King of England?" The Norns had been spinning for I had not meant to say King of England. It had the desired effect. The last of Sigiberht's men launched himself at me. I hurled his master's head at him and as he ducked to avoid the bloody skull, I skewered him on my blade.

Cnut showed that he had kingly qualities for he shouted, "Bar the doors and let none enter!" I saw then how few men there actually were. When the fight had begun there had been less than forty men in the hall and now there were just fifteen of us. All were either hersirs or jarls. All Sigiberht's men were dead. I saw the sentry who had been at the door lying dead. He had wandered into the battle and had no idea who was fighting who. The smiling sentry had died.

Cnut said, "There was treachery here but all those who wished me harm are dead." He sheathed his sword and I saw his mind working, "My father died suddenly. He was not murdered."

Haldi of Svolder said, "But how do we explain the bodies?"

"There was a drunken fight for the men had too much ale. It was begun by Sigiberht. Perhaps my father's heart could not take the shock and, like old Karl Three Fingers, he died in his bed." His face ensured that there was no further comment. He turned to me, "Sven, hold out the Dragon Sword." I did so and saw that it was bathed in blood. There was no metal to be seen on the blade. Even the fuller had not managed to rid itself of the blood. "Every warrior will swear on Oathsword that the story they will tell of this night is the one I have just spoken. You will all become my oathsworn. There were thirteen men and I thought that was an unlucky number. Twelve of them nodded and came to put their hands on the bloody blade and swear that most powerful of oaths, the blood oath. They were oathsworn.

Olaf the Grim shook his head, "I cannot. Denmark must know of your brother's treachery."

Cnut nodded, "Sven, you must also swear." I did as he asked, "You may be right, Olaf the Grim, but it will mean civil war and we might lose both Denmark and England."

"The people should know."

Cnut took the sword from me. "And I too must swear." He did not hold the sword by its blade but did as I had done and held the hilt. I wondered if, like me, he would kiss it like a cross. "I swear that my story will be the story of the death of King Sweyn Forkbeard; the king of two lands, Denmark and England. I am sorry Olaf." He rammed the sword into Olaf's chest. Cnut had grown up. It was not the end that Olaf deserved but it was the right thing to do. A civil war would suit no one. I did not know what Cnut had planned but I knew that I was an integral part of it.

There were plenty of questions the next day as we buried the dead, but Cnut showed that he had steel within him. I had seen changes in him from the diffident boy who had first come to me but I saw real authority both in his eyes and his actions. That this treachery had been planned was clear when all but one of the drekar brought by Sigeberht left as word of the fight spread through the camp. Cnut would have even fewer men to defend his new capital. While the bodies were buried, he sent messengers to the leaders of the five boroughs. He would be crowned and they would attend. He had his own hearthweru and he used them to keep all threats from him. The only one he allowed close to him was me. However, I saw little of him that first day. It was my crew that buried Karl Three Fingers. I chose a place in the graveyard that was close to a yew tree and we made him a coffin, he deserved it. The king would be buried in the church but that funeral would not take place until the lords of the five boroughs arrived. I washed Karl's body; he looked smaller somehow and we dressed him in his mail. Once in his mail, he looked like the great Viking warrior he always had been. With his sword in his hands we hammered the lid down and reverently my hearthweru and I carried the coffin to the grave we had dug. My crew were the only mourners and that was sad for Karl Three Fingers had served his king and country well. My foster father would be sad when he heard the news. I was just glad that the rift between them had been healed, Cnut did not attend either for he had become a real leader and all men looked to him. It was getting on for dusk when we threw the last spadeful of earth on his grave. My crew looked at me.

I wished that my foster father was here for he would have known the right words to say. I sighed and closed my eyes. Karl had accepted Christianity but he still wore Thor's hammer around his neck and when I spoke the words that came into my head, they were not Christian.

"Karl Three Fingers, you were a great warrior and you died as a warrior should with a sword in your hand and truth on your lips. In your dying, you saved my life and I will honour that memory by trying to do as you did." I knew that I was making an oath. The fact that only I knew I was swearing to serve Cnut as a king was immaterial. "Those who tried to disgrace you and slew you are dead. Those who ordered those deaths are yet to be punished but that day will come." The cold winter sun had not been shining for long but in a last flaring of light the castle was illuminated and my shadow fell across the grave. It was a sign and I swear that I felt the presence of Karl as he entered Valhalla. Just as quickly as it had flared the sun fell behind the castle and we were plunged into darkness.

Eirik clutched his Hammer of Thor and as Steana gripped my arm, Eirik said, "*Wyrd.*"

N

Griff
2022

6 miles

Northumbria 1015

Chapter 16

The funeral for the king was held first and Cnut, the putative King of England, waited until the leaders had arrived before he did so. We were all acutely aware that more than half of King Sweyn's army had returned to Denmark and we were perilously short of soldiers. I spent enough time with Cnut before the funeral to know that he saw this as his best chance at a crown. His brother Harald would now be King of Denmark and had Sigiberht's plan succeeded then Cnut would be dead. We needed the warriors of Danelaw to fight for us. The Bishop of Lincylene was the one who spoke over King Sweyn's body before he was laid to rest beneath the stone floor of the church of Gegnesburh.

We still had plenty of food and the funeral feast was worthy of a king but Cnut used it to begin to persuade the lords of the five boroughs to support his claim to the throne of England. One visitor who was accorded great honour was Thurbrand the Hold. Cnut needed the help of every warrior in the north and he put aside his wife's hatred of her captor. As a woman, she was not invited to the feast held to sway the lords to support Cnut. I was elevated to the table with the great lords of Danelaw. It was not a comfortable place for me but I knew that the Norns had spun and the threads that bound me to Cnut could not be broken.

Thurbrand the Hold approached me while Cnut was engaged in a deep conversation with the lords of Lincylene. That powerful city was crucial for it guarded the road to London. "So, you are the man who bloodied my nose, Sven Saxon Sword." I nodded and waited for the threat or the insult. Neither came and he continued when I remained silent, "Had I caught you before you fled, I think I would have had the flesh flayed from your body."

I nodded, "Then I am glad that I obeyed my king's orders and that my clan came to my aid."

"And I hear that you have courted the favour of that old snake, Uhtred of Bebbanburgh."

"And, once again, I obeyed the orders and wishes of my king."

"Who is now dead."

"Aye."

He nodded, "So now we choose between a Danish boy and a failed Saxon." He lowered his voice, "It seems to me that the crown is there to be seized by any who has the strength to do so."

I was not sure if this was a threat but I was not willing to be threatened by someone like Thurbrand. "I think my Prince Cnut should be King of England and there are many others like me who are willing to fight to help him take the throne and the crown." All the time I spoke I looked into his eyes and did not blink. I wanted him to know that I meant every word.

He smiled, "Aye, I know that and that you are a skilled warrior. If Cnut is crowned King of England, Sven Saxon Sword, then much of that will be due to you."

"And will you support his claim?"

He shrugged, "I will think on it. It takes more than roasted beef and ale to persuade me to follow a callow youth. I will sleep on this."

He left and headed for the warrior hall. Since the murder of the king only Cnut and his bodyguards slept inside the castle. If any of the visiting lords thought it unusual, they were wise enough not to speak of it. They might not have believed the story of his father's peaceful death but none were foolish enough to question it. I sat and was lost in my thoughts. That I would not be going to the Tinea was clear for how could I desert Cnut when he had so few men? I would not be given Norton. The parchment signed by Uhtred, King Sweyn and the Bishop of Lincylene was now worthless.

After the lords had all agreed to support Cnut as King of England Cnut sent for me. "Sven, now is the time for you to fulfil your promise to my father and to Uhtred the Bold. You should sail north to the Tinea."

I was stunned. The words I heard were not the words I expected, "But my prince, how can that be? You have less than half the army your father kept and the death of King Sweyn will only encourage Æthelred to return. I have heard that his son, Edmund Ironside, is already landed and is in Wessex gathering support. You will need every warrior you have for he will come north and they will fight for the crown." I did not say all that was in my heart for I did not wish to discourage Prince Cnut. His father had been feared. King Æthelred still had Thorkell and the faithless Danes as allies. It was also rumoured that the Norseman, Olaf the Stout, who recently converted to Christianity and lived in Normandy had offered his support to the Saxon king.

Cnut smiled, "And I am no fool, Sven. You are right, I do not have enough men, and I have sent to my brother and to your foster father for men and ships. The people of Lindsay have promised us horses and I will await your return before I fight. I need Uhtred and his men. When you defeat the Scots then bring the Northumbrian earl back to Gegnesburh and with his Northumbrians, we will defeat the English. I need to find out if my brother was behind this. If he does not send men then I will know." I could see the merit in the plan but I did not like it.

"Thurbrand did not offer his support?"

Shaking his head Cnut said, "No, but he said he would not oppose me. He sits on the fence and will give his support to whoever wins." I began to waver. I could now see the reason for Cnut's decision for bringing Uhtred south would ensure that Thurbrand did not stab him in the back but I did not like it. "However, Sven, you will not take seven drekar but just two." I was about to ask why when he raised his hand, "Uhtred may be unhappy but I think that your drekar and that of Urse the Hairy can do that which Uhtred wants. You will be sailing there early and that will give my brother and your foster father time to send ships to come to my aid and for you to return."

"Uhtred may not like that."

"I think that if he has you and the Dragon Sword, he will be happy. Just return as soon as you can. You may have to forego reclaiming Norton from Egbert but that is a sacrifice you may have to make."

"It is not hard to give up something which seemed like a dream. The Norns are spinning."

He shook his head, "Sven, if I am to be King of England then I cannot be a pagan. The Norns will not be mentioned again in my presence."

I clutched my hammer of Thor for Cnut was challenging the Three Sisters and that would not end well.

He smiled, "I will not force my beliefs on you but keep them hidden, eh? I will send my father's body back to Denmark. He wished to be buried there at Heiða-býr."

"And your wife?"

"When she has given birth to our child, she will need time to recover. I think it is better if she stays here with me for if I send her home what message will that give out?" I nodded. She was almost due to give birth and if Cnut was right then there was no urgency yet. "You and Urse the Hairy should sail as soon as you can."

He was right and I bade farewell with a warning, "Do not think to make war until I am returned or my foster father is here. I do not mean to criticise but you have yet to lead men in a battle."

"And you are my Karl Three Fingers. I will not fight the English."

The Norns were spinning.

I paused before leaving, "And if your brother Harald sends no men to your aid, what then?"

His face showed resolve as he said, "Then I will know for certain that my brother was behind the murder of our father."

I liked Urse the Hairy. He was well named for his arms and legs were so hairy that I guessed, naked, he would resemble an animal. He also had a large drekar and a bigger crew than me. Despite that, he seemed genuinely happy to follow me and serve under me. "It seems, Urse, that there will be just two ships to join Uhtred."

He laughed, "We do not need more to defeat half-naked Scotsmen. The sad thing is that there will be little profit in it for us."

"I think we have made more than enough already. This is a promise we made to a dead king."

Urse always had a smile upon his face but at the mention of the king, it darkened, "You were there when the king died. What happened?"

I looked him in the face and clutched the hilt of my sword, "The king died and those who were responsible now lie dead."

I was not breaking my oath but I still needed Oathsword's support to make the words come forth.

He did not speak for a moment but he stared at me and I know that he was passing my words through his head to hear them again. He nodded, "Thank you. You are our touchstone, Sven Saxon Sword. We know that if you speak then the truth flows from your mouth, no matter how unpalatable. It is better than the honeyed dribble that oozes from some men's mouths. I shall enjoy sailing under your banner."

We headed north until we struck the Humber and then turned east. We had to row and I was nervous until we reached the open sea. I worried that Thurbrand the Hold might choose to take us as some sort of hostage. I knew that the hostages King Sweyn had taken should have guaranteed that Cnut would be safe from attack but if the Saxons had a hostage of their own then it all might change. The journey to the sea was far faster than the voyage to Gegnesburh for the winter rains had raised the levels of not only the rivers but also made the swampy ground a shallow sea. With our shallow draught, we could sail almost anywhere but Lars kept to the main channel. He was too good a mariner to do otherwise. We also had the current with us and we made the sea in one day and felt the choppy motion of the ocean as darkness fell. Both drekar hoisted their sails but kept them reefed and we both hung a lantern from our sterns as we crept our way north. The nights were still longer than the days but we had enough crews to have ten men on watch the whole time. I took one of the watches and steered while Lars slept. It was as I watched the dark shadow that was England pass on the larboard side that I went through all the events that had led to this. Cnut was wrong to think that there were no such beings as the Norns. I had done nothing to place me on my ship sailing north. Every decision was another's. If I had enjoyed free will then I would have sailed home rather than going to Jorvik to meet with Uhtred. I would, even now, be at home with Mary. I still prayed for peace. The hostages were a surety, I hoped, against a major battle but, in my heart, I knew that there would be more bloodshed to come. The first blood that would be shed would be the thirty or so hostages that we had. We lived in a cruel world. It was on the following evening that we spotted the sands that marked the mouth of the Dunum. Mary's home lay upriver from there. The seals that we saw, basking on the sands, were an easy marker for the river. I clutched the hammer of Thor hanging from my neck and said a silent prayer for the Allfather to watch out for my family.

Steana joined me and stood at my side. He was as tall as my shoulder and he said, quietly, "You were praying for mother?" I nodded. "To our one God?"

I shook my head, "No, to the Allfather although I believe that the Allfather and the father of the White Christ are one and the same." His hand went to his cross. His mother had brought them up to be Christians. "Too many events happen that cannot be explained by your White Christ, Steana. My beliefs help me to understand them."

He nodded, "There may be something in what you say for I knew that you were praying."

"It is more likely that you know this because you are my son. I knew when my father was leaving this world and yet he was in Wessex and I was in Agerhøne."

We both watched the land slip away. The basking sands gave way to beaches, dunes and marram grass. We spotted small settlements where people lit fires to make the sea into salt and then the wooden walled town that was Herterpol. We saw the land rise to cliffs with the jagged teeth of rocks guarding them. The land was, even now as winter began to lose its grip, green and fertile. War had not touched this land. I suspect the last real raid on this coast had been the one where I had caught Mary. Since then the Danes and the Norse had raided and taxed Wessex. Danelaw had given way to Northumbria and that had always been different from the rest of the island.

It was late afternoon when we reached the mouth of the Tinea and we hove to. The remains of the Roman wall and their forts could be seen to the north and south of the river. The wooden priory and palisaded castle lay on the north bank but it did not deter drekar such as ours. However, there was little point in risking a night voyage up a river we did not know. There were two branches of the Tinea and we needed the correct one if we were to reach Corebricg, the fort known to the Romans as Coria or, as my wife had corrected me once, Coriosopitum.

165

She was a stickler for such things. We had seen its name on the parchments she and my mother had read whilst searching for the story of the Dragon Sword. We anchored in the middle of the river and kept a good watch while we ate, as we had all the way north, cold fare. It was far from a mundane diet as we used pickles we had brought to vary the taste. So long as we had beer, we were happy. The one thing we missed, here in England, was mead. I yearned for Agerhøne mead. It was the finest mead anywhere. Or so my crew thought.

We rowed without shields lining our sides and the message should have been that we had peaceful intent but the people who lived along the Tinea were wary. Vikings had rarely come in peace and we rowed up a river where the boats that normally fished were tied up along the bank and the places that had walls and gates were securely barred and guarded. We passed the settlement a mile or so from the mouth of the river guarded by yet another old fort and that too was prepared for war. What it told me was that Uhtred had not warned any of our imminent arrival. We were earlier than we had promised but even so…

The village of Corebricg had grown up to the east of the old Roman fort. There were the remains of the Roman jetty and so we tied up there. It meant that the villagers saw us pass and prepared for battle. We were here in peace and so leaving Urse in command of the two ships I went with Eirik and my hearthweru to the gathered warriors. We did not take shields and we wore no helmets. We had no weapons in our hands and I held my palms out to show that we meant peace. There was no wooden wall and the men had grabbed whatever weapons were to hand and now faced us behind small shields that bristled with spears. I knew that my men would find it hard to understand their words. The dialect of this part of the world and the accent often made for misunderstandings. When I saw the priest standing behind their headman recognisable by an ancient torc hanging around his neck, I was relieved. I would be able to talk with him.

The man who spoke was not the headman, he was next to him and was the only one who had a decent shield. He spoke to me in our language. "Viking, halt and state your business." He waved a hand and I heard bows drawn. There were hidden archers.

"Lord Uhtred commanded us to sail north and meet him here. I have been asked to help him to fight against King Malcolm."

I heard the man translate the words. I caught almost all of them but I could tell that my men understood less than half.

"What is your name, Viking?"

"I am Sven Saxon Sword and I serve Cnut." I did not want to use a title yet for it seemed bad luck especially given Cnut's disregard for the Three Sisters. "And who are you that knows our language so well?"

"I am Fótr and I was, like you, a raider. I became a Christian and I have given up the sea this is my home. Lord Uhtred did not tell us that men would come now. The headman is Oswald of Corebricg and he is suspicious. He was told that you and ten ships would arrive but he expected them in a month. Your early arrival has him worried." He gave a sad smile, "It is their experience of our people, is it not?"

I nodded, "And that I can understand but you know, Fótr the Christian, that if we came raiding we would not simply row up your river in broad daylight, tie up and then walk without arms to speak to you."

"You Danes are tricky and use all sorts of tricks. Who is to say that there is not a fleet waiting for darkness?"

"Fótr, you counted the oars?" He nodded. "Then you know that the men I have brought totally outnumber you. If we chose to then this village would be ours and you would have had a warrior's death. What we will do is return to our ships and make a camp. We will enjoy a rest and wait for the earl to send word or to come himself and fetch us."

I heard him translate and Oswald asked his Viking, "How do we know that we can trust them?" I understood his words.

I answered, "You do not know and have to trust us but I swear by my sword that we mean you no harm."

With that, I turned on my heels and led my men back to our ships. Gandálfr said, "Not a warm welcome, hersir."

I nodded, "And understandable. To them, we are wild savages and all that they know of us is pain and death. We are like a wild dog that foams at the mouth and they fear us."

Eirik said, "There is little in the village that we would want. Even the women are ugly."

As we neared Urse and our men I pointed to the half-ruined Roman fort. Many of the stones had been taken to make stone buildings in the village. I said, "We will use the fort as our camp."

Urse nodded, "And Uhtred?"

I shrugged, "They know nothing of us but we are early. Have traps made to catch fish and we will wait."

The villagers kept a wary watch on us. They had armed men with lighted braziers guarding the entrance to the village. Had we wished to attack them then the braziers would have aided us and not the watchers but we enjoyed freshly caught river fish and made shelters in the ruined fort so that, if it rained, we would be dry.

Fótr spent some time in our camp. I think it was to reassure himself that we intended no harm and after the first visit he was convinced. He had been a mighty warrior from his tales. It was not what he told us but what he left out and when I looked at his arms and face I saw scars that can only come from battle. I think the other reason he spent time with us was that he missed the companionship of warriors such as us.

"Are the Scots a problem, Fótr?"

He shook his head, "They raid for cattle but we have caught and hanged so many of them that they do not come unless they are desperate."

"I heard that King Malcolm raids."

He laughed, "He has come once and that was when he was made High King. It is traditional that a High King must make war and have a victory. He came over the border, defeated the rag tag army that Uhtred gathered and then went back home. We were not even summoned so swift was the war."

"And when was this?"

"When his son, Ealdred was but five years old. I had just come to the village so, twelve years ago?" So why had Uhtred needed us to teach Malcolm a lesson? This did not make sense to me.

Three days later five riders approached the village from the north and they rode, not to the fort but to the village. Steana and Snorri were the ones watching and they fetched me immediately. I saw that the five men were warriors and were mailed. Men from the village gathered around them and I saw Fótr point in our direction. A few moments later the five rode towards us. When they reined in, I recognised one as Ealdred, Uhtred's eldest son. He had been with his father when they had sailed from Jorvik with us. He was little more than a youth and I wondered why he had come. He dismounted, "You are early, Sven Saxon Sword, and after the death of your king my father did not expect you until you had mourned him."

"We gave our word and here we are."

He looked at the river, "Yet I count just two ships and not the number we were promised."

"Aye, that is true."

I saw him working out what to do.

"Did your father send you for us?"

My question seemed to help him to focus, "My father was gathering the men of the north, Bebbanburgh, Rothbury and Norham. I came to fetch the men of Corebricg and those of the south and east of our land. The Scots have crossed the border and raided Otorbrunna. My father has raised the fyrd and is marching south from Bebbanburgh. You can fulfil your oath and come with us."

I saw the cross around his neck and could not help teasing him, "Aye, *wyrd*, is it not?" He was a Christian and looked unhappy at my words.

It did not take us long to organise the defence of our ships. We left six warriors and the ship's boys to help the two sailing masters keep them safe. If danger approached, they would simply moor them in the centre of the river. We left in the late afternoon for the Scots had raided for four days before they were discovered. Earl Uhtred knew that they had to be defeated before too many slaves and animals were taken.

Fótr marched for the first few miles with us. We were relegated to the rear. Ealdred led and then Oswald followed with his twenty warriors. Only he and Fótr wore any sort of armour and I wondered if the men of Corebricg were doomed to death.

Fótr nodded to the road that rose and headed northeast, "It is but eighteen miles to Otorbrunna. With the Scots that close we have to fight them. It is good that you are here, Sven Saxon Sword. The men of Corebricg are brave but they are not warriors. The Scots are wild warriors but if you have a shield wall then they can be defeated."

"Will you fight with us?"

He smiled but shook his head, "I would love to fight with fellow Vikings one more time but I live with these people and I must fight alongside them."

"Even though that means there is more chance that you will fall?"

"I am a Christian but I am still a warrior. If I am meant to die then so be it. Perhaps in my death, the Scots will be defeated and my wife and sons will live."

We reached a camp an hour after darkness had fallen. Raylees was just a huddle of five houses close to the burn but we had a place to defend and the Scots had not yet reached it. Ealdred had raised the fyrd and ordered them to meet just five miles from Otorbrunna. It was an armed camp and there were seventy men there but all were like the ones we had brought from Otorbrunna. They were farmers and not warriors. They were from the villages of Bellingham and Wark.

Ealdred handed the reins of his horse to one of his men and approached Urse and me, "My father will meet us here." He hesitated, "Your men are warriors and I would ask you to make your camp closer to Otorbrunna."

I nodded, "You fear that the Scots may try to surprise us."

"They are not that many miles away and while they may still be enjoying the ale and the women of Otorbrunna, until my father arrives I would not risk losing men." He shook his head, "We have few enough warriors as it is. Your two crews may make all the difference."

"Do we know how many men they have and who leads them?"

"You do not bother to count the fleas on the dog."

I shook my head, "It is important to know. I will find out."

"But how? You do not know this land?"

"No, however, I know how to hide as do the five men I will take with me. Gandálfr, gather my hearthweru. Swords and daggers only. Have Eirik bring his bow."

Urse had been listening all the while, "A good idea and I will form a defensive camp. There are plenty of hazel trees for us to make an obstacle."

As I led my men northwest towards the smell of burning that drifted from the north, I realised that the lack of war with real enemies as opposed to cattle thieves had made the warriors softer than they might have been. Uhtred and Thurbrand might be mighty warriors but the men they led lacked the skills that they needed. We did not head along the road but across the moorland, scrub and the many trees that sprouted in small copses. I had never seen Otorbrunna but I knew that there was a burn and that the village lay to the east of it. We headed more easterly as we headed through the dark. It was not as hard to find as it sounds, as we had the smell of burning and the noise of the Scots, in the distance, to guide us. It was a mixture of wood, the food they were cooking and the smell of burning timbers. The increasing noise from the Scots also helped to identify where they were. We moved silently. I had seen Eirik's skills at Haestingas and knew he could be quiet. He had an arrow loosely nocked in his bow and followed behind the others. I led.

I spied their sentries on the road. They had lit a fire and were warming themselves and drinking from a skin. They would give the raiders early warning of any attempt by Uhtred to come to the aid of the village. I knew that my two boat crews were more than capable of surprising the Scots for the attention on the sentries was on the fire, skins and their talk. This was not my raid and I did not know Uhtred's plans. I would gather information and present it to him. We kept moving up the ground as it rose above the stream and the village. The tree line ended and when it did, we crouched down to peer down at the village and the camp. I saw a line of heads mounted on spears. They were defenders who had died. I gritted my teeth as I saw young women and older girls being dragged off. I knew their fate. With the other five spread out we each began to count the campfires and men we saw. Knowing we could compare numbers later on. I had been doing this for many years and I had my own method. The leaders tended to be the better armed and mailed warriors; they usually gathered together. They gave an idea of the numbers. I saw a large fire close to the biggest house that still remained and counted twenty such men. They were the leaders with their bodyguards. That was a large number and if this was our camp then it would have been just four men. I then turned my attention to the other fires and groups of men. By the time I had finished, I estimated that there were well over two hundred men. Adding in the eight sentries on the road we had seen and, I assumed, other sentries, there could be three hundred men. Uhtred would need a good-sized warband to defeat them. I spied helmets and shields but, the leaders and their bodyguards apart, few had byrnies. That made sense for a byrnie was an expensive piece of equipment and few men could afford it. I spied twenty or so horses tethered close to the stream that bubbled through the centre of Otorbrunna.

I had seen enough and I tapped Gandálfr and Faramir on their shoulders. We slid back down the bank and when we were low enough, we stood and headed back the way we had come. On the way up we had passed a dell and when we heard the shout and the scream coming from it, we drew our weapons. I crouched and moved down the slope which was gradually flattening out. There was little light but I saw shadows writhing ahead of me. I had fought in enough raids to know what it was. Three men were raping a young girl. The warrior in me told me to deviate from our present course and get back to our camp with the information we had but the father in me thought of Gunhild. I moved stealthily across the ground knowing that the three men's attention was on their victim. One was between her legs while the other two held her arms. I saw the Scot raise his buttocks in the air and knew what he intended. I covered the last few steps with Oathsword behind me already swinging. My sword bit through his skull with such force that his body was knocked from the girl. An arrow slammed into the man on one side and Gandálfr's sword into the throat of the other. The only sound had been the crack as my sword had sliced through bone. The sentries would have heard only the screams of the girl and they would have known what was happening.

I pointed to the girl and then to our camp. Dreng help her to her feet and I pointed the sword down the slope. It was the silence that undid us. As we passed the road and the sentries, I saw that they were more alert than they had been. The girl's cries had stopped and even had she been dead then the attackers would have made noise and all was silent.

I heard a voice shout something and I gestured for Gandálfr and Eirik to stay with me. I pointed down towards our camp, some miles distant. The girl would not be able to move as quickly as we could. The

Norns had been spinning and the clouds that had hidden the moon were blown away and the darkness of the night became bright. We were some two hundred paces from them but one, keener eyed or soberer than the rest spied the three of us as we walked backwards down the slope. He yelled one word, "Vikings!"

Eirik took advantage of the bright light and loosed an arrow. It was a good arrow but he was lucky for the range was longer than I would have liked. He hit the man who had shouted in the upper leg and he screamed in pain.

"Move."

The others were no longer in sight and Faramir had hastened them. We would have to outrun them. Here their local knowledge came to their aid. They knew this land better than we and I saw them spread out like hunters chasing game.

"Head for the road."

There was little point in avoiding the road and risking being tripped on roots or rocks as we ran across the open ground. When we reached it, I glanced around and I saw no white faces lit up by the moon. We ran down the road that twisted and turned through spindly trees and, after a mile or more I began to think that we had escaped when I heard the hooves on the road. They had sent men on ponies. We had two choices, run into the thin trees and scrubland and hope to avoid them or try to take the horsemen. The moon still lit up the land and I knew that the three of us had to try to take them. We kept running down the road but I was seeking a place to gain some advantage. It was only a slight curve and the elder trees were little more than bushes but it was shelter. I grabbed Eirik and thrust him behind the bush. Gandálfr must have read my thoughts for he stood next to me before Eirik.

"Gandálfr, you take the one on the left, I will take the one on the right. Eirik, you take the one in the middle."

That was all I needed to say for Gandálfr but Eirik did not understand. "What if there are more than three of them?"

Gandálfr laughed, "There may well be but the road is only wide enough for three men abreast. We hit the first three and then take on whoever survives."

The hooves drew closer and I saw four shapes. They rode in a diamond formation and were whipping their ponies. I hissed, "Now, Eirik," when they were twenty paces from us as Gandálfr and I stepped out with swinging swords. The arrow hit the Scot in the chest as the other riders' horses reared at our sudden appearance. The ponies gave the riders speed but not height and I hacked across the arm of my selected warrior to slice through it and into his side. As his arm fell so did he. The fourth rider just had time to raise his sword before Eirik's second arrow knocked him from the saddle. Gandálfr had killed his man.

Sheathing my sword I grabbed the reins of the nearest pony, "Take a pony and we will ride." I heard the sentries as they ran down the road after us. The ponies would ensure that we covered the last couple of miles safely. As we galloped down the road, I saw that the fourth pony followed us. *Wyrd.* We would escape them.

Chapter 17

We found Faramir and the others just a mile from where we ambushed the Scots. We doubled up on the ponies for there was less than a mile to go to our camp. The girl held on tightly to Dreng. Urse and his oathsworn were on guard at our camp and he laughed, his booming voice carrying to the main camp. "Sven Saxon Sword, you go scouting and bring back horses and a girl. The gods truly smile on you."

I dismounted and patted the pony on the neck, "Then they have a strange way of showing it for the camp has almost three hundred men. If they attack before Uhtred comes then we will be hard-pressed to hold them. I will take the girl to Ealdred." I helped the girl from the pony and said, "You did well, oathsworn, rest."

I put my arm around the girl for she was shaking. Had we taken cloaks I would have put one around her but I used my body warmth to give her comfort. Ealdred and the other thegns were gathered around a fire. I saw more men must have arrived after dark for there were faces I did not recognise.

Uhtred's son came towards me as one of the women from the hamlet put a blanket around the girl's shoulders, "Well?" He seemed to ignore the girl.

"There are almost three hundred warriors and at least forty are mailed. They have ponies and horses. We rescued the girl and she may have information. I have not questioned her."

Ealdred smiled, "You have done well, Dane. My father, when he comes, will be pleased. Have some ale and I will speak with the girl." He sat on a barrel as the girl knelt before him. The woman handed the girl some ale. They spoke quietly and I could not understand all that they said. The horn of ale was finished by the time the girl was taken into one of the houses and Ealdred returned.

Ne nodded as though satisfied, "We now know who leads this raid. It is not Malcolm but Findláech, mormaer of Moray. From what the girl said this raid was planned some time ago. My father may have a spy in his court for they knew that we were going to raid across the border when you came north. King Malcolm sent his men to bar the border."

"How does she know this?"

"Her father was the headman. Before he was executed the mormaer took great delight in taunting him and telling him that soon Northumbria would be Scottish once more. After he was executed then the girl was taken hence to be raped. It was a warning to others in the

174

village. Malcolm will pay for this."It was lucky for the girl you arrived when you did.

"The Norns were spinning, my lord." I saw the woman who had given the ale to the girl give me a strange look. "The king comes?"

"He will do but it will take time to gather the rest of the fyrd. This is a way for Moray to garner some easy glory by attacking small settlements before we are prepared. It is fortunate that my father keeps fifty horses for his best warriors. Tomorrow, we prepare to defend this burn for more men will be arriving."

I did not manage much sleep that night. It was not that I was not tired, I was exhausted, but I knew that, as valuable as our scouting mission had been it had also alerted the Scots to the presence of Vikings and if Ealdred was right and Uhtred had a traitor then they would have known the reason. I feared a nighttime attack before the earl and the best Northumbrian warriors arrived. I woke and made water while it was still dark. Urse's men had a fire and were cooking food. He had been awoken by his men and he joined me for pieces of ham fried on a metal skillet.

"The men who watched at night said that the Northumbrians were arriving all night." He shrugged, "They will be in no condition to fight but there will be numbers and the ones you saw will be swollen."

"Their archers and slingers can help but you are right, we need Uhtred. When dawn comes, we will have our men cut down saplings and embed them in the banks of this stream."

He pointed to the water, "The Raylees Burn, that is its name. It may not be deep but the sides are steep. The stakes will make it hard for them to cross. And the bridge? Do we destroy it?"

"No, we use it. Until Uhtred arrives, we fight a defensive battle. The Northumbrians can guard the banks of the burn and our men will block the bridge. I said that the Scots had mail but from what I saw it was not good quality."

He knew what I meant. My mail and his, along with most of our men's, were made from small links. It was more expensive to make but even a bodkin blade could not pierce it. The byrnies I had glimpsed in the firelight were made with larger links and while they could block a sword, a dagger or a spear could penetrate. Some had what looked like copies of Roman armour with overlapping plates. That was only effective when the leather holding the plates held. If they were cut then holes would appear.

Ealdred joined us and I told him what we had planned. He nodded, "Another forty men arrived last night but I fear that my father may not arrive in time. The girl said that they took Otorbrunna three days ago.

They will be ready to move on. They must know where we are and may seek to destroy us while we are weak and then move on to Bellingham."

"We do what we can and then fight hard. I promised a dead king I would do this and a man does not break an oath to the dead."

Ealdred gave me a curious look, "And then you will head south and join Cnut. Your men say he wishes to be King of England."

There was no point in being untruthful, "Aye, he does."

"And that means we may have to fight you."

Again, I could not lie, "Aye, and you would lose." I saw him bristle with youthful indignation. "Ealdred, you are young and, I think brave, but how many battles have you fought?" He coloured. He had yet to fight. "Urse and I have lost count of our battles. I fought at sea in a mighty sea battle with more men on one side than the whole Northumbrian and English armies combined. We have better mail and weapons. We would win and so I hope we do not fight. Your father left hostages and promised to support King Sweyn."

Ealdred nodded, "Aye, but not his son." He meant, of course, Cnut.

It was a slip that Ealdred had not meant to make. Uhtred would not honour the promise and my presence here was unnecessary. Any deaths amongst our men would be down to me and I did not like that thought.

The stakes were in place when the Scottish scouts appeared on the skyline. Perhaps Ealdred had taken my words as criticism for he had the horn sounded and he shouted, "To arms! Stand to!"

He had arranged the men in their own groups. There were four thegns with their men but the bulk of their leaders were gesith, the English equivalent of a hersir. They stood with their men and that was a good thing for men to fight better if they fight for their own people. The shield wall they made along the riverbank was a little ragged. The front row had shields and some of the second but it was hardly a Viking shield wall with locked shields before and above as well as spears bristling. They looked determined enough. The young girl we had rescued had told her story and it had quickly spread. The men who were facing the Scots knew the price their families would pay if they failed and they would defend this burn with their lives.

I was in the front rank with Urse close to the bridge. Our hearthweru made up the rest. We stood on the riverbank close to the south bank of the Raylees Burn and we were eight men wide. We were just eight men deep and I had a reserve line led by Eirik. He had wanted to fight alongside me but I needed someone with a cool head to lead the reserve warriors. Their task would be to fill the gaps created by men who fell.

The Scottish scouts disappeared leaving just two of them on ponies to assess our defence. The army arrived sometime later. The mormaer rode with his twenty horsemen and directed his men to their positions. Even as we had been assembling at the bridge, I had seen knots of men arriving. We had reinforcements but not enough. The billhooks, wood axes and ancient swords were not enough to hold an army that outnumbered us.

The enemy formed four lines. The first line was made up of slingers and archers. They would, I knew, advance down the gentle slope and try to hurt the defenders as much as they could. There were not enough shields to guarantee that our defenders would survive. The next rank was made up of the Scots who had helmets, shields, and long spears. The second rank was a real mixture but the best of these warriors were in the centre and would be coming for us. The last rank was made up of the mormaer and his best men. The bodyguards would be there. Their standards were also in the rear rank. That seemed strange to me. We did not use them but if we had then, like Oathsword, they would have been in the fore. After a blessing from a priest, the Scots advanced down the gentle slope and I took heart from the fact that the line was uneven. They did not have enough discipline.

The slingers raced down the slope for they were the young warriors and they were followed closely by the archers. Ealdred shouted, "Archers and slingers, wait for my command." It was the right order. There was a moment to launch the missiles and that would be when the Scottish archers nocked an arrow for then they would be still. Some of the Scottish slingers began hurling their stones as they ran. It was foolish as was clearly demonstrated when one fell as he did so. Laughter from our side of the burn emboldened our men and angered theirs. The stones they threw struck shields and helmets. One lucky stone felled an unlucky boy slinger amongst the men of Bellingham.

"Loose!"

The stones and arrows from our side rose as one. Ealdred must have been a slinger at one time for he judged the moment perfectly. Many of their archers fell. The arrows and stones in reply resulted in some of our men falling but the duel was won by the first decisive encounter. The Scottish archers and slingers soon took flight to run behind the mormaer's third line.

In the distance, to the south, I heard a horn and wondered what it meant. In theory, it could only be Northumbrians unless King Malcolm had been cunning and used the Mormaer of Moray as a diversion. I shook my head to clear it. I wanted to be back at Agerhøne with Lodvir and my foster father. They did not deal in tricks and subterfuge. Being

177

with men like King Sweyn, Uhtred and Thurbrand was making me doubt everything. All I had to do was that which I knew best, fight. I braced Saxon Slayer against my right foot and ensured that the shield was as comfortable as it could be.

The Scots were almost out of control even though it was a shallow slope. The reason was clear. Ealdred's archers and slingers were bringing down men and the Scots knew that while they outnumbered us their best chance of victory was to close with us so that missiles could not hit them. They would take their chances with the stakes and Danish spears. I watched as some men ran so fast that when they tried to stop at the burn they could not and three impaled themselves on the stakes. They would have a long, slow lingering death. I concentrated my attention on the mailed men with spears as long as ours, as they slowed to form a shield wall. These were not simple raiders or warriors for the season, these were men like we were. These were trained warriors who knew their business. They had gathered the bodyguards and best warriors to form them into one unit to try to break what they must have seen as their biggest threat, us. One problem they had was that our line overlapped the edges of the bridge. They could only cross six men abreast and the two men on the flanks, Snorri and one of Urse's men, would have no opponent but could strike with impunity at those on the bridge. The other problem was that the bridge was wooden and not intended to take up to sixty mailed men.

The warriors at the fore realised the problem and began to adjust their lines and that slowed them. Stones rattled against mail and shields. Our archers realised the futility of sending arrows at mailed men but the slingers could get lucky and hit flesh or perhaps smack a helmet so hard as to render the warrior disorientated. One slinger managed to hit a Scot full in the face and he tumbled to the side. As luck would have it, he fell into the burn and lying face down he would have that most ignominious death of any warrior, drowning. As they marched across the bridge, I saw it shake. It would not take much more damage.

"Brace!" I would worry about the bridge when the time came. We had to stop them from knocking us from the edge of the bridge.

They ran the last four steps, pulling back their spears to ram them at us. They must not have fought many Vikings before because when they struck, we did not do as they expected and fall back. Instead, we thrust at them at the same time as they did. It was a test of every warrior's individual courage. If you had good reactions as I did, my hearthweru, Urse and his oathsworn, then you could block a spear with your shield whilst ramming your spear at the best possible place, where your opponent was weakest. That varied from warrior to warrior. As the

Scottish spear slid off the boss of my shield, I saw that his shield was not square on and there was a gap. The man had mail but the rings were not the size of a halfpenny but a shilling and Saxon Slayer slid through a ring and into the warrior's gambeson. The head shattered the ring and with it the integrity of the mail. The head entered the right side of the Scottish warrior's body and his face told me that he realised he was a dying man as the sharp spearhead drove deep into his body. The warm blood gushing down his side was a harbinger of death. His spear clattered to the bridge and his dead body was only held in place by those pushing behind. When the rest of the six men in the front rank fell to our eight spears three of their bodies fell into the burn and the rest pushed hard behind to get to us. It was too much weight for the bridge and the northern end collapsed into the water. The water was not deep, a man could wade across it but they now had an obstacle, the half of the bridge still attached to the south bank and if they tried to climb it then there would be a wall of spears awaiting them. In addition, some of those who fell landed face down and with the weight of mailed men upon them, drowned.

As the enemies before me disappeared I glanced to my right and saw Scots in the burn duelling with Northumbrians on the bank. It was an even struggle. The trouble was the collapse of the bridge meant we could not cross easily and go to their aid by flanking the Scots. It was then I heard the horn again but this time it was to the north and on the other side of the burn. I saw Lord Uhtred's standard as he led his horsemen to charge into the rear of the Scots on the Scottish left flank. In terms of numbers, we were still outnumbered. I guessed that the dismounted warriors of his warband from Rothbury, Bebbanburgh and Norham were on foot and still marching to reach us. The disparity in the numbers was offset by two things; Lord Uhtred led horsemen using spears like lances and their best forty Scottish warriors were now in the burn and trying to clamber out. The first eight all died quickly and the rest, seeing the horsemen, chose an exit on the north side of the bank.

This was a decisive moment and as Urse looked at me I raised Saxon Slayer and shouted, "Forward!" I shouted in Danish but my intention was clear and we slid down the broken bridge and used the dead bodies as soft steppingstones to climb up the other bank. Uhtred's sudden appearance had shaken the Scots and the north bank was undefended.

Once we stepped onto the drier ground I yelled, "Wedge!" We would still be outnumbered and if the Scots chose to target my men we would lose more men than I was willing to lose. Urse and Gandálfr stepped behind me and a wedge of eighty men began to march up the slope. We were not the Scots and we had discipline. I used a well-known chant to keep us in step and to raise our spirits.

Bluetooth was a warrior strong
He used a spear stout and strong
Fighting Franks and slaying Norse
He steered the ship on a deadly course
Njörðr, Njörðr, push the dragon
Njörðr, Njörðr, push the dragon
The spear was sharp and the Norse did die
Through the air did Valkyries fly
A day of death and a day of blood
The warriors died as warriors should
Njörðr, Njörðr, push the dragon
Njörðr, Njörðr, push the dragon
When home they came with byrnies red
They toasted well our Danish dead
They sang their songs of warriors slain
And in that song, they lived again
Njörðr, Njörðr, push the dragon
Njörðr, Njörðr, push the dragon

In theory, the Scots could have outrun us but the horsemen were there to spear any back that they saw. The weaker warriors, the ones without mail just ran and risked death but the mailed warriors and those who were oathsworn, could not simply run. They formed knots of men and tried to retreat in good order. Their Mormaer and his men had mounted their horses and that, too, was a mistake. Men on foot know that their leaders can run any time they like. Vikings never fought on horses. The ones that did were called Normans. These were brave warriors and gathered around their clan leaders to sell their lives dearly. My wedge was cutting a swathe through their ranks until we found the eighty men of a clan led by a greybeard. They stood defiantly close to the top of the slope where I had first spied the Scottish scouts. Our chant still helped us and we pulled back our spears as one. I knew that the Scots who still had spears would be bracing them but I saw swords and axes rather than spears poking out from behind the shields. The old man cursed me in his language, I guessed it was Gaelic. I had my hammer of Thor and the spell tucked into my kyrtle. I had paid our volva for it. Had Mary known I would have been in such trouble. The spell would protect me from his curses. He rammed his spear at my head, perhaps thinking that my open-faced helmet was a tempting target. I flicked up my shield and the spear gouged a line along my helmet. He was older and his reactions were slower. My spear forced its way through the overlapping metal plates and into his body. My shield pushed his body over and there was a wail from his oathsworn as I pulled out my bloody spear. They had let down their clan chief and they hurled themselves at me, frenetically trying to be the one to avenge me. I was the point of the wedge and while I had to face stabbing spears, swinging axes and savagely curved swords, they had to face the spears of the men behind me who were able to stab and skewer them with ease. Although our pace had slowed, we were still moving forward and the Scottish oathsworn fell. We slipped and slid over bodies greasy with blood.

It was at that moment that the mormaer realised he had lost the battle. Perhaps the old man and his men were the best he had left and their destruction heralded his own. He had the horn sounded and even those who were still fighting us heeded it. They turned and fled. This would be Uhtred's greatest victory and he and his horsed men rode like hunters to pick off, seemingly at will, those who tried to flee. When we reached the crest of the hill we stopped. We were weary beyond words and men who discarded armour, weapons, shields and helmets would easily outrun us.

Urse raised my right hand and shouted, "Oathsword! Oathsword! Oathsword!" The chant was taken up not only by the men who had followed me but I saw Fótr and the men of Corebricg as they, too, stopped their killing and saluted me.

While the bulk of the Northumbrians chased and harried the defeated Scots, we stripped the bodies of the men we had killed and took the mail, rings, coins, bracelets and weapons. The bodies we left for the villagers to pillage. They would burn the dead and spread their ashes over their fields. The Scots would have done some good. I expected that Uhtred would ride as far as Otorbrunna before he stopped. We were weary and would go no further. I believed we had done more than was expected of us. Had we not been there then the Scots would have taken the bridge and the village before Uhtred reached it. The earl would have lost this part of his land. We had suffered but not as much as we might have; just two of Urse's men were dead although Dreng and Snorri amongst others had wounds. As we went back to the village Gandálfr and Faramir bantered with the two wounded hearthweru. It is in the nature of warriors to do so. Urse and his warriors carried their dead back to bury them by the burn.

Eirik was in a happy mood for he had killed a mailed man and taken the coins from a Scot who had a purse that jingled. "It is good that we

took those ponies, hersir, for we have much to take back to the drekar."
I nodded, absentmindedly. He took that for doubt and asked, "We will
be returning to the river and the drekar will we not?"

"Aye, of course, but I am unsure where we will sail then."

Would Uhtred keep his promise and go with me to Norton to take
my land from Egbert? For my part, I wanted to get to the drekar and my
son but after that I was unsure. Cnut needed me more but this whole
adventure had been to get Mary the home that her heart desired.

The women of the village had butchered one of the Scottish ponies
that had been killed and were cooking it with wild herbs they had
gathered. They were adding pickled fruits kept in jars after the autumn
harvest. The precious pickles were a sign that the village was thankful.
Such delicacies were kept for special occasions. The food would be
well flavoured. I saw the woman who had taken in the girl from
Otorbrunna. They kept looking at me and when the girl caught my eye
she smiled. I could not help but think of my daughter and my heart
ached to see my family again.

The first men to return were the men on foot. They carried with
them the wounded as well as the treasure they had taken. I saw Fótr and
the men of Corebricg. They carried their dead and wounded too. The
Viking came over to us and took off his helmet, laying it on his shield
along with his spear. "I wished that I had been with you by the bridge.
To see a shield wall used so well..." he shook his head, "and the wedge
you led advancing through that warband took me back to my time as a
real warrior. Have you ever watched such a wedge, Sven Saxon
Sword?" I shook my head. "Me neither. I have been in one but as we
ran after you all that I saw was a mailed arrow that marched as one. It
was as though you had all drilled for days."

Urse laughed, "Until we came north with the hersir my men had
never fought alongside him. It was the sword that melded us into one."

I shook my head, "But I did not even get to draw it."

Urse said, "You and the sword are as one, Sven Saxon Sword. I am
glad that I came with you for I now understand the real power of the
weapon. It is like all such magic swords. It needs to be wielded by the
right man and you were chosen to carry it."

Fótr said, "I am a Christian and I should not believe it."

I looked at the warrior, "But you do."

"God forgive me, but aye. When I led the men of Corebricg I knew
that because you and the sword were ahead of us that we would win.
The men of Corebricg are not great warriors but today they fought as
though they were. Perhaps there can be magic in White Christ's world."

I nodded. Mary had told my mother and me many stories of Jesus and as Eirik helped me to take off my byrnie I said, "My wife's father was a priest and she has read the stories from the Bible. From what I have heard the White Christ used magic. Did he not walk on water? Make water into wine? Feed the five thousand with five loaves and two fishes?"

I saw the warriors, both Christian and pagan take that in and while we cleaned our mail and sharpened our weapons all were silent. I was silent because I knew that the sword had been made by a Christian king to convert a pagan one. Was the sword a bridge? Was it intended to join those we called English with the Danes? When I reached Agerhøne it would be another conversation I would have with my wife.

It was getting on to dark when the horsemen returned. Ealdred had ridden with his father but he was not with him when they led their weary horses down the slope. There was no body draped on a horse and I wondered where the young Northumbrian was. The horsemen led their mounts to the water and allowed them to drink from the stream. They did so upstream from the battle. There the water was clear. Downstream the water was bloody even now.

The woman who had taken in the girl appeared to be an important person for when she shouted that food was ready all obeyed. Uhtred and his oathsworn headed towards us from the horse lines. I was pushed by my men and the villagers of Raylees to be given my bowl of food first, even before Uhtred. The woman ladled the choicest pieces of meat into my bowl and it brimmed to the top. The girl gave me a large piece of griddled bread. Both smiled at me.

"Thank you," I smiled back and although they might not have understood the words, they both beamed back at me.

Uhtred pushed his way into the line and then followed me to sit on the stacked stakes we had taken from the burn to make crude benches. Urse joined us while our hearthweru formed a circle around us. "You came north early, Sven Saxon Sword." He had a strange look on his face and I wondered what it meant.

"Perhaps the Norns were spinning, Lord Uhtred."

"You know I am a Christian and do not believe in such things."

The stew was hot and I held the spoon out to let it cool as I laughed and said, "You might be a Christian Lord Uhtred but you believe in the Norns. I can see it in your eyes."

He had the good grace to nod and to laugh, "My son is grateful that you did come. I left him to command at Otorbrunna. I am grateful. I was tardy reaching the battle and I am not certain that we would have held the bridge without you."

Urse snorted, "That is beyond doubt. Your Northumbrians are brave, Lord Uhtred, but they would have lost the bridge and you this part of your land. You would have bled to retake it."

I could see that Urse's words had annoyed the earl, "You were supposed to bring more ships than you did."

"But not for some time." The stew was delicious and I wanted to eat it and not go over what might have been. "We came early and we have saved your land." I dipped some of the griddled bread into the liquid and ate that before I said, "The Scots heard that you intended to attack them. You have a spy in your camp."

He nodded, "I know and my son told me. He was a priest, we found him in Otorbrunna and he has paid for his treachery with his life."

I wiped the last of the stew from the bowl with the last of the bread. "When you spoke with King Forkbeard you said that the attack was to keep your borders safe. Moray is far from here. It seems to me, Lord Uhtred, that had you not said that you would attack the Scots then there would have been no need for eight ships to sail to your aid."

I had been ruminating about the request for warriors since we had arrived and perhaps a full stomach or the victory had helped me to think a little clearer. Whatever the reason my words struck like a well-aimed arrow. He reacted before he could think and his widening eyes and open mouth warned me that the next words he would say were a lie. He recovered his composure quickly, "I had word that King Malcolm was planning something and it seems I was right. Anyway, I thank you and Norton shall be yours."

That told me that he had intended to renege on the arrangement. The fact that he then assiduously avoided conversation with me and spoke, instead, to the leaders of the warband who, having been served their food made their way through the barrier of bodyguards to speak to their earl. They were ascribing the victory to his timely arrival almost as though it had been planned. There were no men left waiting to be served and I headed back to get some more. I liked the taste of horsemeat.

The women were putting food in their bowls and I put mine back in the satchel. I would not want them to go hungry. The woman frowned and said, "More?"

I shook my head, smiled and then lied, "No. To thank you. It was good." To emphasise my meaning for I did not know if they would understand them, I rubbed my stomach and made a yum, yum sound. They laughed and I was happy that we had saved the girl before she had been violated. If nothing else our journey north had achieved something of which Mary would approve.

The woman looked as though she wanted to say something but did not have the words. She took my arm and led me, much to the amusement of Urse the Hairy and my hearthweru to Fótr. She began to speak quickly to Fótr whilst jabbing a finger at me. Had I done something wrong? He nodded and then asked her questions. Seemingly satisfied she turned and put her hand into the purse around her waist. She took out a small woven piece of wool and I felt a shiver run down my back. It was a spell. She kissed it and gave it to me. Then she hurried back to the other women and their food.

Fótr shook his head and touched the cross about his neck, "It seems that being with you, Sven Saxon Sword, drags me back to a pagan world I thought I had left. My wife will scold me if I tell her all that has happened."

"What was all that about? I know that she has woven a spell for me and that makes her a volva but …"

"She dreamed." This time it was my turn to clutch my Hammer of Thor. "Aye, it was about you. She saw a fleet of ships and it was burning. It was a Danish fleet; she saw the dragons. She watched warriors being slain and ships burned. She made the spell to protect you."

"Did she see me in her dream?"

"Aye, she saw your drekar with you at the prow holding a sword that looked like a dragon."

She had never seen the weapon drawn so how did she know that it was a dragon sword? The Norns had sent the dream to her, or perhaps the Allfather.

"What does it mean?"

Fótr leaned in, "Sven I have learned much while we eat. I am Northumbrian now but you have been betrayed. One of Uhtred's oathsworn boasted of how Edmund Ironside, King Æthelred's son, visited Bebbanburgh at the end of last year. They agreed to trick King Sweyn into sending his best men north so that they could take the king at Gegnesburh."

I shook my head, "I did not like King Sweyn but he was too clever and cunning a general to be taken like that."

Urse the Hairy had been listening and he said, "But he is dead and it is the whelp who leads our army. Sven, you know Cnut better than any. Can he deal with an enemy army?"

I knew the answer even had I not had the dream. The dream was just confirmation from the spirit world. I turned to Gandálfr, "Have our goods packed on the horses, we leave this night and march to Corebricg. Even now we may be too late but we must try."

They all raced away and I clasped Fótr's arm, "I thank you and I am in your debt."

"You may be too late."

I nodded, "And yet I must try. I thank you, Fótr. You are a shield brother and I hope we never have to meet in battle."

He smiled, "If we did then I would have the glorious end all true warriors seek."

It became clear to the whole camp that even though it was dark we were leaving. Uhtred strode over to me, a worried look upon his face, "What is the matter, Sven Saxon Sword? Why do you leave? You are exhausted and it is a long march to the Tinea."

I looked the Northumbrian in the eyes and gave him an honest answer, "You know why, Earl Uhtred, I go to save my king and as many of my oar brothers as I can from a treacherous attack."

I knew that the barb had hit home, "He is not a king. He is not even a prince."

"In my eyes, he is a king and I will take a crown for him, one way or another and if it is England that we win then beware Earl Uhtred for I do not like treachery."

"I could hold you here."

I laughed, "And you would die. You will not risk that, my lord. You have gambled that Edmund Ironside will win and that you will be rewarded. You have outwitted both King Sweyn and Thurbrand the Hold but one person you will never outwit is me for I know you to be the snake you are. You have used me and men only do that once. Say farewell to your son."

He suddenly looked fearful, "You would have revenge on him too?"

"No, for he has not betrayed me." I drew Oathsword, "The vengeance I shall have will be visited upon Edmund Ironside and you, Earl Uhtred of Bebbanburgh, when next we meet."

Chapter 18

He had no choice but to let us leave for the whole army, his oathsworn excepted, cheered us as we marched south. Had he ordered us to be slain then none would have obeyed. It was a small victory but a victory, nonetheless. We were already tired but the ponies we had taken lightened the load and we did not march in mail. Even so, the journey of eighteen miles took all night and we reached our ships, exhausted, at dawn. Part of me had worried that Uhtred might have done mischief and sabotaged them but I was according to him too much credit. Edmund Ironside was the planner; Uhtred was just a plotter.

I sent Eirik to run ahead and warn the ships of our approach so that by the time we reached the river the two sailing masters were preparing the ships for sea. While the crew took their places, I left the ponies as a gift for Fótr. His wife and children were relieved when I told them that he lived still. "Tell Fótr that the ponies are a gift and I hope that they remind him of a time we fought side by side."

"He is a good man, hersir."

"I know."

As I went back to my ship, I knew that his wife would be confused. He had not fought alongside me in a shield wall but we had fought together and Fótr would understand. I let Lars steer the ship down the river and I stood at the prow lost in my thoughts. While most Christians would assume the dream meant nothing, I knew that if a volva had dreamed it then there was significance. When Sweyn had been king then the ships had all been both guarded and bound together for protection. He had used horsemen to keep watch on the land to have early warning of an enemy. Would Cnut be as vigilant? I knew the answer, for the dream of the volva had told me that ships had been burnt. Cnut had sent to Denmark for more men and ships yet none had come by the time I had left. I was not surprised that Harald had ignored it but I wondered why my foster father had not sent some ships. There were more questions than answers. Urse and I would sail as quickly as we could to get to the Trent. We would both row and use the sails to get the best speed we could. Half the crew would row until they were tired and then the other half would take over. We would all rest when it was dark and we sailed south just with the wind for power. The hardest part proved to be the Tinea but once we reached the open sea we flew. We had the luxury of an hourglass and we spied the mouth of the Humber just twenty-eight hours after leaving Corebricg. We hove to in the wide estuary and we all donned our mail. Urse believed in the dream as did the two crews and a warrior who sailed into a battle without mail had a death wish.

I led and we headed up the Humber to the Trent. We knew the length of the journey for we had done it both ways. The wind gave us some help but it took seven hours to reach the Trent and when we did, we spied a drekar heading north. We were still in the Humber and after we had reefed sails and sculled oars to keep us steady, I shouted across to the captain, Einar Foul Fart, "Why the rush?"

"There has been treachery for we were surprised by an English attack in the dark of night. Thorkell the Tall led the English to fall upon our camps. Many crews were slaughtered as they tried to flee. We barely made it."

I cupped my hands and shouted, "But you made it. Why did you not help Cnut?"

I saw him shrug and wave. "We lost. The Norns have spun Sven Saxon Sword."

Were we too late? I cursed those who had abandoned Cnut. I saw the cleverness now of Edmund's plan and saw Thorkell the Tall's hands all over it. He knew that if I was at Cnut's side, he would not be able to surprise him. The temptation of Norton and my oath to Sweyn had sealed Cnut's fate. I was both flattered and angry. We passed more ships fleeing north. To be fair to their crews they looked to have battled and lost men; some had barely eight oars a side. Gegnesburh lay twenty miles upstream. As we headed south and drew to within ten miles of what King Sweyn had hoped would be the new capital of a Danish England, I saw a spiral of smoke in the distance. Something was burning and it could be the fleet. Was Cnut still alive? How many men remained with him? I waved Gandálfr to join me. We only had half the crew rowing and I needed to speak my thoughts to another.

"We have lost our base in this land, Gandálfr, and the question is how do we extricate the prince?"

He voiced my fears, "If he is still alive."

"We have to believe he is or else why would the Northumbrian woman have the dream?" He nodded. "We will be outnumbered when we reach Cnut and he will be assailed. We need a plan to ensure that we do not reach him only to die at his side." I suddenly realised that no ship had passed us for a mile or so. Eight drekar looked to have escaped and that meant there were many more ships left at anchor. "We need to secure ships as close to Gegnesburh as we can and hold them. We will take the outboard ships and cross the others like a bridge. You and the hearthweru along with our ship's boys can do that."

"Hersir, our place is at your side."

"Your place is where I deem it necessary." My voice was filled with anger and I was taking my frustration out on Gandálfr, it was not fair on him and I relented, "I need you and the others to secure a ship so that I can take the rest of the crew with me. You four are more than capable of holding a drekar."

"I am not happy for we should be guarding you but I will obey your command."

I turned to Lars, "Get the sail reefed. In a perfect world, we would lower the mast but I do not want Thorkell and Edmund to know we are coming to Cnut's aid.

Lars shouted, "Reef the sail." He turned to me, "We are not getting much benefit in any case and this way we can sail quicker downstream. When we land do you want me to turn her around?"

"If you can but I need the ship's boys to help my hearthweru prepare a ship for any that survive."

"We will be swift."

I went to the prow with Gandálfr and saw light glinting off metal and even at that distance heard the din of war. There was a battle going on and it looked to be to the north of Gegnesburh. There were ships between the battle and us but I needed to be as close to the fighting before we landed. I looked up and saw that the sail had been reefed. Steana grinned and gave me a wave when he caught my eye. I had barely spoken to him since we had boarded. I prayed that his first time away from Agerhøne would not be his last.

I stood at the prow clinging to the forestay. I could now see the battle. Cnut was hemmed in on three sides and had moved north from Gegnesburh; his father's dream of using that as the new capital of England was, like the wooden buildings, in ashes. I saw that the English were on the side closest to the river and were three hundred paces or so from the Danes who were falling back. Thorkell and his men were to the east on the far side. They were driving the Danes towards the more numerous English of Edmund. We had to get ashore and I viewed the banks. The ships here were all in pairs, tied to the east bank. The men of Wessex who followed Edmund Ironside had attempted to destroy the ships. They had failed for instead of damaging the outer drekar first they had tried to sink those close to the banks. The men of Wessex were not sailors. The result was that the innermost drekars were still tied to the bank and half-submerged but they could be used as a bridge.

I shouted, "Larboard oars in." At the same time, I signalled Urse, who was following, to emulate me. We bumped next to a drekar I recognised as **'Stormbird'**. It had thirty-four oars and was a decent size.

I had already told my men what we intended and, after donning my helmet and taking my shield I stepped over the gunwale and crossed over the sunken drekar, *'Crow'*. I climbed across the flooded deck and hauled myself to the bank. While I waited for my men and Urse's to join me I viewed the battle which had moved another two hundred paces further north and had now passed *'Crow'*. Cnut's ever-shrinking band was in danger of disintegrating. The one slight advantage we would have would be that we would be striking into the rear of the men of Wessex and those at the rear had no armour. The ones with armour were at the fore and even as I watched I saw the warriors led by Thorkell begin to surround Cnut and his men from the east.

I drew Oathsword. This would not be a battle for a spear. Pointing my blade at the men of Wessex I said to Urse, "Two wedges and we drive towards Cnut. The aim is to make a corridor through which the prince can escape."

"A good plan."

"Let us use the shock of silence and steel in the back. We shout only when we are close to Cnut and need to alert him to our presence."

He nodded. It was not in our nature to fight silently but in this case, we needed to whittle down the numbers quietly so that we could reach those with mail byrnies and close to Cnut to give us a chance to extricate as many of the army as we could. Even as we began to march, I reflected that Thorkell could have guaranteed victory if he had placed his warriors to the west of Cnut and cut off his escape to the ships. His mistake was Cnut's only hope. We could not chant and we were moving quickly. For that reason, our wedge was not as tight as it might normally have been; it would have to do. The first Saxons to die did so silently although it would not have made any difference if they had cried out for the din of battle made it impossible to discriminate between the sound of a cry of exultation and one of the pain of death.

With my shield held high, I pulled back the Dragon Sword and rammed it up through a Saxon's body. As I pulled it out, he fell and I stepped forward to repeat the strike. The men of Wessex just died thinking that the shield pressing into their backs was that of another Saxon. I slew eight and was less than twenty paces from the front of the Danish line when men turned and saw not Saxon shields but Danish warriors with bloody swords.

"We are undone! Turn and face!"

The noise of battle was so great that only a few men heard and they turned. The Danes protecting Cnut saw the heads turn as did the prince himself. I raised my sword and shouted as loudly as I could, "Oathsword!" When the two crews I led, repeated the cry then all heads turned and Cnut led his men towards us. He must have shouted an order but all I heard was the roar of my men.

It became harder as we now faced men who were mailed but the difference was that it was they who were now hemmed in between two sets of Danes. The men led by Cnut had been almost destroyed and now they spied hope. They fought with renewed energy while the men of Wessex saw victory snatched from them by what they would deem a treacherous attack in the rear. A Saxon housecarl armed with a long two-handed axe roared at me and raised his axe above his head. As he began to swing it down towards my helmet, I rushed at him and, holding the shield angled above my head drove Oathsword up through his mail. The mail was not the loose rings of the Scots we had recently fought but was made of the smallest mail rings wrapped around the smallest dowel. My sword did not slide through easily and I wondered if it might be defeated by the work of the weaponsmith. I pushed extra hard, my muscles complaining and burning. Lodvir's training came to my aid and I drove the tip through the mail and into his padded undershirt and up through his body. His axe shaft fell against my shield and I pushed his body from me.

The falling Saxon revealed a thegn whose right side was to me and his sword was raised to end the life of Ulf Olafsson. The Saxon's attention was on Ulf who was also fighting one of the thegn's bodyguards. This time I swung Oathsword down across the thegn's raised arm. I broke the mail and my sword sliced down to the bone. I must have hit tendons for the sword fell to the ground and the thegn turned to look at me. I drove my sword into his face. Ulf slew the bodyguard and with their thegn dead the warriors who remained panicked and began to flee south, back to the burning buildings of Gegnesburh. They could not make much progress because the rest of the army of Wessex barred their way but it did allow Cnut and those who still fought with him to reach us.

I saw that Cnut's helmet had been struck and his mail was blood-spattered but he grinned when he saw me, "When I heard the cry. 'Oathsword', then I knew we would be saved!"

"You are not saved yet, my prince. Lead your men towards the river. We have four drekar and we can help you to escape."

He looked behind him and saw the bodies of his oathsworn lying there. "And the rest?"

"They are warriors. I save the future King of England. I cannot save the rest."

He nodded, "Very well. Sound the retreat."

One of his men had been wounded but still carried the horn. As he blew five shrill blasts a Saxon raced at him with an axe and split the man's skull in two. I whipped Oathsword across his neck and his blood showered those coming to get us.

"My prince move swiftly for each moment of delay costs us men we shall need if we are to take this land back."

I looked behind me and saw that my wedge was now a semicircle. As Prince Cnut led his men through the gap Urse and I had made I shouted, "Back, but steadily. Let us tell them who they fight!" I started to chant the clan's chant. The first one I had used in Wessex.

We are the bird you cannot find
With feathers grey and black behind
Seek us if you can my friend
Our clan will beat you in the end.
Where is the bird? In the snake.
The serpent comes your gold to take.
We are the bird you cannot find
With feathers grey and black behind
Seek us if you can my friend
Our clan will beat you in the end.
Where is the bird? In the snake.
The serpent comes your gold to take.

It gave us the beat to march back in line. It was so familiar to us that even when we fought, we could still sing and there is something disconcerting to a warrior when he fights someone who can sing and smile as he slays them. Oathsword's edge had long gone but it was a well-made sword and I broke bones as I brought it down on weary arms. I hit one Saxon on the top of his helmet and the dent was so deep that the man fell at my feet. We lost men but the Saxons lost more and as we fell back over clear ground the Saxons had bodies to contend with. More than three quarters of Cnut's army was still two hundred paces from us and fighting to join us but when I saw arrows flying from behind us and heard the rattle of stones on Saxon mail and shields then I knew we were close to our ships.

As Gandálfr and my hearthweru joined me I halted. His voice came from behind me, "You have reached the ships, hersir. Let us board."

Without taking my eyes from the Saxons who saw Cnut slipping from their grasp I shook my head, "When the Prince is aboard *'Sea Serpent'* then we will board. I want to give as many men as possible the chance of life."

192

I brought my sword across the side of the head of a Saxon who had
lost his helmet. As he fell at my feet Gandálfr said, "But you risk your
life without cause!"

"The Norns have spun, Gandálfr, and I was sent here for a purpose."

"Brothers, let us show these Saxon what Oathsword's hearthweru
can do." My hearthweru suddenly launched themselves at the advancing
Saxons. The best four warriors on my drekar, they all had sharp
weapons and had yet to fight. Their attack took the Saxons by surprise
and the four of them sliced, hacked and stabbed through a wall of men
who had been fighting for hours. The effect was dramatic. The Saxon
attack not only stopped but they began to fall back. More survivors
from the disaster reached the drekar and it was due to my hearthweru. I
had chosen well.

Steana's voice sounded shrilly above the din of war, "Father, the
prince is safe!"

"Fall back! Especially you four berserkers!"

My men all fell back and thanks to Gandálfr's attack we reached the
riverbank and the sunken drekar without hurt. I sheathed Oathsword and
picked my way across the flooded ship. I saw that the men led by Cnut
had taken the oars of *'Stormbird'*. Einar the Fat was a hersir and had
taken the steering board. He shouted cheerily, as I passed him, "I owe
you a life, Sven Saxon Sword, we all do. If you ask us, we will sail over
the edge of the world!"

I nodded and said, "Let us get back home first before we make such
promises."

I saw Cnut standing next to Lars. My sailing master had managed to
turn the drekar so that we were pointing downstream. I looked and saw
that Urse's sailing master had managed the same and Urse was aboard.
It meant we could lead the line of survivors home. I waved to show him
that I was still alive. When Gandálfr and my hearthweru clambered
aboard we were ready to sail but I saw that there were many more men
we could take.

"Use your bows to allow as many men as possible to be saved. We
will need them to fight again."

My weary warriors dropped their shields and began to string bows. I
saw that our attack had shaken the enemy and Danes were racing for the
lines of ships. Further downstream the Saxons had not managed to
damage them. If the Northumbrian woman had not dreamt then many
more men would have died. We had not saved all but more men would
live thanks to her intervention. I could not help but clutch my Hammer
of Thor. I saw warriors helping wounded shield brothers over the

sunken *'Crow'* as arrows slammed into Saxons who did not manage to raise their shields in time.

Einar the Fat shouted, "Sven Saxon Sword, we are full. I dare not risk us sinking."

I nodded, "Take your oars."

'Stormbird' would have to turn and to enable that to happen we needed to move. Lars shouted, "Loose the sail." As the wind filled the sail we headed, with the current, downstream.

Passing Urse I shouted, "Follow us and keep close."

Like us, his men were using bows and as we passed drekars that were rapidly filling with the defeated Danish army of Prince Cnut, they kept the Saxons from closing too quickly. Looking to the west I saw that we were too late for many men. They had formed a shield wall and were dying as Thorkell the Tall's men hacked and sliced into them. They were all enjoying a warrior's death but it was a waste. They were the men that Cnut would need to either take the Danish crown or fight for the English one. It was getting on for dark when we passed the last of the moored drekar. Behind us was a line of fifteen ships. Not all were full but thanks to the dream more had been saved than might have been expected. More importantly, Cnut lived. When we reached the Humber, we hove to so that the crews could attend to wounds. We had a hazardous voyage to reach Denmark and we would need every hand we could on the oars. Those ships that were undermanned were sent replacements from those like mine and Einar the Fat's that were overloaded. We allowed the drekar to drift under reefed sails to the mouth of the estuary.

Cnut stood at the stern with me. He shook his head, "I should not have let you go to Uhtred the Bold."

I nodded, "Prince Cnut, you did not just let me go, you ordered it."

He looked to the south, "Vanity, Sven, I thought that we had defeated the Saxons. I see now that they are more cunning than I gave them credit for."

I had been the prince's teacher and this was not the time for a sympathetic shoulder but another lesson. "Prince Cnut, you forgot to be vigilant."

"The men of Lindsay gave us horses and promised us men, I thought to raid."

"Without me at your side?" He said nothing, "Did any reinforcements come from Denmark?" He shook his head. "Then you should have dug ditches, planted stakes and waited until they did come."

He said nothing for a while and then said, "I sent my family back to Heiða-býr. When they had gone, we had a feast. Thorkell and his men fell upon us."

This was worse than I had expected.

He looked at me, "I once said I needed you as my father needed Karl Three Fingers. I now see that is truer than I thought. Will you help me, Sven Saxon Sword?"

I knew that my words would affect the rest of my life, "To do what, Prince Cnut?"

He sighed, "I am a prince without a land. I would have you help me to carve one out."

Dawn was just breaking ahead of us and I waved a hand behind, "With this handful of ships and broken men?"

He gave me a determined look, "When I sent my wife home, I also sent the treasure we had taken. We shall buy an army."

"And then?"

"And then I shall speak to my brother and ask if we can share the throne of Denmark."

I knew the answer to that without consulting a volva. I said nothing. I could not see much hope of achieving Cnut's dreams of a crown but I also knew that the threads that bound us meant I had no choice in the matter. My fate and that of Prince Cnut were irrevocably bound together.

I nodded, "I will help you, Prince Cnut, but I fear it will be a long journey we take together."

He beamed, "With the Dragon Sword, Sven, all is possible."

Just at that moment, the sun flared above the horizon in the east and behind us, the land of the Saxons was bathed in sunlight. There was hope and the Norns had spun.

Blood Sword

Epilogue

Agerhøne 1014

We had to bury two men at sea before we reached our home and
that upset Prince Cnut more than the deaths of the many hundred who
had fallen at Gegnesburh. I think it was because they lingered for two
days before they died and their slow death was painful to watch. Both
were, like Cnut, Christians and would not take a warrior's death. After
they were slipped over the side, I went to Cnut for I could see the effect
it had on him.

"They died for me, Sven. Am I worthy of the death of such brave
men?"

"That depends upon what you intend to do. Why do you wish to be
a king?"

"What?"

"It is a simple enough question, my prince. Is it the title and the
crown you seek for if that is the case then their deaths were not worthy
ones?"

"Of course not but I was born the son of a king."

I pointed to Siggi and Snorri, "And those two are the sons of a pig
farmer. Is that how these things work?"

He frowned and stared astern, "I would be a king for I believe I
would be a better king than King Æthelred and I would be better for the
people there."

"Then that is a worthy reason but you must keep that thought ever
in your head. So when we visit with your brother do you think he will
allow you to rule jointly?" I asked the question because I wanted to
know if Cnut had realistic ambitions.

"In all honesty, I do not but I am my father's son and as he did not
name an heir then I have as much right to the crown as Harald."

"Except that his oathsworn were not slaughtered on the Trent and he
sits on the throne and wears the crown upon his head."

"Then my hope is that he will grant me a share of Denmark's
treasury and support me when I try to retake England from Æthelred
and his family."

"And that will take time. We would need two hundred ships. We
have a handful. I know that more will escape but not many. You need a
reputation to draw men to your standard and that means raiding." I
pointed east, "There are many places you could raid: the lands of the

Wends, Pomerania," I pointed south, "Frisia, Frankia, even the lands of the Arabs. Are you prepared for that?"

He gritted his teeth, "I am. I will find a safe haven for my family and then begin."

"Good then I will do all that I can to help you," I gave him a wry smile, "first I have to face Mary and tell her what we plan."

As we neared Agerhøne I saw that the other drekar of Ribe and Agerhøne were drawn up on the beaches. I had not mentioned it to Cnut but I had no reason that I could come up with why my foster father had not come to Cnut's aid. So many sails approaching the harbour drew all to the quay. Families looked anxiously for their menfolk to wave. Most were relieved but we had incurred deaths and those women and children who did not see their man hung their heads. My mother and I had been such a pair when my father, Bersi, had been killed in Wessex. I understood their pain. Mary stood with our two children and while her smile was a thin one it was there. Gunhild and Bersi, my son, beamed. Jarl Sweyn Skull Taker stood and waited for me and Prince Cnut to land. He was the jarl and all other greetings would have to wait until we had spoken.

He approached Cnut first, "I was sorry to hear of your father's death, Prince Cnut. I did not always agree with him and his decisions but he was a strong king and I admired him."

Cnut retorted so quickly and so angrily that it took even me by surprise, "Then why did you not heed my request to aid me? With your ships, we might have won and England would, even now, be mine."

My foster father was calm in the face of the onslaught, "I understand your emotion, Prince Cnut, but know that I would have sailed to help for my foster son was also in danger…"

"But…"

He looked at me, "But I did not know. The first I heard was six days since when Aksel the Swede told me that ships had returned to Heiða-býr and that he had heard you had asked for ships. As you can see, we were already preparing our ships and would have sailed today but yesterday a ship came and told us that you and your army were destroyed at the Battle of Gegnesburh. I can see now that it was not true and for that I am grateful." He lowered his voice, "If you sent a ship to ask me then either it sank on the way or there was treachery. Whose drekar did you send?"

"It was Ivan Blue Tooth."

My foster father nodded, "He was in Heiða-býr with the other ships sent to your brother."

"Did my brother not ask men to come to our aid?"

Sweyn shook his head, "Just the opposite. He ordered all ships to stay in Denmark and not to go to your aid. Aksel told us that."

Cnut's face looked as though someone had punched him. He nodded, "Then I am sorry that I thought ill of you. I apologise." He turned to me, "Until I can gather enough men to visit with my brother could I stay in your home, Sven?"

"Of course."

Jarl Sweyn Skull Taker looked worried, "You do not intend to make war on your brother, do you? Civil war would help no one."

Cnut smiled, "I know I was foolish and lost a battle I should not have done but since then I have appointed a counsellor who will guide me. Sven Saxon Sword and Oathsword shall be at my side and such foolishness as Gegnesburh are in the past. The callow youth will be moulded and shaped by the warrior who saved so many at Gegnesburh."

I saw my foster father swell with pride and, as Prince Cnut's words had carried to those waiting, saw the smile on my wife's face replaced with a scowl. I sighed. The Norns had spun and my life was now so complicated that I would not even contemplate trying to unravel the knots. I would endure the scolding knowing that my fate was decided by powers greater than me. Whatever happened to Cnut would also happen to me. *Wyrd.*

The End

Norse Calendar

Gormánuður October 14th - November 13th
Ýlir November 14th - December 13th
Mörsugur December 14th - January 12th
Þorri - January 13th - February 11th
Gói - February 12th - March 13th
Einmánuður - March 14th - April 13th
Harpa April 14th - May 13th
Skerpla - May 14th - June 12th
Sólmánuður - June 13th - July 12th
Heyannir - July 13th - August 14th
Tvímánuður - August 15th - September 14th
Haustmánuður September 15th-October 13th

199

Glossary

Beardestapol – Barnstaple
Beck- a stream
Blót – a blood sacrifice made by a jarl
Bondi- Viking farmers who fight
Bjorr – Beaver
Burgh/Burh-King Alfred's defences. The largest was Winchester
Byrnie- a mail or leather shirt reaching down to the knees
Cantwareburh- Canterbury
Cent – Kent
Chape- the tip of a scabbard
Corebricg – Corbridge
Denshire- Devon
Deoraby – Derby
Drekar- a Dragon ship (a Viking warship) pl. drekar
Dun Holm Durham
Dyflin- Old Norse for Dublin
Eoforwic- Saxon for York
Føroyar- Faroe Islands
Fey- having second sight
Firkin- a barrel containing eight gallons (usually beer)
Fret - a sea mist
Fyrd-the Saxon levy
Galdramenn- wizard
Gegnesburh – Gainsborough (Lincolnshire)
Gighesbore – Guisborough
Gippeswic- Ipswich
Hamtunscīr -Hampshire
Hamwic- Southampton
Heiða-býr – Hedeby in Schleswig- destroyed in 1066
Herepath- the military roads connecting the burghs of King Alfred
Herkumbl- a badge on a helmet denoting the clan
Hersir- a Viking landowner and minor noble. It ranks below a jarl
Herterpol – Hartlepool
Hnefatafl – a Viking game a little like chess
Hoggs or Hogging- when the pressure of the wind causes the stern
or the bow to droop
Hremmesgeat – Ramsgate
Hringmaraheior – Ringmere

Hrofescester- Rochester, Kent

Hundred- Saxon military organization. (One hundred men from an area led by a thegn or gesith)

Isle of Greon- Isle of Grain (Thames Estuary)

Jarl- Norse earl or lord

Joro-goddess of the earth

kjerringa - Old Woman- the solid block in which the mast rested

Knarr- a merchant ship or a coastal vessel

Kyrtle-woven top

Ligera caestre – Leicester

Lincylene – Lincoln

Lydwicnaesse- Breton Point, Exmouth

Mast fish- two large racks on a ship designed to store the mast when not required.

Meðune –River Medina in the Isle of Wight

Midden- a place where they dumped human waste

Miklagård - Constantinople

Northwic-Norwich

Njörðr- God of the sea

Nithing- A man without honour (Saxon)

Northantone, - Northampton

Ocmundtune- Oakhampton

Odin- The 'All Father' God of war, also associated with wisdom, poetry, and magic (The Ruler of the gods).

Østersøen – The Baltic Sea

Otorbrunna – Otterburn

Oxnaford - Oxford

Ran- Goddess of the sea

Roof rock- slate

Saami - the people who live in what is now Northern Norway/Sweden

Sabrina - The River Severn

Sandwic – Sandwich (Kent)

Scree - loose rocks in a glacial valley

Skumasþorp- Scunthorpe

Seax – short sword

Sennight - seven nights- a week

Shamblord - Cowes, Isle of Wight

Sheerstrake - the uppermost strake in the hull

Sheet - a rope fastened to the lower corner of a sail

Shroud - a rope from the masthead to the hull amidships

Skald - a Viking poet and singer of songs

Skeggox – an axe with a shorter beard on one side of the blade

Skreið- stockfish (any fish which is preserved)

Skjalborg- shield wall

Snekke- a small warship

Snotingaham - Nottingham

Stanford - Stamford

Stad- Norse settlement

Stays- ropes running from the masthead to the bow

Strake- the wood on the side of a drekar

Tarn - small lake (Norse)

Teignton- Kingsteignton

The Norns- The three sisters who weave webs of intrigue for men

Thing - Norse for a parliament or a debate (Tynwald in the Isle of Man)

Thor's day- Thursday

Threttanessa- a drekar with 13 oars on each side.

Thrall- slave

Trenail- a round wooden peg used to secure strakes

Úlfarrberg- Helvellyn

Ullr-Norse God of Hunting

Ulfheonar-an elite Norse warrior who wore a wolf skin over his armour

Verðandi -the Norn who sees the future

Volva- a witch or healing woman in Norse culture

Walhaz -Norse for the Welsh (foreigners)

Waite- a Viking word for farm

Wiht -The Isle of Wight

Withy- the mechanism connecting the steering board to the ship

Wintan-ceastre -Winchester

Woden's day- Wednesday

Wyrd- Fate

Wyrme- Norse for Dragon

Yard- a timber from which the sail is suspended

Historical Notes

The dragon sword is a blade of my own imagination although King Alfred did give a sword to the illegitimate son of Prince Edward, the king's son. Aethelstan became the first king accorded the title King of England. As readers of my books will know swords are always important. This series will reflect that.

A word about Denmark, the maps and the place names. If you look at a map of modern Denmark, you will see that Ribe is not where I place it. Names change over the years and you will see, as the series progresses, the reason for some of the changes. The Heiða-býr of King Sweyn is also no longer there. It was destroyed sometime after King Sweyn died. There are some ruins where it once was but as the Danes built using wood they are not as substantial as the Roman ones would have been. The Battle of Svolder did take place but the island from which the allied fleet sailed is not marked on any map as Svolder. My research indicates that it was north of Øresund which is close to Copenhagen. There are two islands that fit the detail and I have used the one called Anholt which is a triangular island and would have fitted the events of the battle. If any of my Danish or Norse readers have better information then please let me know.

The raids on Hampshire, Devon, East Anglia and Kent are all documented by the monks who chronicled the Danish raids. The events happened almost exactly as I wrote them. History has helped me to weave a story that has many unbelievable stories. The fiction is the clan of Agerhøne. Thorkell the Tall is reputed to have been Cnut's foster father but as Cnut is not mentioned until 1014, I have used that lack of information to make up a story. The rescue of Ælfgifu is pure fiction and there is not a shred of evidence that she was held captive. However, she does eventually marry Cnut and as her family were killed on King Æthelred's orders I thought it was a reasonable storyline.

Some of the events I write about are incredible such as King Æthelred paying gold to the Danes and, in the same year, butchering every Dane in his kingdom including the sister of the Danish king. It beggars belief but, apparently, happened. The bodies of the dead were discovered some years ago. Ulfcetel Snillingr was also a real character and he almost managed to destroy the Danish fleet. Oathsword's part in saving the fleet is also fiction.

The murder of the Archbishop of Canterbury happened the way I wrote it and I did not make up the name Thrum. Thorkell did change sides after the bishop's murder. King Sweyn's campaign to take England happened almost exactly as I wrote it. King Sweyn chose his putative new capital because it was in the heartland of Danelaw. The raids on the Danelaw were not pursued as vigorously or as violently as those in what was essentially Wessex, Mercia and Kent. There the people suffered badly as a result of the Danish raids.

The major battles such as Hringmaraheior, Lundenwic and Gegnesburh all happened. The results were as I wrote them but the details are of my own invention. I used the tactics and battle plans as used at the time. Uhtred was earl of Northumbria. He offered hostages to King Sweyn and bent the knee as I wrote. He changed sides as soon as Sweyn died and married one of King Æthelred's daughters. Thurbrand the Hold is also a real character. Both will figure in the next book in the series so no spoilers here!

The battle of Raylees is pure fiction. Uhtred did fight a number of battles against the Scots but I needed to have Oathsword away from Cnut's side when he was defeated.

The saga will continue until Cnut becomes King of England… and perhaps a little further. Who knows?

- **King Cnut- W B Bartlett**
- **Vikings- Life and Legends -British Museum**
- **Saxon, Norman and Viking by Terence Wise (Osprey)**
- **The Vikings (Osprey) -Ian Heath**
- **Byzantine Armies 668-1118 (Osprey)-Ian Heath**
- **Romano-Byzantine Armies 4th- 9th Century (Osprey) -David Nicholle**
- **The Walls of Constantinople AD 324-1453 (Osprey) -Stephen Turnbull**
- **Viking Longship (Osprey) - Keith Durham**
- **The Vikings- David Wernick (Time-Life)**
- **The Vikings in England Anglo-Danish Project**
- **Anglo Saxon Thegn AD 449-1066- Mark Harrison (Osprey)**
- **Viking Hersir- 793-1066 AD - Mark Harrison (Osprey)**
- **National Geographic- March 2017**
- **British Kings and Queens- Mike Ashley**

Griff Hosker April 2022

Other books by Griff Hosker

If you enjoyed reading this book, then why not read another one by the author?

Ancient History

The Sword of Cartimandua Series
(Germania and Britannia 50 A.D. – 128 A.D.)
Ulpius Felix- Roman Warrior (prequel)
The Sword of Cartimandua
The Horse Warriors
Invasion Caledonia
Roman Retreat
Revolt of the Red Witch
Druid's Gold
Trajan's Hunters
The Last Frontier
Hero of Rome
Roman Hawk
Roman Treachery
Roman Wall
Roman Courage

The Wolf Warrior series
(Britain in the late 6th Century)
Saxon Dawn
Saxon Revenge
Saxon England
Saxon Blood
Saxon Slayer
Saxon Slaughter
Saxon Bane
Saxon Fall: Rise of the Warlord
Saxon Throne
Saxon Sword

Medieval History

Blood Sword

The Dragon Heart Series
Viking Slave
Viking Warrior
Viking Jarl
Viking Kingdom
Viking Wolf
Viking War
Viking Sword
Viking Wrath
Viking Raid
Viking Legend
Viking Vengeance
Viking Dragon
Viking Treasure
Viking Enemy
Viking Witch
Viking Blood
Viking Weregeld
Viking Storm
Viking Warband
Viking Shadow
Viking Legacy
Viking Clan
Viking Bravery

The Norman Genesis Series
Hrolf the Viking
Horseman
The Battle for a Home
Revenge of the Franks
The Land of the Northmen
Ragnvald Hrolfsson
Brothers in Blood
Lord of Rouen
Drekar in the Seine
Duke of Normandy
The Duke and the King

Danelaw
(England and Denmark in the 11th Century)
The Dragon Sword
Oathsword

Blood Sword

Blood Sword

New World Series
Blood on the Blade
Across the Seas
The Savage Wilderness
The Bear and the Wolf
Erik The Navigator

The Vengeance Trail

The Reconquista Chronicles
Castilian Knight
El Campeador
The Lord of Valencia

The Aelfraed Series
(Britain and Byzantium 1050 A.D. - 1085 A.D.)
Housecarl
Outlaw
Varangian

**The Anarchy Series England
1120-1180**
English Knight
Knight of the Empress
Northern Knight
Baron of the North
Earl
King Henry's Champion
The King is Dead
Warlord of the North
Enemy at the Gate
The Fallen Crown
Warlord's War
Kingmaker
Henry II
Crusader
The Welsh Marches
Irish War
Poisonous Plots
The Princes' Revolt

Blood Sword

Earl Marshal
The Perfect Knight

Border Knight
1182-1300
Sword for Hire
Return of the Knight
Baron's War
Magna Carta
Welsh Wars
Henry III
The Bloody Border
Baron's Crusade
Sentinel of the North
War in the West
Debt of Honour
The Blood of the Warlord

Sir John Hawkwood Series
France and Italy 1339- 1387
Crécy: The Age of the Archer
Man At Arms
The White Company
Leader of Men

Lord Edward's Archer
Lord Edward's Archer
King in Waiting
An Archer's Crusade
Targets of Treachery
The Great Cause

Struggle for a Crown
1360- 1485
Blood on the Crown
To Murder a King
The Throne
King Henry IV
The Road to Agincourt
St Crispin's Day
The Battle for France
The Last Knight

Blood Sword

Queen's Knight

Tales from the Sword I
(Short stories from the Medieval period)

Tudor Warrior series
England and Scotland in the late 14th and early 15th century
Tudor Warrior

Conquistador
England and America in the 16th Century
Conquistador

Modern History

The Napoleonic Horseman Series
Chasseur à Cheval
Napoleon's Guard
British Light Dragoon
Soldier Spy
1808: The Road to Coruña
Talavera
The Lines of Torres Vedras
Bloody Badajoz
The Road to France
Waterloo

The Lucky Jack American Civil War series
Rebel Raiders
Confederate Rangers
The Road to Gettysburg

The British Ace Series
1914
1915 Fokker Scourge
1916 Angels over the Somme
1917 Eagles Fall
1918 We will remember them
From Arctic Snow to Desert Sand
Wings over Persia

Blood Sword

Combined Operations series
1940-1945
Commando
Raider
Behind Enemy Lines
Dieppe
Toehold in Europe
Sword Beach
Breakout
The Battle for Antwerp
King Tiger
Beyond the Rhine
Korea
Korean Winter

Tales from the Sword II
(Short stories from the Modern period)

Other Books
Great Granny's Ghost (Aimed at 9-14-year-old young people)

For more information on all of the books then please visit the author's website at www.griffhosker.com where there is a link to contact him or visit his Facebook page: GriffHosker at Sword Books

Printed in Great Britain
by Amazon

81670604R00129